"Great characterization of Esau and very good writing."

Donna E. Pudick, author, educator.

"Mr. Newman is a capable wordsmith."

Ellen Traylor, best-selling author of biblical fiction.

"Mr. Newman is a serious student of the Bible and the commentaries. An entertaining historical novel about an enigmatic Biblical character."

Rabbi Mendel Krinsky.

Esau: The Bible's Mightiest Villain

A Historical Novel by

Alexander Newman

Joshua Tree Publishing

• Chicago •

ESAU: THE BIBLE'S MIGHTIEST VILLAIN

A Historical Novel by
ALEXANDER NEWMAN

Published by
Joshua Tree Publishing
• Chicago •

JoshuaTreePublishing.com

13-Digit ISBN: 978-1-941049-30-3

Front Cover Image Credit: Bliznetsov
Back Cover Image Credit: Jag_cz

Printed in the United States of America

DEDICATION

To Margarita, with love.

PREFACE

Most people familiar with the Bible remember the story of Esau, who sold his birthright to his brother Jacob for a mess of pottage. However, that story does not capture the whole essence of Esau. Peel away his brutish mask, and a fascinating, nuanced, and ultimately tragic portrait emerges. Far from being a simple evil savage, Esau was endowed with enormous spiritual power, which he wasted in the pursuit of violent and sensual vices. How did he become the mightiest villain of all time, a synonym for both evil and martial prowess, instead of the greatest beacon of light? This novel will lead you to the answer through his life of adventure, battle, love, and betrayal. This is a work of fiction, but fiction grounded in the respected biblical commentaries such as *Midrashim* and in historical research. Despite being told from a fresh vantage point, the story is faithful to the original, including names and events from the Bible; the rest is an amalgam of legends and fiction. If the conflicts in this book seem familiar, it is because the struggle of Esau and his descendants against the sons of Jacob is everlasting. It has shaped much of human history for more than 3,000 years, and it continues to unfold today.

Alexander Newman

Some Characters

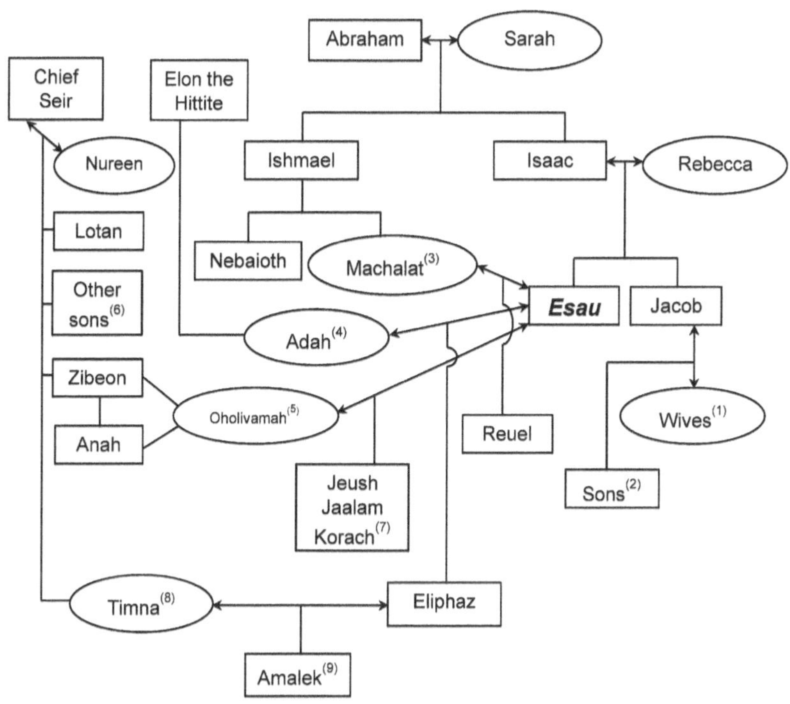

Notes:

1) Wives of Jacob: Leah, Rachel, Bilhah, and Zilpah.
2) Sons of Jacob: Reuben, Simon, Levi, Judah, Zebulun, Naphtali, Issachar, Dan, Gad, Asher, Joseph, and Benjamin.
3) Third wife of Esau; original name Basemath.
4) Second wife of Esau; nicknamed Basemath for a time.
5) First wife of Esau; nicknamed Judith for a time. A product of an illicit union of Zibeon and his son Anah's wife.
6) Other sons of Seir: Shoval, Anah, Dishon, and Etzer.
7) Korach is an illegitimate son of Eliphaz and Oholivamah.
8) Timna is an illegitimate daughter of Eliphaz and Seir's wife Nureen.
9) May his wicked name be erased from memory.

CHAPTER 1

The arrow found its target: the deer's brown eye. The buck staggered for a few moments, bobbing his antlers and kicking the sand, and toppled over. Esau smiled: not bad for a fifteen-year-old whom nobody had taught archery. As he went through sparse pine forest to retrieve his trophy, looking around for a place to build a fire, some distant voices brought him to a halt.

He scanned the woods, but all he saw was trees, dry needles, and white stones. A few scattered patches of red anemones, which sprouted for a couple of months in the spring, enlivened the desolation a bit.

Esau crept toward the sounds, bypassing fallen tree branches, until he detected something gleaming at a distance. There! A multitude of soldiers in battle attire stood in a field behind the forest, about five bowshots away, their brass helmets glittering in the midday sun. He wrinkled his forehead. Where did they come from? How did he miss their arrival?

Esau edged closer, tiptoeing from tree to tree, trying not to brush against the sap, sinking his sandals into a soft carpet of needles. He gasped when he made out the red banner and realized that it belonged to King Nimrod of Babylon, the first and the most famous of all the kings in the world.

Esau stopped to think this over. What is the king doing so far away from home in my wilderness? Hunting? After all, people call him the Mighty Hunter before the Lord. But if Nimrod is indeed here, it would be too good to be true. This would spare me a three-week journey to his kingdom!

He squinted again and rubbed his neck. If I could kill the king and take his prize, I would become the new Mighty Hunter. But I want a different title. The Mighty Warrior? No, there are plenty of those. I want to be called . . . The Mightiest.

The Mightiest.

I can defeat the king, no doubt. All these guards around him, all their shiny weapons and helmets—they don't matter here. He is not going to hunt with his clanging entourage.

Esau soon grinned with content, as a man dressed in different clothes than the rest strode into the woods accompanied by two others. Esau slunk toward the three men, dashing and halting, caressing the needles away from his face. He stopped at the edge of a large clearing, with the Babylonians on the other side of it.

The group paused and changed the course back into the forest. The field ahead, of low grass and occasional thorn bush, offered little cover. No, let them come here.

Esau stepped on a dry tree branch, and the sound echoed among the midday calmness. He stepped on it again, dropped on the hard-packed sand and peeked, swiping the dust off his face.

The soldiers stalled, exchanged gestures, and headed toward him through the clearing, observing every bush, every rock, and every anthill ahead, almost gliding above the ground. Nimrod, if it was indeed him, was leading the way, bow and arrow at the ready, treading with poise and confidence, yet not making a sound. His companions kept their fancy composite bows on their backs and their swords in the scabbards, ready to grab whichever weapon they needed in an instant.

Esau ducked behind a massive rock and held his breath, feeling fortunate that the king and his men faced the sun. But when he saw Nimrod and his two guards spread out, his heart sank.

If they continued on this course, they would soon surround me, he realized. Instead of killing Nimrod, I'd be killed myself before getting anywhere near the king. I'm trapped. And why is it so hot all of a sudden?

The rustle of footsteps was getting louder, but after a pause Esau heard whispers and spied the Babylonians changing their course yet again. They were so close that he could see every worn leather strap on the sides of their muscular legs and the dust on their short red battle tunics. Someday I'll wear a red uniform of my own design, he resolved in passing.

Esau wavered for a little while, wondering if it was indeed Nimrod in front of him. The king was supposed to be dark-skinned, and so was this large strapping man in a shiny brown long-sleeved leather tunic decorated with the figures of wild animals—and no body armor. That's good enough.

He tossed a flat stone close to the ground, aiming to avoid the bushes. As expected, the stone did not tumble but hit the ground and slid.

The men turned toward the sound, with their backs now facing Esau and bent like the bows they were carrying. The two guards set out to investigate, while the leader remained in place, erect, with an arrow notched on his bow.

Esau tried to calm his heart, remembering how he had wrestled a bear cub to the ground last month. He aimed an arrow at the back of the king's head and released it.

Nimrod started to turn around, and the arrow only nicked him. The king shrieked and loosed his own arrow without aiming. He missed.

Esau grabbed the sword and ran toward the king, flitting between the thorn bushes and ignoring their stinging. Nothing else mattered until he covered the dusty distance.

He noticed Nimrod loading another arrow with his stubby bejeweled fingers and skipped sideways; the arrow smacked a tree behind the clearing. The king reloaded but did not have a chance to aim: a thrust of the sword sliced his neck. The arrow flew past Esau, and the king froze in place without making a sound, his mouth open, his head stiff, his widened dark eyes staring at the attacker.

Esau knocked off Nimrod's golden helmet incrusted with precious stones and grabbed his long braided hair. Protecting himself with the king's body, Esau lumbered toward the guards. Seeing them up close, he felt insignificant in comparison, but he kept going, his eyes narrowed, his lips flattened.

"Kill him, kill him!" screeched the king. His soldiers—the older man on the left and the younger on the right—wavered.

Esau pushed Nimrod with all the force he could muster toward the older guard. He then rolled on the ground toward the younger one and stung the soldier's leg with his short bronze sword, cutting through the sandal straps.

The soldier sprung back and looked down in horror, as if ten hissing vipers were coiled in front of him. Backing away, he stumbled upon a rock and spread his arms.

Esau leaped from the ground and thrust his sword into the man's now-exposed abdomen, just below the short scale armor, twisting the blade to prevent it from being trapped within the wound. The soldier screamed, swaying on his feet, and slumped to the ground. His pointed bronze helmet rolled away, but Esau did not linger to watch.

The older and more confident guard put down Nimrod's body and unsheathed his well-polished sword. His curly silver beard glinted in the sun like a coat of chain mail; his elaborate uniform and the heavy leather armor on his shoulders were decorated with gold insignia. He must be a general, Esau figured.

The general waited to attack, and the two combatants stood still, watching each other. The vile-smelling Babylonian wiped away the sweat from his brow and touched his large bulbous nose with his free hand.

Esau scowled, thinking about what that meant. Was the man afraid to fight? This old warrior with a scar-crossed cheek? Did he think he could run away? Where? Back to the soldiers to inform them that he failed to protect his king?

The guard stepped over Nimrod's body, yelled something, and made a forehand swing. Esau swiveled out of the way and deflected the strike, which only slit his white woolen *simlah* cloak. The guard followed with a backhand swing that was also parried. After the combat continued for several minutes, the men paused to catch their breath, and the general allowed his bloodshot eyes to meet Esau's.

The silver beard quickly shifted his glance, but it was too late. The sword of Esau cut through his right arm, and the Babylonian dropped his weapon. The second thrust sliced through the general's neck; his legs wobbled and gave way.

The victor turned away from the crumpled mess and tottered back to the younger guard. He was still alive, struggling to breathe, trying to stop the bleeding by pressing his blood-soaked hands on his stomach. His eyes filled with tears were pleading for mercy, and he was mumbling something.

"Why are you here?" Esau demanded in a harsh voice, gasping for air, too. The man did not answer, and Esau pounded on the wound, spraying himself with blood.

"We were . . . looking for you. We knew you hunted here," the guard stammered and coughed, his short black beard becoming brown.

"You traveled all this distance—for me? Why?" Esau took another deep breath, swatting away flies.

"He was . . . jealous . . . of you. He dreamed that you would . . ." mumbled the soldier through the bloody bubbles.

"Dreamed what? That I would kill him? Was he a prophet or something?" demanded Esau.

The soldier did not answer. His body arched up and then slackened; his eyes stared at the sun without flinching.

Esau returned to the king's body. Nimrod was lying face down, one of his sandals dug deep into the ground as if trying to find a refuge there. The older guard was also dead. Esau frowned: no answers today.

A pair of black vultures descended on the king's body and tried to peck at it but stopped in their tracks and backed down. Instead, they flapped their wings and waddled toward the general. Esau shooed them away. The bodies were his.

He felt an unfamiliar smell of death that he could not describe. It was not just a smell of human blood and feces, but that of finality, hopelessness. Esau wasn't sure whether he was elated or sad; he was smothered by the exhaustion. But there was no time to sort it all out. One last task remained.

He picked up Nimrod's shining helmet, admired the rubies and sapphires glimmering in the sun, sighed, and threw it back. He turned to the prostrate body and labored to strip off Nimrod's tunic, trying to protect the leather by lifting the king's torso upside down and letting the blood drain away. Done! He ran his fingers over the tunic and buried his face into it, expecting the smell of a sweaty hide, but the aroma of an apple orchard greeted him instead. He grinned.

His hands and legs still trembling, Esau was unable to take another step. He stood at the clearing, devouring the sweet desert air. A beetle landed on his ruddy face, but Esau did not stir. A thought crossed his mind that were the rest of the soldiers to appear then, they could have overpowered him without any difficulty.

He looked at Nimrod's listless head again. Not a single gray hair. Hmm.

A chittering ground squirrel ran in front of Esau and startled him—just in time. Through the stifling stillness of the day, he detected the unmistakable sounds of heavy footsteps. Moving toward him.

CHAPTER 2

Carrying Nimrod's garments on his shoulder, Esau wobbled back to Hebron for days, or so it seemed. Scorching afternoon sun or not, he trudged through lifeless, blistering wasteland. Trying to strengthen himself, he recalled two great things that happened on that day: an adventure with a betrothed girl in the morning and this improbable victory in the afternoon.

He stopped to take the last sip from his leather pouch. A glance at the king's tunic brought him back to his thoughts.

How was I able to kill the great Nimrod, who could convince his entire generation to rebel against the Lord? Who started building the Tower extending into the sky? Whom his subjects idolized as a deity? The Mighty Hunter, who never missed a shot? Until now. It's funny that the only person on the face of the earth who had opposed building the Tower was my own grandfather Abraham. And now I've completed his struggle with the king.

A pair of old toothless leathery shepherds with a drove of bedraggled sheep gave him a puzzled look and followed his dusty steps. Esau felt too tired to even think about killing them; all he could do was stagger along.

With water gone, the road got blurrier and blurrier. A headache replaced his musings, and he felt ready to faint. Wishing that the night would arrive already, he closed his eyes to feel a brief respite of shade. A pair of huge stones ahead offered some cover, and he hastened his steps. That's when he lost his footing and fell into something.

***

Esau cracked his eyes open to the sight of three giggling young men with knives in their hands staring down at him. Something sharp was poking at his back. He felt his arms and legs: nothing broken. He closed his eyes, exhaled, and let his limp head drop on the muddy bottom of the pit. If there were snakes and scorpions here, they would have attacked already, he thought. At least it's cooler down here.

The youngsters exchanged whispers, elbowed one another, and threw some pebbles at Esau, but he did not twitch. When one of them finally descended and started poking at his body, Esau grabbed his foot and toppled him. With a sword against his throat, the lad pleaded for mercy.

Esau looked up and screeched, "Get away from here or he's dead!" The two young men did not stir, still peering down.

"I have some gold, and I'll give it to you—but move!" offered Esau.

The young outlaws looked at one another, and one of them said, "Throw it to us and let him go, then we'll talk."

"So you could take off and leave me here? No, thanks," replied Esau. "Let me out, and *then* we'll talk."

"Fine. Throw your sword to us, handle first, and push him out of there," said the same man. "Your bow, too."

"I'll throw the weapons to you, but I must get out first," insisted Esau.

His captors agreed, and soon all four of them were above ground. The three ruffians surrounded Esau, one of them pointing an arrow at its owner.

Up close, the outlaws did not look that young—all of them were a bit older than Esau. Or did it only seem so because all of them were missing some teeth? They wore the same clothes as he did, only dirtier.

"So where's the money, redhead?" demanded the man holding the bow.

"It's either here, at the bottom of my *simlah* pocket, or down there in the mud. I cannot feel anything with my fingers," said Esau. He invited one outlaw to come closer to the edge and looked down into the hole with him. He then took off his cloak and handed it to another. "Check it out yourself."

With the two robbers distracted, Esau skipped behind the man fumbling with the cloak. In the blink of an eye, he wrapped the *simlah* around the man's arms and shoved him onto the man still staring down below.

Both outlaws yelped and dropped into the pit, while Esau snatched a knife from the ground and threw it into the third one. The knife only nicked the target, but the bowman lost his balance, which allowed Esau to rush forward and punch him on the chin. The man collapsed and dropped the bow. Esau kicked him a few times, picked him up, and tossed him to join his comrades.

"See you later, morons."

***

After making it back home, Esau tried to wash the blood off the leather but could not. He smelled the aroma of the food being prepared in his brother Jacob's room next door, stuffed the trophy under his unmade bed, and stumbled towards the food. The blood would have to wait.

Jacob was cooking something red. Whatever it was, it would do.

"Give me some of that red, red stuff," Esau demanded, taking a whiff. "I am ready to die of hunger."

Stirring the food, Jacob cast a long disapproving look at his brother. "You don't know what this 'red stuff' is all about, do you? Do you even have a clue about what happened today?"

Hearing only silence, Jacob continued, "Our grandfather died. And where were you? Hunting, I presume." He pointed to Esau's torn and blood-covered clothes and straightened his own pristine white *simlah*.

Esau's mouth slackened. So, the old patriarch is dead at last, he thought. I expected him to live longer that 175, if he was so righteous. But anyway, it means that my fifteen years of pretending are now over. I'm free from under the old man's thumb! Maybe that's why I felt so liberated today and accomplished these two great things.

"Never mind where I was, just give me some of this red . . ."

"I cannot give it to you. This is a dish of red lentils, the traditional first meal of mourners. Cooking it for our father to comfort him," Jacob frowned, putting down the silver ladle.

"Lentils?" Esau's eyebrows shot up. "Why? There are so many things you could eat that do not require so much cooking."

"Lentils are round," explained Jacob in a patient voice, "and they represent the circle of mourning that comes around to everybody in the world. Lentils have no mouth, just as the mourners are silent. We've studied all this together, don't you remember?"

"Well, we've studied a lot of things. All those religious commandments . . . I don't know why we bothered, since we don't even have to observe them. Good thing I've skipped some of that." He took another whiff.

"Yes, the commandments will be given to our descendants centuries later, when they will become binding. And yes, we don't have to observe them yet, but it's the right thing to do."

"Oh, forget the lectures. Just give it to me! I'm exhausted! I cannot even lift my arms to hold a spoon! Pour it in my mouth!" Esau sat down on a bench and opened his mouth wide.

Jacob sprung back. "Esau, you are my twin and older brother," he said, pushing his words through a locked jaw and tensed lips. "But you are just a brute! Look at yourself sitting here with a mouth agape. And you and your progeny are supposed to become the heads of our clan when our father passes away? To offer sacrifices on behalf of all of us in the future, as we've studied with you? Oh, I forgot, you must have skipped that, too."

Esau closed his mouth and smiled. "Jacob, what's the problem? Am I too hungry for your taste?"

"Stop it! I'm talking about sacrifices—a serious business! That job will demand absolute perfection. As you should know, if the priest offers them while drunk or with his hair uncut for more than thirty days, he would incur a death penalty! And where is perfection in you?"

Jacob stood silent for a minute, flaring his nostrils, and resumed in a soft voice, "Esau, we have two options. You could wait until I'm done cooking this dish for our father, and I'll make you another one after that. Or, I could serve you this food right now—pour it down your throat, if you wish—but first you'd have to sell me your birthright! I'll give you all the gold I have in exchange."

"Birthright?" sneered Esau and glanced at the food once again. "What good is it to me? To offer some sacrifices all my life for the rest of you? Why? Are we all not going to die anyway, as our grandfather did? It's a silly symbol that's not real to me. What *is* real is my dying of hunger. Yeah, you can have the birthright . . . just don't forget the gold!"

Jacob beamed for an instant and erased the smile. "Brother, I'm glad you've agreed, but I know that you can change your mind at any time. Swear by our father's life that the birthright is now mine!"

"Fine, I swear, I swear," grumbled Esau, and they shook hands.

Jacob pulled out an ornate wooden chest hidden underneath his bed and retrieved the gold, showing Esau that none remained inside. They finalized the sale in the traditional fashion, by sitting down to eat. Esau polished off most of the lentils and the bread, chasing it down with Jacob's aged red wine. Having licked the bowl clean, he tapped at the fancy silver wine goblet, catching the last drops of wine.

He smirked, "How foolish can you be, my little brother, to give me all your gold and feeding me a good meal—for nothing, in exchange for some symbol! In truth, you've just relieved me of a boring chore I wouldn't want to do anyway. That's another great turn of events today!" Seeing Jacob's puzzled look, he added, "Never mind."

***

Later that day, Esau disappeared for a while to his favorite hideout, a cave at the base of a hill in the badlands outside Hebron. The rocky soil around the cave was so hard that nobody could track his footprints there. The cave contained everything he needed: a large leather flask with water, a blanket, and lots of food, mostly dried fish, insects, and pork. Esau knew that he was not supposed to eat many of these things, but who was going to check up on him?

***

General Ereechar lingered over the three bodies and shook his head. He turned to one of his commanders and ordered, "Bury them here—we can't carry them back. And remember: it was a hunting accident. A wild boar mauled the king while he was trying to protect a young injured soldier. Got it?" He took a deep breath and continued, "We are going to Hebron. First thing in the morning."

Chapter 3

All through her pregnancy Rebecca complained about discomfort, a constant commotion in her belly. She reasoned that she must have been carrying twins, or even more than two babies, because she always felt violent kicking at some odd times. She kept telling her husband that whenever she approached a house of study established by Abraham, the kicking was on one side; whenever she passed a temple of idolatry, she felt it on the other. It was as if her offspring wanted to get out and go there without waiting to be born.

What was happening? Her handmaidens did not have a clue, and Rebecca avoided the local soothsayers. She decided to visit the academy established by Noah's son Shem and Shem's grandson Eber, the most respected place where the ancient wisdom was preserved and taught. Perhaps old Shem could pray to ease her pain, Isaac suggested.

***

The academy, perched on top of a hill, dominated the area. It did not have a fence, and its doors were wide open. The simple whitewashed plaster walls were devoid of any decorations but were crack-free. Guardrails protected the edges of the flat roof, as they did in Isaac's house. Rebecca's two handmaidens helped her off the donkey equipped with a padded saddle, and she hobbled inside.

Her eyes narrowed from all the stark white; even the stone-paved floor, which lacked a single speck of dust, was pale. An old man with a long white beard dressed in a flawless robe of snow and gold came out to greet her with outstretched arms. His firm steps echoed through the empty hall.

"I am Shem," he announced, "I know why you are here, Rebecca. I have received a prophecy regarding you. Please come in!"

He invited the startled woman to sit on a plain but comfortable couch. After offering her water and swearing her to secrecy, he revealed the message: "You are carrying twins. They will be the forefathers of the two great nations that are destined to battle one another until the end of time."

"Two nations? And they have started fighting already? I knew there was a reason for my pain. But which one is more important? Which one will prevail?"

"They will alternate in greatness," Shem explained in a quiet voice, stroking his beard and looking down. "When one is raised high, the other will be cast low. But in the end, the older will serve the younger. This is all I can tell you. Please ask of me no more."

***

The midwife glanced at the bloody footstool and recoiled at the sight of the first twin. The baby was full of red hair—like he was wearing a dark orange cloak—and even had teeth! His parents named him Esau ("complete").

Even at the very beginning of his life, with his eyes still closed, Esau was fighting someone. Was he angry at his mother—or trying to prevent the birth of his brother? Neither the parents nor the midwife could understand how all this could be possible. Yet somehow the baby did manage to hurt Rebecca, and she could bear no more children afterwards.

The second baby that emerged looked normal, but he was grasping Esau's heel, which also surprised his parents. They named him Jacob ("the heel").

***

Rebecca stomped into her husband's room, "We need to talk!"

Isaac got up from his studies, gave her a wide smile, and invited her to sit on a bench with a padded blue cover. He sat down, too.

"Rebecca, by the look on your face it's about him again? What has he done now?"

"I don't know, but the king's people were asking for him earlier, when you were away. So, he must have done something! And I find it more and more difficult to deal with him and his hot temper." She took a sharp breath.

"I'm sorry it hurts you, my dear, but he is just a boy! Maybe he did something silly. That's the way he is . . . You know we've done all we could to prod him toward the way of the righteous," said Isaac, flinging his arms open.

"I know, I know. The boys have studied under you and your father. Who could've asked for better teachers? Then we've sent them both to a house of Abrahamic learning."

"Yes, the only place other than the Shem and Eber where . . ."

"Well, it did work for a while, I grant you that. But after they turned thirteen, everything changed. Jacob is a gentle and diligent boy, while Esau is turning into a coarse and wicked man. We can't keep ignoring this any longer—don't you see?"

"But Esau is still studying, isn't he?"

"Who knows. He uses every opportunity to slink away and go out into the field—and then lies about it. And I can't believe how clever and convincing his lies and excuses are!"

"Like what?"

"See, you haven't heard." Her eyes sparkled. "One day, I was told, he came to the study hall covered in blood and explained that he had fought off a robber on the road to school. They sent him back home to clean up and get bandaged. He promptly washed off the blood of a rabbit and escaped to hunt—he later admitted to that. Meanwhile, the other students were looking over their shoulders for weeks on their way to school. Another time he said that you had stumbled and fallen, and that he needed to watch over you. He was excused again, and off to the field he went."

"Rebecca, I know how clever he is. I've heard a few stories myself. Everybody knows about his golden tongue that can convince anyone of just about anything."

"Anyone?"

"Well, take our Hebron judge. I was told he loves our son's ability to extract truth from people. When a case seems hopeless, the judge invites him to question the litigants. Esau always comes up with a way to trick the guilty man into confessing."

"Hmm . . . Anything recent?"

"A few months ago, the judge requested that Esau help get a confession from an accused murderer who claimed innocence. Esau asked the suspect not whether he had killed anyone but what weapon he had used, and listed some choices. The man was taken aback, lost his nerve, and admitted to the murder. And just a couple of weeks ago, Esau made a thief confess. He did it by asking about his accomplices, rather than whether he himself had stolen anything. The man blurted out the name of his partner and thus incriminated himself."

"So, he's even smarter than I thought," Rebecca clenched her teeth and shot glances around the room.

"And there must be a reason Esau was born with this brilliant mind. Maybe he has his own lengthy path toward righteousness. If we are too harsh with him, we might scare him off that path for good." Isaac tilted his head.

"You really believe that?"

"Rebecca, may I remind you of Ishmael, my own older brother? Was Ishmael not a wild man in his youth, just like Esau? Was he not a hunter, a bandit, a degenerate even, a shame on the house of Abraham? And yet he later repented from his evil ways."

Rebecca paused and breathed out, "There's something else."

"What?"

"His new hunting clothes. I asked where he got them from, and he said he bought them at the market."

"And you didn't believe him, I take it. Why not?"

"Well, have you looked at them? They are amazing. I've never seen even kings wearing attire like this. Forget about buying it at the market. All they have there is simple garb like woolen cloaks, tunics and head scarves. I shop there; you don't! Everyone keeps asking who made that tunic."

Isaac remained silent, as Rebecca continued, "Then there are those blood stains . . . not on the sleeves but around the neck, as if a man was ritually slaughtered wearing these garments. Creepy."

Isaac sighed and tightened his lips. "I know of only one man who wore such clothes—King Nimrod. Wasn't he recently found dead not far from here? People said it was a hunting accident. You think it's true?"

"No. I've heard that two shepherds had seen a red-haired man carrying some blood-stained leather clothes in the desert. Do you know of any redheads other than Esau? He's nicknamed Edom—red—for this very reason! But why would he do that? How *could* he do that?"

"I don't know, but . . ."

Just then Esau walked in, dressed in his hunting leather, carrying a limp fawn on his shoulder. Isaac and Rebecca sat still, their eyes not leaving him for a second.

At long last Rebecca uttered, "Esau, where have you been? The king's guards were looking for you."

"Which king's guards, mother?"

"Son, stop it! How many kings do we have? The King of Hebron, of course!"

"I don't know why they would . . ."

All of a sudden Rebecca screamed and pointed to her husband's feet. Isaac looked down. A large black desert cobra was coiled on the mud floor, rearing its head toward him.

Rebecca gasped, "No!"

The snake waited to strike, as if deliberating Isaac's fate. Esau pulled out his sword, and the cobra turned its head. He glowered back, waited for a short time, and sheathed the sword.

Rebecca panted, "Why?"

Esau howled, "Out! Out, you snake! Out!"

The serpent slithered in his direction, shuffling across the floor, stopping to hiss and bob its head. Esau stood still in silence, watching the black menace circling around his legs, rubbing its scales against the side of his sandals, and flicking its forked tongue along the hem of his tunic. The cobra gave him one last hiss and wriggled out the front door.

The three of them exhaled and gazed at one another. Esau left without saying a word, his forehead covered in beads of sweat.

Rebecca wheezed, "What was that? I thought the wild animals were not supposed to attack the righteous."

"I thought so too," echoed Isaac. "Maybe I'm not so righteous—or maybe we just needed to see this before we continued our conversation."

"What do you mean?"

Isaac got up, came closer, covered her hand with his, and said, "There is another reason to be extra patient with him. I've always sensed that Esau had this immense spiritual strength. It's wild, primal, but it exceeds mine and Jacob's! And I've had a revelation that confirmed my hunch."

"What?"

"It's true. He possesses a very, very rare gift. His soul is not of this world but of the older, mightier world that preceded ours. That world collapsed because it could not sustain the intensity of its own spiritual light. But some of its fragments remain embedded in our world, and Esau is one of them."

"Whoa . . . Are you saying he is some kind of angel in disguise?"

"No, no. I said that he has more energy of spirit than anyone else. Anyone! But his energy is raw, untamed—like that of a wild stallion. If it could be harnessed to good ends, he would achieve what is impossible even for the most virtuous. He would become the greatest spiritual beacon of all time! Understand now? Do you think any of us could have done what he just did?"

"I don't know who he is or who he'll become," Rebecca yanked back her hand, "but I do know that he isn't studying—he is just fooling you."

"Fooling me how?"

"Well, when he returns home from school, you always question him on what he has learned that day, right? But how can you be sure that he isn't recalling a snippet of something he picked up outside the study hall?"

Isaac did not say a word, looking sideways.

"I'll tell you more," she continued, pulling on a loose thread of his robe. "He keeps asking you questions about some arcane details of religious observances, such as tithing, yes?"

"Yes, a separation of one-tenth of the increase in someone's agricultural wealth. It has to be given to the poor or to the priests. What about it?"

"I once overheard him asking you whether a person was obligated to separate one-tenth of salt, or of straw, as a tithe. Even I know that it isn't needed for those trivial items. But he asked you, what about the items that were enhanced by salt and straw? The value of salted food or of the bricks laid in mortar that contained straw is not trivial. Should the value of salt or straw be computed based on their worth alone or on the worth of the items they enhance?"

"Yes, it was a good question." A brief smile crossed Isaac's face.

"You see? To you, such questions show a great mind striving to learn. To me, he's just trying to conceal his cunning nature. He also keeps feeding you the savory stew you like so much, to endear him to you even more!"

Little did she know how Esau's savory stew would help change the lives of both her sons forever.

***

Esau did not get far from home when he ran into the king's patrol squad. Six armed guards on foot.

The leader yelped, "It's him!" and the guards surrounded Esau.

He looked this way and that—there was nowhere to run. Spears were facing him on all sides.

CHAPTER 4

Esau had never been inside the king's palace, and he kept gazing at high ceilings, wall tapestries, and elaborate plaster carvings. One day I'll live in a home like this, he decided.

Esau noted with satisfaction that the king was not much older than he was and that the exquisite linen robe and gold jewelry could not obscure his small frame. The contrast with two hulking guards who towered over the throne was amusing.

The king addressed his kneeling prisoner, "Esau, the Babylonians have visited us asking for you. What have you done to offend them? Were you involved in any way in the unfortunate death of King Nimrod, perhaps?"

"No, your majesty. How could I? I don't know what they want with me."

The king averted his eyes away from Esau's stare and mumbled, "We have to . . . eh . . . work with them. You'll be held in my palace until they arrive to question you."

"But your majesty, I'd wait here for weeks! Could I perhaps be kept at home under guard until they come?"

"No! Would you prefer to be shipped to Babylon? That's what they demanded! It took us much effort to make them relent. Take him away!" the king ordered, straightening his robe. "Oh, wait!" he said when Esau was at the door.

"Your majesty?"

"What's the story with Abraham and Nimrod? They said you were after your grandfather."

"Yes, the two of them had a history. My grandfather was born in Ur of the Chaldees, in Nimrod's kingdom. When he was a young boy, he argued against worshipping idols. Nimrod threw him into a fiery furnace to punish him."

"But Abraham obviously didn't die there?"

"Right, he emerged unscathed from the furnace. This miracle had made him into a legend and brought a multitude of followers to him. Quite a few of them followed him here."

"I know that. Go!" The king sunk deep into his throne and crossed his arms.

***

Esau examined his very first jail cell, puzzling over the notes carved into the wall stucco. The dirty mud floor and the wooden bed reeked; there were no windows, only a door with bronze bars and a heavy lock. He sighed. At least he had plenty of time to think.

When his parents came to visit him later in the day, he asked them to bring him a change of clothes and hide his leather garments. They obliged.

***

A month later the palace guards roused Esau and brought him upstairs to a large room filled with soldiers and servants. A heavyset middle-aged man wearing a golden crown and a purple robe decorated with sparkling stones sat on a massive armchair, flanked by the guards in the familiar red uniforms. The King of Hebron sat to the side. Another contrast, Esau mused.

"I am Ereechar, the new King of Babylon," a thundering voice announced. "Get up and come closer."

Esau bowed his head and approached in silence.

"We understand that you might know something about the heroic death of King Nimrod. Do you?"

"I'm sorry I don't, your majesty."

"Don't lie to us!" the king's voice ruffled his curly black beard. "People saw you carrying his leather garments and later wearing them."

Esau glanced around the room. The animal heads mounted on the walls stared at him. I might join your company soon, he thought. There's no way out of this one.

"I have to confess my sins to your majesty," Esau muttered. "I was hunting in the wilderness and came across three slain men. I don't know how they died. I was fascinated by the leather garments on one of the bodies and took them. I didn't know it was King Nimrod . . ."

"You didn't, huh?" the Babylonian roared, and the rest of the room joined in laughter. Esau prepared for the worst.

"I'll tell you what," said the king, still grinning. "Let's say I believe you. You had neither a motive nor ability to kill them. It was a hunting accident."

"Thank you, your majesty," Esau squeezed out, wondering what kind of a snare awaited. He looked up into the king's brown eyes capped by shaggy eyebrows. The eyes did not smile, even as the mouth did.

"You are still a thief, and you deserve to be punished. But I am a merciful ruler, and you could escape with your skin if you give us something in return."

"What could I possibly give your majesty?"

"Your service. We'll pardon you if you join our army as an officer. Otherwise . . ."

Esau prostrated himself on the stone floor. "Thank you, your majesty. Your mercy knows no bounds. But if it pleases you, may I add a condition to your generous offer?"

"What? You? A condition?" The king's jaw dropped.

"Yes, your majesty. Just a one-year deferment to complete my religious studies. I would be honored to be of service then—I'm making a solemn pledge to do." Esau closed his eyes.

The Babylonian sat blinking for a few moments and started laughing again. "Religious studies? That's a new one!" he bellowed.

"Please, your majesty!" Esau prostrated himself again. "I owe all my skills to those studies. I was nobody before I started them. I will be stronger and of much more use to you when I'm finished. One year is all I ask." He peeked up.

King Ereechar turned to his men and roared, "You know what? I like this redhead's audacity! We need more men like him. Maybe he'll become as great as his grandfather."

He turned back to Esau, "Fine! I'll give you a year, but after that, you're mine! Or you're dead. Understand? Just remember, you can't hide from us. And bring me back Nimrod's clothes. Out!"

After Esau left, the king said to his advisors, without as much as a glance toward the ruler of Hebron, "He didn't even take the golden helmet! The jewels on that helmet alone are worth more than this entire wretched city! He must have known he couldn't sell such gems without us finding out. A smart young man!"

***

The first thing Esau did upon returning home was to don his leather tunic under his *simlah* cloak. There is no way the king gets it back, he decided. He told his parents about the deal he had struck with the Babylonian and left for some fresh air. He missed it so much! But instead of going hunting, which lost all the fun since he started wearing his new clothes, Esau went to Hebron market.

Strolling about, Esau came up to a stall where bronze vessels were sold and observed the merchant's movements out of the corner of his eye. After some time, he asked the trader to show him a vase from the back and grabbed a small pitcher from the rug-covered wooden display. Hiding it in his cloak, Esau thanked the merchant and ambled away.

He noticed another young man who didn't seem to belong in the crowd of shoppers. Tall, strapping, and handsome, he reminded Esau of himself. Following the lad, Esau saw him grab a bronze knife when the merchant wasn't looking and gliding away, shielding the prize with the sleeves of his cloak. A fellow thief!

Esau trailed the young man until he left the market, stepped into a path between two mud-brick houses and disappeared. When Esau turned to leave, he recoiled at the sight of the youth blocking his exit and extending a knife to his face.

"Why are you following me?"

"Easy, easy! Just wanted to know where you'd go with that knife you took."

"What knife?"

"The one you're holding, with a decorated bone handle! But don't worry, I am a thief like you!" Esau said with a broad smile, extending his arms with open palms.

The lad dithered a bit but put the knife away. The two of them examined each other with the hands on their hips.

"Look," said Esau, chewing on the lower lip, "I replaced my first heavy *simlah*, which got ripped in a fight, with this one. It's made of the thinnest wool fabric I could find, to move around faster. I also had the front of it redone by adding wide folds and a large interior pouch. A much better place to keep the stuff you take and the weapons, too. Here!" He pulled out the pitcher.

"Nice. But aren't you cold in this thing at night?"

"Nah. I still have a tunic underneath, like everybody else, and I just don't get too cold."

The lad tilted his head back and smiled, "I am Ardon."

"Esau. Some people call me Edom."

"So, Esau, what do you do with the stuff you take? Surely you can't hope to resell it in the same market! And the nearest other market is in Be'er Sheva, a day's walk."

"Doing it for fun. Relieves the boredom. And you?"

"Me too."

"So, are you a Hittite, like most people here?"

"Yeah. And you?"

"I'm not sure where I belong," muttered Esau. He looked down. "Listen, let's work together. It would be much easier if one of us distracts the merchant, while the other grabs the stuff."

***

After the two of them grew tired of hoarding things, they decided to try something different. Walking apart, they trailed an old man who was careless enough to expose much gold in his money bag. Ardon tripped him up in a less-crowded area of the market, and both of them rushed to help the man to his feet.

As Ardon wrapped his arms around the victim and pretended to struggle lifting him up, Esau cut off the money bag.

By the time the man realized the money was missing, they were gone.

This was their biggest take yet, they agreed, but they soon discovered that they did not have the market to themselves. In front of their eyes a boy snatched some money from a shopper's hand and dashed away.

The little thief managed to outrun the shopper but not them. Esau grabbed him by the throat and pinned him against a large fig tree, drilling into his eyes with an unblinking glare.

The boy, a full head shorter than Esau and Ardon, struggled to get away but couldn't. He took the money out of his tattered shawl and threw it on the ground, but Esau did not fall for that ruse. Ardon picked up the silver.

"What do you want from me?" wheezed the boy, his eyes darting to the sides.

"That was a risky trick you did," replied Esau. "You're going to get caught one of these days. You'll do better with us."

He removed his hand. The boy tried to sprint away, but Esau grabbed him and yelled, "Stop! Think! Think!"

The boy raised his eyes at Esau from under his forehead and pushed back his straight black hair. "What would you want me do?"

"We'll think of something. Do you want to go with us or not?"

The boy nodded, and Ardon asked, "What's your name?"

"Dekel."

"We are Ardon and Esau."

Looking at the boy's rags and his dirty face, Esau asked, "Have a place to stay?"

"No."

"Then the first thing we need to do is to get a tent for you," said Esau. He did not feel like inviting this youngster—or Ardon, for that matter—into his private cave. "Here's how we are going to do it."

***

As the sun was reluctantly leaving the sky, the last shoppers hurried to get home, and the merchants were busy packing their wares. The three young men watched a trader roll up the black goat skins around the poles and place them in a donkey-driven wagon. He was the only one selling the tents, since most families made their own.

They followed the trader to his home, also a black goat-skin tent, where he left the rolled-up skins in the wagon and took the donkey inside. The adventurers waited in darkness until snoring started to resonate in the calmness of the night.

"The tent is very heavy and difficult to move in the dark," whispered Esau, "so let's drag it away and hide it for now."

They pulled the skins off the wagon and chuckled. That was easy! But then Dekel stumbled over one of the rolls and fell, shrieking and cursing in the process. Everyone halted, and a few minutes crawled by. Nobody came out of the merchant's tent, and they carried away the loot.

"How are we going to find our way back in the dark?" squealed Dekel.

"Boys, if you plan to lead this life of ours, you'd better learn to walk at night. The darkness is our friend, right?" His two companions followed Esau without saying a word.

Suddenly, Dekel shrieked, "Ahh! My foot!"

"Quiet! What happened?" asked Esau.

"I broke my ankle, or something," sobbed the boy.

This changed things. Esau couldn't leave Dekel there; he had no choice but to allow his new buddies to share his hideout, which happened to be nearby. With Ardon's help, Esau carried Dekel to the cave. There wasn't anything valuable there anyway, Esau consoled himself.

Once inside, he lit a fire and some candles. He took a closer look at Dekel's foot: it was bruised and swollen. Esau ran his hands all around it, and Dekel did not scream.

"Your foot isn't broken," concluded Esau in a confident voice, patting Dekel on the shoulder. "Let's bandage it, and you rest here for a few days. Try not to step on it—use this stick as a crutch. You'll be fine in no time. For now, sleep near the entrance, to shorten your trips outside."

"Thanks! But may I stay here with you after I get better?" Dekel stopped sobbing.

"Yeah—for a while. Just be careful not to have people follow you here."

"Of course not, and I won't be much of a burden. But you'll be here with me, right?"

"No, I won't. I have a proper home in the city."

Nobody wanted to sleep. Ardon and Dekel kept asking Esau about his life. To change the topic, he said, "Well, if you want, I can teach you how to walk in total darkness."

"Sure. How?" asked his companions.

"When you walk outside at night, you take a stick, a tree branch or anything like that and sweep the ground in front with it. If you've ever seen a blind man walking with a cane probing the ground—that's how you walk."

"So you'd scare away any snakes and scorpions?" asked Dekel.

"Yeah. Also, you don't lift your feet. You shuffle them forward and then to the side, kind of like you do with the stick. And you softly step on your toes first and only then you shift your weight on the heels."

"Why?"

"So that you don't stub your toe and don't step into a hole, even if your stick missed it. And if you do hit a rock or a tree root, you'd be touching it with your toes first and have a chance to stop."

"But you could still run into a tree branch, or something above ground," objected Ardon.

"Yes, you could, but I'm not finished. You also sweep the space in front of you with your hand, using the same motion as with your stick and feet. Again, groping like that would allow you to touch any obstacle rather than hitting it."

"That would be a slow walk," murmured Dekel.

"Sure. But you'd avoid the accidents like the one you just had."

"What about walking inside when you get up at night?"

"Dekel, you could walk like this anywhere—even in a house full of furniture, if you've ever been to one. You'd never bruise your shin on a bench again."

"Esau, how do you know this at your age? Is your father a soldier?" asked Ardon.

"No, but he is a holy man," answered Esau. "And I just pick up things."

"It seems you can also see in the dark," said Dekel.

"Well, better than most people."

"Like an animal?"

"Yeah, like an animal."

***

A loud shriek woke up Esau. He peered into the shadows behind the flickering fire and made out Dekel's figure at the entrance. The boy was calling for him, pointing outside.

Esau got up and lit a candle. He stopped cold when he saw glowing eyes and heard the howls.

"Are these wolves?" Dekel trembled. "All around us?"

"Yeah, looks like a pack of evening wolves," said Esau.

"What are we going to do?" Dekel sobbed. "So many of them!"

"Relax!" ordered Esau. "I'm dressed for it."

"What?"

"Watch!" Esau stepped outside, spread out his hands, and barked, "Vanish, wolves! Vanish!"

But the fiery eyes only got closer, and Esau could now detect the hazy silhouettes surrounding the cave. He stood with outstretched arms, as if trying to push the beasts away.

One wolf came up so close that Esau could smell its foul breath, hear its muted growl, and see the twinkles on its snarling teeth. I guess my clothes aren't working on them, he thought. He felt the handle of his sword, but with Dekel clinging to his side and Ardon clutching a dagger behind him, there was little room to maneuver.

Esau took a deep breath and . . . the predators halted and backed away, still snarling. Soon they blended back into the emptiness, allowing the cicadas to take over the night.

The shaken young men stoked the fire and sat around, staring at one another.

"What happened? Why did they leave?" asked Ardon.

Esau did not answer.

"They listened to you! They did!" cried Dekel. "I know they did! Tell us why! Tell us!"

"Fine," said Esau after enduring endless badgering. "You are my friends, and you deserve to know. But not a word about it to anyone else! Swear to me!" They swore and looked at him with anticipation.

"See this leather tunic under my *simlah*? It's a special garment that makes animals listen to me when I'm wearing it."

"But . . . how? Where did you get it? Who made it?" wailed Dekel.

"Ever heard of King Nimrod and his hunting clothes?"

"No."

"Then I'll tell you. According to the legend, God Himself had made these clothes for Adam in the Garden of Eden. They fit to perfection anyone who puts them on." He took off his *simlah* cloak to demonstrate—there was not a wrinkle in the leather. "But even a bigger miracle is that their owner can attract and control all animals, as I can do now. Maybe even people, I'm not sure yet."

"So how did the king get them?"

"I've heard that after Adam's death, the clothes were cherished and handed down from father to son. Ten generations after Adam they found their way to Noah. You know about Noah and the ark he was building to survive the upcoming flood, right?" Ardon and Dekel nodded.

"Noah brought the clothes into the ark and never left them out of sight. But after the year-long flood ended, he and his family had to help hundreds of animals disembark. In the chaos, he lost track of the leather, and his son Ham stole it from under his nose. My kind of guy!" He smirked. "Then Ham hid the treasure for many years, until he gave it in secret to his son Cush, who later passed it on to his own son Amraphel."

"But how does Nimrod fit into all this?" asked Dekel.

"Hold on. Nimrod is just a title, Amraphel's title. He's the one who started wearing Adam's clothes again. And as long as he was wearing them, his power over people knew no limit. He inspired them to build the Tower of Babel—remember that one? In the process, he earned the title of Nimrod. It means the 'Mighty Hunter before the Lord,' that is, a skillful trapper of minds and a mighty rebel against God."

"And then Nimrod became a king?"

"Yeah, after the Almighty intervened and scattered the Tower's builders, they formed separate nations. They ended up going to war with each other, and Nimrod's people prevailed. They proclaimed him a king—the first king in history!"

"And all that because of his clothes?"

"Yes. I'm sure any hunter, leader, or general could only dream about owning them."

"And now you do. But how could you possibly have gotten these garments? Did you have to fight for them? Steal them?" Dekel's eyes were all whites.

"Well, that's another story. I think we've had enough for today."

Esau went back to sleep, leaving his friends bewildered.

Chapter 5

Esau and his companions reclined in the cave after a good dinner. Esau scooped up and released a handful of dust and asked, "Why are we wasting our time at the market, when the real treasure is out there?"

As they turned toward him, he continued, "Look, we live along the Hill Road, which goes through the crests of the mountains. Caravans pass by every day. I hear this road isn't as busy as the Coastal Route or the King's Highway, but it's right here, in front of us."

"Are we going to become highway robbers now?" mumbled Dekel, ruffling his hair.

"And kill people? The caravans have armed guards!" added Ardon.

They are just boys, Esau smiled to himself. Killing is easy! They still don't know how Nimrod died.

"Don't be afraid. It's not that different from what we've been doing. Let's say we distract the guards, grab the stuff and disappear. Just like you grabbed the money off that man's hand when we first met you. Umm?" Esau gave Dekel a long stare.

"They'll catch us!" Dekel shivered.

"Not if we outrun them. These caravans travel for months at a time, and the guards go on foot or ride donkeys or camels. If we had good horses, we'd get away."

"Esau, look at us—are we bandits?" Dekel's voice was louder now. "You've been caring for me all this time, bringing me food and water, and keeping me company in this cave. But now you want me to risk my life? For what? Don't we have enough fun now?"

"Dekel, since when have you gotten so fearful?"

"I'm not afraid!"

"Esau, are you saying we need horses to do it?" Ardon jumped in. "Are horses faster than camels? And is getting them worth the trouble? There are plenty of camels around."

"For a short while and on some types of ground, yeah, horses are faster."

"But where would we get them? Aren't they bred in Egypt?" Ardon asked.

"Yes, the Egyptians breed them, and the Hittite traders bring them up north for resale. They use the Coastal Route, not our Hill Road, because horses need to travel on a flat plain. All we have to do is to steal some."

***

After trudging through a desert road to Ashkelon, the three adventurers spent much of the next day observing the Coastal Route. Most caravans had hundreds of donkeys tethered to one another, carrying all sorts of loads. The weary animals dragged along much slower than men on foot. The security guards indeed rode camels or walked; many of them were Egyptians, easily identified by their dark skin, shaved heads, and the black paint around the eyes.

Later in the day the companions eavesdropped on the conversations at a local tavern and chatted up the traders and the tavern owner, an attractive middle-aged woman with a ready smile and sharp eyes. They learned that the caravans traveling from Egypt carried grain, papyrus, aged wine, lentils—and gold. They also learned that a caravan of horses would pass by the next day and that it normally stopped overnight near Ashdod, the next city to the north.

The following morning the aspiring horse thieves found a shady spot under a grove of acacia trees and waited for the caravan. Here it was!

No fewer than a hundred horses were tied to one another with leather cords; they were led by traders accompanied by at least a score of guards on camels. The three companions followed the caravan until it arrived at an inn located outside the cream-colored walls of Ashdod.

***

The tavern owner put down the dirty dishes and summoned her youngest son.

"Follow these three young men, keeping some distance away. You've met Haydar, right? If you see them snooping around his caravan, tell him—you'll make us some money."

The boy left in haste and soon caught up with Esau and his men. He followed them until they turned off the road behind the horse caravan. His mother was right, as usual.

***

When in Ashdod, Haydar always stayed at the same sprawling inn, where he and his men could count on a good meal and a strong drink. Instead of untying the horses in the evening and retying them in the morning, he preferred to arrange them in a spiral, tied to one another overnight. Other than saving time, this kept the animals from wandering away in the dark.

It was getting late, and the guards herded the horses inside the corral. As Haydar dug into a dish of lentils and goat meat, a familiar-looking boy came up to him. The boy straightened his dusty shawl, bowed, and introduced himself.

"Sir, back in Ashkelon, we saw three men who seemed interested in stealing horses, and they followed you here." The boy glanced at Haydar's food.

"Show them to me and I will give you the reward," Haydar croaked, holding the fork with a chunk of food in it.

"Yes, my lord. I'll be nearby."

Without saying anything else, Haydar turned away and resumed his champing. The boy kept his eyes on the food for a while.

The guards locked the gates of the corral, and the three of them that remained outside lit the fires all around the fence. The boy was hiding behind a large fig tree, peering into the darkness beyond the flames, when he gasped.

"Looking for us? We saw you following us on that donkey," scowled Esau, pressing the knife against the boy's throat.

"I . . . I wasn't!"

"No? Then what are you doing here?" The boy was silent, trying to bite his lips, but Esau still noticed their tremble.

"Is there a reward for informing on us?"

"Y-yes."

"Hmm . . ." Esau deliberated for an instant. "Here is what I want you to do. If you help us, you'll return home in one piece, maybe even get that reward. If you don't, we'll burn down your smiley mother's tavern and kill all of you. Understand?"

With the eyes ready to pop off his face, the boy nodded, being careful not to cut his own throat in the process. The thieves left the would-be spy and crept closer to the corral.

"Do horses sleep standing up?" whispered Dekel.

"Indeed they do," said Esau.

"But how is this possible? I cannot sleep standing up."

"Because you are not a horse, although you act like one sometimes. Yes, horses can lock their legs in place and sleep upright. Go now!"

Dekel skulked to the gate and smashed the crude lock with a shovel they had found. After a few tries, he broke the lock and took off before the startled guards could react.

The innkeeper's boy sprinted towards them, yelling, "I saw him running over there!"

Two guards took off in the direction he was pointing, leaving the third one with the horses. The man was peering into the darkness in their wake.

Esau tiptoed behind the guard and hit him on the head with a rock. The man was still standing, and Esau hit him harder. He then cut the leather cord separating the first six horses from the rest and led them out. Rudely awakened, the horses required some persuasion, which Esau supplied in abundance.

The thieves disappeared into the night, stopping only to muzzle the horses. Esau was leading the way in the dark through rocky streets with his sweeping groping motions. It got easier once they reached the main road.

***

Early next morning the King of Ashdod was looking at the sagging tapestries on the walls of his palace past a kneeling Egyptian visitor.

"Your majesty, last night some thieves stole six of my horses from a locked corral outside the city. They used a local youth to divert our attention. If it pleases the king, may a posse be formed to go after them?"

"And why should we do this? You've chosen to stay outside Ashdod's walls to avoid paying our caravan taxes. You Egyptians are cheap," thundered the king, examining the cowering sweaty figure in front of him.

"Let me prove it otherwise, your majesty. I will pay five silver shekels for each horse returned to me."

The king stared at the trader without saying anything, tapping his swollen fingers on the carved arm of his chair. Seconds dragged by.

"I meant, ten silver shekels per horse," hastened Haydar, but the king did not utter a word. "Please . . . I don't have any more money, and I'd be in trouble if I arrived without these horses that were paid for. Please . . ."

The king looked up at the ceiling, flicked his fingers to the servants swaying the ostrich-feather fans around him, and summoned the commander of his army. As the stout general waddled in, the king said, "Send a squad of your cavalry after the thieves who stole the horses from my friend Haydar the Egyptian. Bring the thieves and the horses to me."

"Yes, your majesty. But one of the men from the squad has sent a message this morning, begging to allow him to be late. His wife is having a baby." The general shrugged.

"Then let him catch up with the five of them later. It will take your people some time to figure out which way the thieves went, anyway. But once you do, they should be easy to find. There aren't too many places to hide in the desert."

Chapter 6

Esau and his fellow thieves were smiling and joking about their perfect heist. Since none of them could ride a horse, they plodded on foot, leading two animals each. They retreated off the road anytime they noticed other travelers, which required stepping with care between pits, rocks, and thistles.

As they approached Lachish, they saw five mounted soldiers clad in leather armor galloping behind. The young men got off the road again, expecting the horsemen to pass by, but the soldiers followed them.

"Keep calm!" said Esau through gritted teeth, putting his arm on Dekel's shoulders. "We bought these horses for our father, remember?"

The riders stood in a perfect line among sparse wormwood shrubs, their spears extended toward the youths. The commander glanced at the six horses without saddles and grinned, "Walking along with the stolen horses! That's some thieves!"

"Who are you?" demanded Esau, frowning.

"The royal guards of the King of Ashdod! And you, scum?"

"We are . . . from Lachish. Just bought these horses for our . . ."

"Bought?! Do you have a bill of sale then?" The guards chortled.

Esau hissed, "Yes, we do have it," standing with his feet spread apart and his head kept high, as if defending the desert behind him.

"Then show it to me," the commander exclaimed, still grinning. "Come over here!"

Ardon and Dekel stood on wooden legs, as Esau came closer to the commander and started searching the front of his cloak. The other horsemen surrounded Esau, spears at the ready.

"Look deeper, perhaps it's fallen inside your underwear!" yelled one of them.

Esau shrugged his shoulders, raised his hands palms up, and gave the guards a broad smile. They burst out laughing. While they were rocking in their saddles, Esau yanked out a sword, rushed forward, and struck the commander on a side of the knee.

The man screamed and tumbled off the horse, his foot caught in the stirrup. He thrashed about, screaming and kicking up dust.

With a backhand strike, Esau hit the leg of the horseman closest to him, who flung back, lost his weapon, and slid to the ground. As the guard moaned in pain, Esau grabbed the reins of his horse and with both hands thrust it toward the third trooper.

The horses collided but didn't topple; they swung around, which exposed the back of the third guard to Esau's strike. The man spread his arms and fell backwards, losing both the reins and the spear; his horse galloped a few paces away.

The two remaining soldiers were now facing Esau, standing side by side. The rider on the left threw his spear at the young thief, who managed to rotate his body and evade it.

The guard then pulled out his sword and nudged his horse toward Esau, who skipped to the right and then forward, ducking under the horse of the other guard. As he did so, he ripped into the rear leg of the horse and so toppled both the horse and its rider, but in the process the foot of the falling man hit Esau on the back. Esau fell to the ground face down, and the sword slipped from his hand.

He jumped up, the sand still on his face, only to find the remaining horseman holding a sword to his chest. Hemmed in by the fallen horse and the guard struggling behind him, Esau realized he could not evade the attack—and he could not deflect the strike without a weapon. His legs refused to move. Was it the end?

But the rider stalled and dropped the sword. His eyes widened, and he fell forward, a glistening knife in his back. Behind him stood Ardon.

Cringing and cursing, the three companions finished off the wounded and looked at one another.

"How did you do this?" Dekel asked.

"I have a gift," breathed out Esau. He turned to Ardon, "Thank you, brother—you saved my life!"

"And you saved ours. We'd all be hanging if they arrested us."

"True." Esau paused to catch his breath. "But there is no turning back from this life now, do we agree?" Ardon and Dekel grimaced but nodded.

"But on the bright side, this is an unexpected bounty," puffed Esau. "Take their weapons, armor, money, and the horses that aren't injured—and let's get moving! Thanks to them, we are well-equipped now."

"Esau, look!" screeched Dekel.

Another equestrian was hurrying toward them, dressed in the same uniform as the other five. He halted his horse, glanced at the carnage, and turned around.

As he galloped away, Esau wished he had a bow and arrow in his hands—or at least could ride a horse as well as the man disappearing into the dust.

***

The three outlaws practiced riding horses and working with their new weapons. After a taste of trying to ride sitting on the horse's spine, Esau made a simple cushioned saddle for each of them out of thick blankets. They kept the horses in a paddock, which they built a few bowshots away from the cave. Esau did not want the horses to be too close, in case someone stumbled upon them and then found their hideout, but he still needed the corral to be visible from the cave. They attached a tablet to its gates with a warning:

These horses are in quarantine, suspected of a contagious plague. Do not touch them if you want to live.

After a few weeks of practice, Esau told his fellows, "I think we are comfortable riding now. Time to take the next step. Remember, we need money, not merchandise. We have enough of that in the cave—there's little space left here." Esau kicked over a fancy copper pot.

"Stealing money might not be easy," mumbled Ardon, putting the pot back. "From what I've heard, merchants like to sell one set of things and buy something else with the proceeds—the stuff they could sell back home. They never seem to carry much money."

"Makes sense," agreed Esau and looked outside. "Then we should find out more about this trading business. Meanwhile, there are plenty of travelers passing by, and they must carry at least some money. Let's start with the easy work."

***

The new bandits practiced robbing travelers in the desert until they felt comfortable enough to handle caravans. They spent days hiding in the hills above the Hill Road, trying to figure out what the passing caravans carried and where the valuables might be hidden. The caravans were smaller than those along the Coastal Route, yet protected the same way. Each one had at least six guards; one was riding in front, one in the rear, and four in the middle, two on each side. Scores of guards accompanied some larger caravans.

Esau decided on a trial raid along the part of the road that crossed over a *wadi*, a seasonal stream of water. It was summer, and the soil in the *wadi* turned to slick, dried mud. As Esau explained, horses rode better than camels on such smooth surfaces, while camels' paws provided better traction on sand.

On the day of their first caravan job, Ardon pointed to a caravan with scores of donkeys loaded with compact bags but with only six guards on camels. Esau nodded.

A *sudra* covering much of his face, Ardon rode up to the right side of the caravan near the front. Without dismounting, he struck one of the donkeys on the back of its neck with a sword. The donkey sagged, and the tethered animals stopped. Ardon rode out into the *wadi*, with the two guards from the right side and the front guard trailing him.

Once the three guards left, Esau and Dekel confronted the caravan's leader and the two other merchants traveling in front. The startled traders did not resist when the attackers motioned them to dismount, grabbed the two bags that were on the leader's donkey and the merchants' money bags, and rode away in haste. The remaining three guards went after them.

As Esau had expected, he and Dekel were able to ride faster than their pursuers—until Dekel's horse stumbled on a rock and threw him off. Esau cursed, returned to Dekel's horse and grabbed its reins. Seeing that his companion was not seriously injured, Esau dismounted, still preferring to fight on the ground, and waited behind his horse; limping Dekel soon followed behind his.

Two spear-wielding guards attempted to outflank Esau and Dekel, while the third stood facing them. Esau shoved the stolen bag off his horse and grabbed the seat. He managed to deflect a spear thrust with his improvised soft shield and caught the spear on the rebound, yanking it with all his might and pulling the rider off the camel.

Mimicking the maneuver Esau had used on the Ashdod guards, Dekel lunged toward the second rider and struck the side of the camel's leg. The camel jerked and kneeled, and the rider almost fell off. As he struggled to dismount, Dekel pierced his body.

While Esau and Dekel were finishing off their opponents, the third guard hesitated, trying to control his frightened animal. He rode off after Esau dashed toward him.

"You did great, Dekel! You're learning," said Esau.

***

The three raiders met back at the cave. Having emptied the bags on the ground with great anticipation, they saw . . . Egyptian lentils! Had they risked their lives for two bags of beans? But perhaps the money bags would make it worth it?

They looked inside—and threw the bags back on the ground. They started to chuckle, then roar, backslapping one another, expunging all the worries, all the suppressed fears, all the disappointments of the day, until the tears came.

"You said the leader would carry the most valuable merchandise!" exclaimed Dekel, pointing to the hill of beans.

"Well, this was our first time—and we've survived! We'll be more successful in the future." Esau picked up a lentil and threw it sideways.

"At least we now own a camel," Dekel shook his head, still grinning. "And two more spears."

"Maybe we need a change of tactics," said Ardon. "Riding away with the guards in pursuit is risky, no?"

"Yeah. We need more people to overpower the guards, rather than trying to escape," Esau agreed.

"Guys, do you realize that we are all killers now?" asked Dekel, losing his smile. "We started with stealing goblets—and what have we become?" He cradled a handful of beans in his hand.

"I told you, there was no turning back," said Esau with a grim glare. "But it's too bad we keep leaving so many witnesses alive."

CHAPTER 7

Esau was leading a donkey carrying a veiled woman sitting on a small ornate rug. The two of them looked like a typical married couple and aroused few suspicions. The woman was quiet, and Esau recalled his very first romantic adventure on the morning of the day he vanquished Nimrod.

***

He was fifteen, still living with his parents. A ravishing girl, accompanied by a well-dressed young man, caught his eye in the town market. She was about his age. A fancy red headscarf could not hide her long dark hair, and a simple white linen dress could not conceal her shapely figure. Esau followed her home and had been watching her tent from the nearby bushes for days.

Only an old man in a white shawl was living with the girl. Esau concluded that she was betrothed but not fully married, because the same young man from the market was coming to escort her whenever she left the tent. Esau was well familiar with the local marriage customs, which dictated that the bridegroom chose a trusted friend to accompany his bride anywhere she went.

The fact that she was someone's future wife was not a problem at all. Esau recalled from his casual studies that the nobles, the mighty men of the generation before the Flood used to kidnap the brides from their chambers and violate them on their wedding days, before their husbands could take them. I will outdo the nobles of yore, he promised himself then. Am I not a noble of sorts myself, a mighty man, a grandson of Abraham? The girl is mine by right, even if she doesn't suspect it.

Every day, he saw the same routine unfold: the old man departed in the morning with his donkey, and the girl was left all alone. But how to approach her without arousing suspicions? If she cried out loudly enough, Esau knew he would be in trouble—the locals would have no mercy. He devised a plan.

The girl washed her clothes once or twice a week and dried them on a line strung between the trees behind the tent. She did the washing the day before, and Esau enjoyed the scene. He returned at night and stole the most beautiful object he could find in the dark—the same red headscarf that she had worn to the market. Early that morning he came back to his hiding spot and watched the old man leave. He stashed his weapons and walked toward the tent, the scarf in hand.

It was a typical nomad's tent made of black goat skins, divided into two parts arranged along the front and separated by a curtain. The part near the entrance was the men's space; the women's space was farther back.

Esau rang a copper bell at the entrance and lifted the door flap; the girl peeked out from behind the curtain. Standing outside, he greeted her and asked, "Dear lady, is the scarf I am holding yours or not? I found it on the road nearby, while traveling to a house of religious study."

The girl beamed but did not move. Esau knew that according to the local customs a betrothed girl was not supposed to speak one-on-one with the men other than her relatives or her chaperone. She surely was not supposed to be alone with other men inside a tent. But she's trapped now, he reasoned. What could she do? Ask me to drop the scarf on the ground and leave? That would be impolite—also against the customs.

"Yes, it is mine," she muttered with a slight smile. "Thank you!"

A mother and a young boy emerged from the nearby tent, stared at Esau, and walked in his direction. He forced himself to stay put with an outstretched arm and greeted the neighbors, who passed by looking at him.

After more hesitation, the girl emerged from behind the curtain and approached. She took the scarf, offered thanks again, and lowered her gaze. Did she blush? A faint smile lingered on her lips, and her front foot pointed toward him, even as her body was turned away. All the good signs!

"Could I have a drink of water before I go?" Esau asked in his sweetest voice. "It is so hot today."

He knew the girl could not refuse this universal request for hospitality, and indeed, she turned around and went back to her room. Esau followed her into the tent.

She came out from behind the curtain with a pitcher and stopped in her tracks, spilling some water on her bare feet. Esau held his breath.

She handed him the pitcher, looking away. He drank and handed it back. As she was taking it, he grabbed her hand and pulled her toward him. The pitcher fell to the ground with a soft clang.

"My lord, I am betrothed," she whispered, looking at the entrance while trying to push him away.

"I know," he said and kissed her, holding tight her shivering body. He dragged the girl behind the curtain. She tried to resist, but her movements lacked strength, as he stripped off her clothes. She did not scream.

***

Since then, Esau used his wit and golden tongue to pick up Canaanite women. He set up the stolen black tent in the nearby wilderness, secluded but still close to town, and stocked it with a comfortable mattress, oil lamps, and jugs with wine and water.

He preferred married women now. Nobody guarded them, unlike single girls and betrothed brides, and they could move around with ease. After all, a lady of the house was expected not only to cook, but also to buy food staples. There were other advantages in dealing with married women, Esau learned. Canaanite girls were open to all sort of perversion, but they were as protective about their virginity as a mother bear of her cubs. And married women were more experienced.

His favorite hunting ground was still the town market, which was located near the city gates, and it was an easy trip from there to his tent. Given enough time, every local woman could be seen there. As Esau strolled among female shoppers, he kept track of the attractive ones.

One day he ran into a gorgeous young woman accompanied by two maids. Esau could not take his eyes off her innocent delicate features, slender figure, soft pale skin, and long black hair. Loitering nearby, he waited until the blue dress she was examining slipped from her bony fingers and rushed to pick it up before the maids could.

"Let me help you, my lady. Someone as refined as you should not soil her hands picking things off the sand," he purred.

The woman raised her large brown eyes and thanked him, smiling. She was so graceful!

He dusted off the dress and handed it over, "Here, my lady. It would look marvelous on you—as anything would, I am sure!"

She smiled again, lowered her head and looked up. He thought that the look lasted a bit longer than a casual glance, or was it his overheated imagination? The maids pretended not to hear all this.

The next day he saw the woman again, walking through the market in the new dress, alone this time. Was it a signal?

Esau went up to her and said, "Good morning, my lady! What a great turn of events—I am privileged to behold your beauty yet again! I knew the dress would look great on you!"

She looked straight into his eyes with a faint smile. "Thank you for your advice, young man. It was certainly a good purchase!"

"Are you seeking to buy something today as well?"

"Yes, perhaps a handbag to match the dress."

"I know just the place," crooned Esau and led her to the merchant.

"What do you think about this one?" asked the woman, holding a woven red leather pouch and glancing at him sideways.

"It would be a nice match. You have an exquisite taste, my lady."

She dropped the bag, and Esau caught it in the air. As he handed it to her, their hands met, and he held her long thin fingers for a second. She took away her hand and paid the merchant.

"It's a beautiful day today—almost as beautiful as you, my lady," breathed Esau. "It would be a privilege to accompany you back home, if you so command. I have a donkey tied up around the corner, unless somebody has stolen it."

"Yes, thank you. I hope the donkey is still there," she said with a sparkle in her eyes.

He helped her mount the donkey and covered her with a travel cloak. She did not protest when the donkey's measured steps took them to his tent instead.

Her name was Rulaat, and she was the wife of a wealthy merchant selling olive oil. Her husband traveled often, and in his absence Rulaat amused herself by shopping, fine dining at home, and meeting with her friends of similar means. Esau could relate to her loneliness. He told her his real name; he did not know why, as he had never done so with other women.

They spent some time together drinking aged wine, eating and getting to know each other. At last, it was time to go—or so she thought.

"Rulaat, I cannot let you go, not just yet."

"But I have to! I should have already been back by now. My servants will get concerned and start looking for me," she demanded, standing near the exit.

"Don't worry about that," he replied, slouching on the mattress.

"No, you don't understand—I *have* to go!" She pointed a finger at Esau. "Take me back. Now!"

"Sit back down," he ordered. "I told you, you can't go yet."

"Are you kidnapping me?" Her eyes widened and her dainty hands started to tremble, which Esau noted with satisfaction.

"Just stay here with me for a day or two."

"Are you mad?! I cannot stay here in this filthy tent, eating this filthy food, sleeping on this filthy mattress!" she shrieked. "And I told you, they'll be looking for me! Let me go, you low-life!"

She looked so attractive now, he thought and said, "The mattress was rather nice with you on it. Anyway, you don't have a choice, do you? Which way would you run from here?" He stretched his lips into a smile.

Rulaat peeked outside toward inhospitable wilderness extending in all directions and broke down. Esau felt awkward watching this beautiful lady tear herself apart.

"I will do whatever you want—please let me go," she sniffled.

"Oh, we just went over this. You need to stay here a while."

"And then you'll kill me?"

"No! Why should I? You'll be delivered to your beautiful home alive and well. Just do as I say."

Esau kept an eye on her during the day and restrained her at night. She did not attempt anything reckless, but neither there was the merry companionship he had hoped for. It was all quite tense, as if he was guarding a prisoner of war. What happened to her gentle flirting and her sparkling eyes? She did not eat, she did not smile, and she needed her perfume in the stifling heat. They just went through the motions, as she looked away, and by the end of the second day Esau realized that the bloom was off the rose.

"Rulaat, it's time to say goodbye," he announced. "You are not happy here, and I am not a cruel person. I'll take you back tonight."

"And how am I supposed to explain my absence?" she asked, sitting on the far corner of the mattress.

"How should I know? Spin a story about being kidnapped by some gang as you were returning from the market and then escaping. You women are better liars than I am."

"And if my husband wants to investigate further?"

"Tell him you have no clue about who those people were or where they came from. From what you've told me, he'll convince himself there is nothing he could do and just let it go."

"I've heard of some kidnappings in the area," Rulaat conceded. "It's worth a try." She paused and adjusted her dress. "And what prevents me from telling him that *you* kidnapped me?"

"Well, if you could come up with a good explanation of why you insisted on going to the market alone after meeting me there the day before, and how you ended up here without a fight, go right ahead. Remember, your maids have seen us talking." Rulaat did not reply.

That night, Esau dropped her off. She gave him one last defiant look and walked inside, as he slinked into the darkness.

***

Esau joined Dekel in the cave for a few days and then resumed his trips to the market, first covering his face with a *sudra* and later dispensing with it. One day he bumped into Rulaat walking with a paunchy balding man wearing fine white linen clothes. Their eyes met for a split second, and she stiffened, latching onto the man's arm.

"What is it?" Esau heard him ask.

"Nothing," replied Rulaat. "I just stumbled."

Chapter 8

All of Hebron was buzzing with the latest news: a coup in Babylon claimed the lives of King Ereechar and his closest advisors. Esau walked around smiling; he even stopped robbing travelers for a while. Life was good.

But soon after a drought arrived at Canaan and with it, famine. Isaac's animals were losing weight subsisting on parched hillside grass. It was time to move to a more verdant place. Isaac ignored the advice of his servants to relocate to Egypt, where food always seemed to be in abundance, and moved to Gerar instead. It was a town in south Canaan, a couple of days walk from Hebron, where his father Abraham had once sojourned.

Living in and around Gerar, Isaac took up farming and met with unexpected success, managing to reap back-to-back hundredfold harvests while his neighbors suffered. He became so wealthy that his fortune dwarfed that of Abimelech, the king of Gerar. Not wishing to outshine his sovereign, Isaac moved to Be'er Sheva.

Esau and Jacob accompanied their father during all these journeys; Ardon and Dekel followed their leader. Because Esau could now afford to buy anything he desired, he was less and less interested in plunder and drawn by other pursuits.

His favorite entertainment was to walk into a roadside inn and start a brawl with the men dining there. He always came out on top, regardless of the number of his opponents.

One evening Esau wandered into a remote inn where he had never been before, although he had heard that it was frequented by some tough clientele. The truth of it became evident the moment he walked in.

The place was littered with shards of pottery, and the decorations consisted of the mounted heads of wolves and leopards. The diners did not look like regular travelers—they were a rugged, disheveled, and loud bunch; some had more teeth than others. All seemed to be packing knives or daggers underneath their dirty *simlah* shawls.

Esau sat down in the corner, at the end of a long wooden table bearing countless knife wounds, and ordered strong barley beer. He glanced around the room and realized that he might be over his head in this establishment.

Right on cue, a large man in a torn and tattered shawl landed in front of him and scowled, "Hey, how come your hair is so red?"

He's just a drunk, concluded Esau, and replied in an even voice, looking away, "That's the way I was born."

"Well, I think your hair is just too red and too long. How about I trim it a bit?"

The drunkard pulled out a knife and tried to cut off a lock, but Esau sideswiped his arm and slammed it against the table, rattling the dishes at the other end. The man groaned, and Esau grabbed the knife from his hand. A nice sharp blade, he noted in passing.

Holding the back of the man's filthy neck and the knife against his nose, Esau leaned over and growled, "How about I cut off some of *that*?"

The man didn't say a word as he tried to escape deeper into the bench with his teeth showing and his eyes ready to abandon the face. Several other ruffians came closer, brandishing darkened blades.

"Back away—or I'll kill him!" yelled Esau and put the knife to the drunkard's throat, glaring at the others.

One of the men facing Esau looked stronger and was dressed better than the rest. His rugged face, ringed by long gray hair, was marred by a thick scar on the forehead. "Go ahead, finish him," the man smirked, running his fingers along the tip of his dagger. "I have more men to spare, but you, son, have only one life."

Esau did not reply. The chieftain crooned through stretched lips, "Just give me the knife, and we won't harm you, I promise!"

"Fine. But please don't hurt me!" Lips trembling, Esau took away the knife and extended it toward the leader, holding the weapon on an open palm.

"Good boy." With a crooked grin, the leader stretched his hand toward the knife.

In a flash, Esau ripped into the chieftain's arm above the wrist and lunged forward, slicing his neck. The bandit froze in place, and Esau slashed the opposite side of his neck. A sharp blade, he observed again.

The rest of the gang gasped and backed away. The chieftain tried to raise his dagger, but his injured hand could not hold it.

As he bent down to pick it up, Esau kicked him on the chin. The bandit fell backwards, hit his head on the edge of the table and slid to the floor.

The blood spurting from both sides of his neck started to make his hair look like Esau's. The man grunted and grabbed onto the bench, trying to get up, but sagged to the floor instead.

Still holding the knife, Esau spat on the chieftain and looked around the room. Eleven of them. The brigands backed even farther away under his fierce stare.

"Sit back down!" screeched Esau through the dry throat. Turning to the innkeeper, he threw some silver pieces on the scarred counter. "Beer for everyone!"

The men warily sat down. Sipping his beer, they just gazed at him.

He announced, "I am Esau from Hebron. I've taken down some major scores with my men back there. Want to join me?"

The men glanced at the chieftain, who had stopped twitching, then at one another and started to nod. Nobody seemed to be in the mood to challenge the newcomer.

A few more rounds helped, and Esau learned that the gang robbed caravans and raided faraway villages, never staying in one place for long. Their former leader planned all the hits.

One wiry man with a scruffy black beard and leathery face seemed a bit brighter than the others. He said, "My name is Areef. Don't you remember me from before? The pit outside Hebron? Hey, you aren't *that* Esau—a son of Isaac?"

"I am."

The outlaws put down their beer and stared at him. One of them croaked, "But he's the richest man around! People say that the dung of Isaac's mules is better than the gold and silver of Abimelech. Why do you need *this*?"

Esau shrugged his shoulders. "I love this life. I don't want anything else."

Someone exclaimed, "If I had all this money, I wouldn't rob anyone. I'd just sit here drinking and whoring!" After Esau gave him a stern look, the man burped, "Sorry."

Esau asked, "Is there a plan for tomorrow?"

"Yes, an afternoon caravan job on the Coastal Route. An Egyptian one," replied Areef.

"Carrying what?"

"Probably the usual Egyptian stuff: grain, linen, flax, ox-hides, lentils, dried fish, and papyrus in large bags; maybe different perfumes, glass vases, and painted pottery in small bags," Areef rattled on. "But it's the caravans going *back* into Egypt that carry more valuable things." The others nodded.

"Such as?" Esau looked around the table, trying to engage someone else.

But the men stared into their mugs in silence, and Areef answered again, "Such as precious stones and cosmetics, like the black eye paint that you see on all the Egyptians, animal skins—things like that."

"So what do you do with all that loot, once you get it? Resell it somewhere?" Esau asked, looking away from Areef.

"Yes, our chief, er, former chief, would send us to different markets to sell the stuff. I hate it—I'd rather rob than peddle," said one outlaw, leaning on the creaky table.

"I know what you mean. We once robbed a caravan and discovered that all it carried was beans. That wasn't what we expected!" Esau paused. "I'll tell you what—forget about selling the grain at the market. We'll have more fun than that!"

He watched the faces around the table. The men seemed to like what they were hearing. "Let's do tomorrow's job," he concluded. "I'll see you all in action. But this time, we'll take the most valuable stuff, nothing else."

***

Later that night Esau told Ardon and Dekel about the events at the inn. They seemed unimpressed.

"Are we sure we want to go on a major job with a bunch of people we don't know? Mostly drunkards and low-lives, from what you've told us," hedged Ardon.

"Oh, please. Remember, the last time there were only three of us, and we did it. This time there'll be fourteen, not counting the man guarding the tents," said Esau. "Accept it: we are now a part of a large gang."

****

Early next morning the outlaws departed westward to Gaza. The ambush went without a hitch. Outnumbered, the Egyptian guards offered no resistance. But the caravan carried only food and fabrics—not what Esau expected. He pulled the caravan leader away for questioning.

With hunched shoulders and bowed head, the trader mumbled, "My name is Dershah. We are Egyptian merchants, selling food and other staples throughout Retenu, the land you call Canaan and Syria. Before we return, we buy precious stones like lapis lazuli, turquoise, and agate, sometimes also cosmetics, and carry them back to Egypt. That's all, my lord. Please have mercy!" He looked up.

"How about gold and silver? Ever carry those?"

"No, my lord. Only the royal scribes appointed by Pharaoh himself can handle that trade. We can't touch it."

"But do you know at least *when* they transport the gold?"

As Dershah dithered and rubbed his shaved head and cropped gray beard, Esau grabbed him by the throat. "Answer me if you want to live!"

"Please, my lord . . . I don't know! But perhaps I might hear something if I run into the scribes later." Esau did not loosen his grip, and the trader added, "I will . . . I will let you know when I learn anything."

"When will we see you next?"

"In four months."

"How can I trust that you'll show up?"

"My lord, that's my business. I know no other trade. Please have mercy!"

Esau took away his hand and stepped back, allowing Dershah to catch his breath. He addressed his gang, "Let them go, but take their money bags."

"Are you sure you want to do that?" asked Areef. "In the past, we would've killed them all on the spot."

"Let's see if he proves useful. Give him a chance—we can always kill him later if he doesn't deliver," answered Esau in a quiet but stern voice. "You are with me now, and you'll have to learn to use your heads rather than brute force."

***

Four months passed, and the gang accosted Dershah's caravan again.

"My lord, I am grateful for your sparing my life the last time," said Dershah, staring at the ground. "As you can see, I'm here—I've kept my word."

"What have you learned about the gold caravans?" Esau held on to the handle of his sword.

"Actually, quite a bit. They travel every two months, going from Memphis to Geval, carrying the payments for the cedar timber that has been delivered by ships."

"Slow down. The people of Geval first ship you the timber and then you pay them by sending the valuables in caravans?"

"Yes, my lord."

"That's what we call trust. What sort of valuables?"

"Anything they ask for. Gold and silver, of course, but also fabrics, ox-hides, food." Dershah paused and looked Esau in the eye. "The next caravan will leave Egypt in five days."

"How will it be guarded?"

"I'd think two to three scores of soldiers, at least. At least!"

"Where do they stay on the road?"

"They don't lodge in roadside inns or in towns along the way. Worry about an ambush. They prefer finding an open spot off the road, pitching their tents there, and guarding them well."

"Smart." Esau's eyes sparkled. "When will they get here, if they leave Memphis in five days?"

"Takes me about a month to get here. Same for them, I'd think."

"Thanks, Dershah. We'll be in touch on your next trip. Have a safe voyage and keep your money this time," said Esau.

"What should I tell my people, since you are not robbing us?" asked Dershah as Esau was leaving.

"Tell them you've bought us off with your own money."

Chapter 9

Areef was staring at the pot of cooking beans, the compliments of Dershah, without saying anything. He was shifting on top of his small carpet, touching his neck, and adjusting his cloak.

"Stop fidgeting, Areef. What's wrong?" asked Esau.

Areef took a deep breath and replied, without looking at him, "Esau, are you sure we should take on a caravan guarded so well?"

"We wanted gold, didn't we? Wanted to escape the tedium of selling stolen grain at the market? Here is our chance."

"Yeah, but . . . the Egyptians would vastly outnumber us. Plus, they are professional soldiers, better trained and equipped than us here." He pointed to their ragtag gang. "How . . ."

"Is that what's eating you? Trust me, we can handle this." Esau looked around at the others. After some waffling, the outlaws nodded. Esau continued, "But we'd have to disappear afterwards—for a long time. Either the Pharaoh would be after us, or he'd hire one of the local kings to do it for him."

He took Ardon and Areef aside and said, "Listen, I am well aware that we cannot even hope to defeat the Egyptians in open combat. I'd like to tip the scales in our favor. Any ideas?"

Not receiving an answer, he rubbed his chin for a while and then said with a wide grin, "Hey, perhaps we could poison them somehow—wipe them out all at once! Do you guys know where we could get some good poison?"

"I know a physician near Ashdod who has all sorts of medicinal things. I bet he stocks that, too," said Areef.

"Ashdod again? Hmm . . ." Esau exhaled through puffed out cheeks.

"A problem?" asked Areef.

"No, no problem. Let's pay him a visit tomorrow."

***

The next morning Esau and Areef left to see the physician, riding through the familiar dusty road through the wilderness. They passed a herd of goats on the way, with no shepherd in sight.

"Wait!" said Esau. He got off the camel, grabbed a kid from the herd, and shoved it into a large leather bag. Nobody ran after them, and they continued on.

"Here it is," Areef pointed to a plain mud-brick building on a side of the road.

"Is this physician a friend of yours?" asked Esau, observing three donkeys tied near the entrance.

"No, not really," answered Areef. "Why?"

"Well, we might have to . . ."

A clean-shaven young man in his teens met them at the door and showed them inside with one of his long arms protruding from the sleeves of his cloak. He recognized Areef and called his master, as Esau looked around the shop. The shelves were crammed with jars, small boxes, sieves, and grinding implements of all sorts. Some strong smell lingered in the room, and Esau rubbed his eyes.

An older man came up to them and hugged Areef, as they kissed each other's cheeks. He was wearing a red turban and a red cloak—to better hide the blood stains, Esau thought. As pleasantries followed, Esau examined the man's narrow face, his short white beard, and intense dark eyes. Yeah, this is how a physician should look.

"My dear Areef, how can I be of help? Is anybody sick in your . . . company?"

"Oh, no, thanks. My friend here is a livestock owner. He needs your assistance."

The physician turned to Esau, who did not miss a beat. "We've had some attacks on my cattle by wild beasts. Also, thieves have been stealing animals."

The physician's eyebrows zoomed up in a curve. "So, is anybody injured?"

"No, no—I want something else," said Esau with a faint smile. "I need some poison to kill both the beasts and the thieves."

"Oh, I partly understand," the physician's eyebrows came down. "You want to set poisoned bait for the beasts. But I'm not quite sure what you are planning for the thieves."

"Still working on a plan," grinned Esau, "but first we wanted to see if you had any good poisons for our needs."

The physician offered a polite smiled in return. "I most definitely do."

"Then why don't you show us? We are looking for the most lethal poison, and we'll need a lot of it."

"Good poisons are very expensive," the physician gave Esau a long sideways stare. "But here is what I have—from all corners of the world."

He led them to a dusty shelf in the back. "In this jar is the poison of the blue-ringed octopus, which kills very quickly. This one here is dried belladonna. If a man eats a single leaf of it, he'll die. This little jar contains hemlock, brought from far north; a tiny amount is deadly. Do you need to see more?"

"Yes, show me all," said Esau.

"This powder, even more expensive, is called Gu. It is brought from a faraway eastern country. The travel there takes several years."

"What's in it?"

"That's the most amazing part. They put various venomous animals—snakes, scorpions, centipedes, spiders, toads—in a large vessel and let them fight it out. After a while, they see which one has survived. Then they take the victor and grind it up into this powder."

"Nice. What else have you got?"

"This liquid is derived from rotting meat. If ingested, the man becomes paralyzed and dies soon. This one is made from ground apricot kernels."

Esau noticed that the physician skipped two small flasks and asked what was in them.

"These, my friends, are two extremely toxic substances, probably an overkill (he smiled again) for your needs. One is derived from the wolfsbane plant. A man could be poisoned after just touching its leaves. He would suffocate in agony. The other one is called the king of poisons. It is very, very expensive, but probably the most lethal one here."

"Just how expensive is this king of poisons?"

"A weight of one hundred silver shekels."

"For this little jar?"

"Yes. But it is worth it . . . to some."

"And what does it do?"

"The victim dies soon after suffering from excruciating abdominal pains."

"Sounds about right. I want this one. But let's try it out first."

"On whom?"

"I have someone . . . something . . . with me. Do you happen to have some milk around here?"

The physician brought out a small pot of milk, placed a tiny amount of the poison in it, and put the flask on the counter. Esau took the milk and went outside.

The goat kid soon started rolling on the ground, bleating and swinging its legs for a few minutes.

Esau returned to the shop and said, "I'll take it."

"Do you . . . umm . . . happen to have the money with you?" The physician's eyes opened wide. He moved his hand toward the counter.

"Of course not—but thanks," answered Esau and snatched the flask.

He and Areef turned around to leave, and the physician ran after them, grabbing Esau by the sleeve. Esau gave him a stern look, but he did not let go. The young assistant joined his master, ready to latch onto another sleeve.

Without warning, Esau pulled out a knife and stabbed the physician twice in the abdomen. The man gasped and hunched down on the floor. The assistant tried to back away but stumbled, and Esau stabbed him also.

Before leaving, they took the rest of the poison containers and checked the shop for any other useful items. They found some money, but most of the jars and flasks were unmarked, so they were of little use.

Esau opened the heavy entrance door and halted. A young woman with a bow was standing in front of him, her arrow pointing at his chest.

Esau greeted her, but she did not reply. He tried again, "I am sorry about what happened here. Things just spun out of control."

As seconds passed, he kept his gaze on her. Although a long white shawl and a headscarf covered her figure and head, he could see that she was slender and very attractive, even with that vengeful look on her face.

"They were my brother and my father! Now you'll pay for what you've done!" She had a beautiful voice, too.

Areef stuck his head in the door and sprung back. He clung to the wall for dear life.

Esau purred, keeping still, "My dear, if you shoot me, he'll kill you. Do you want to die, too? I think two unfortunate deaths are enough for today." He exhaled bit by bit, sensing that the longer she aimed at him, the less were the chances she would shoot.

All of a sudden, she said, "Put everything back, turn around and leave." The furrow on her forehead relaxed a little, and Esau was now certain she would not shoot.

He edged toward her and crooned, "I can't do this. As you've overheard, our livelihood depends on having the poison. Anyway, what good is it to you now?"

She backed up a step and rearranged her aim. "Don't come any closer, or I *will* shoot!" Esau did not expect such determination in her voice.

"Fine, fine. I am putting it all on the counter over here. Watch!" He pulled out a couple of jars and turned around, his heart racing with excitement.

She's not going to shoot me in the back, Esau told himself as he moved farther away from the entrance. Come on, girl, move inside! But she did not stir, waiting for Esau to empty his bag, and he had to comply.

"Now what?" he asked. She hesitated, this fierce woman, even more attractive than she appeared at first. Esau remained in place, admiring her delicate narrow face framed by long black hair visible underneath the headscarf, her long thin nose, and slightly curved lips. Her slender fingers showed no signs of fatigue. And still no answer.

"Listen, I know this is all traumatic to you, and I am truly sorry about what happened. I wish it had turned out differently. Let me make it up to you."

"What can you do for me? Bring them back? You are bandits, not sorcerers!"

"We could help you make a living with us. If you like adventure, that is. Think about it: a princess among the thieves!"

To Esau's surprise, the woman seemed to be considering this option, and he pressed on, "Do you have any other relatives in the area?"

"No."

"Well then, unless you can run this shop by yourself, you would be better off with us. If you know anything about medicine, you'd be of great help."

"You won't hurt me?" Her face betrayed no emotions at all.

"I give you my word," said Esau. He couldn't believe the way things were going. "And I, mine," chimed in Areef, who tore himself away from the wall.

"Bury them first. We can't leave them here!" she commanded and lowered her bow.

The men dug a simple grave behind the shop and placed the slain men there. They introduced themselves.

"I am Anadil," was all she said. They grabbed what they could, locked up the shop and gave her the keys. Then they put Anadil on one of the donkeys and left.

***

Exhausted by the events, the three travelers dragged back from Ashdod under the afternoon sun. Not a word was spoken until Esau asked, "Look, Anadil, maybe you didn't mean to join us and agreed to go without thinking. We are not cruel people, and you are free to leave if you wish."

She did not reply. Her delicate lips formed such a warm smile that Esau was captivated.

He tried again, "Where did you learn how to use a bow? It's my good fortune that I've never found out how well you could shoot. But at least your form is proper."

"I can hit a bird's head a hundred paces away," she blurted.

"Oh? How did you manage to gain such skill?"

"I was training."

"To what end?"

"To join a gang. I always dreamed of being in a gang."

"What?!" Esau and Areef almost fell off their camels. "You always wanted to be at outlaw? You?"

"Yes, I did," she insisted in a quiet but firm voice. "I'll tell you more some other time."

"Hope you won't be disappointed with our life," said Esau, still chuckling. "It's not all that glamorous."

They passed a score of camel-mounted soldiers in the familiar uniforms, carrying a banner of the king of Ashdod. Guards on a routine patrol, meaning no harm to us, Esau hoped. But the soldiers stopped and turned around.

"Yes, it's him!" exclaimed one of them. The soldiers surrounded Esau and his companions and ordered them to dismount.

"Put away your weapons and kneel, all of you!" ordered the patrol's captain.

The travelers complied and placed their weapons on the searing sand. The commander got off the camel and stepped with confidence toward them. Lifting up Esau's chin, he demanded, "So you are the horse thief who killed five of my men?"

"No, my lord, I've done nothing of the kind! There must be some mistake! We are peaceful travelers from Gerar."

"Really?" The captain glanced at his soldier, who nodded. "Lying scum. The king has a bounty on you."

"My lord, it wasn't me. It was the others in the gang. I just stand out the most with this hair. Perhaps I could share some information with you if you be lenient with us."

"Speak! But don't think you'd talk your way out of this."

Esau mumbled something, and the captain cracked his lips, "What? Speak up!"

"I can tell you where they are if you let me go," whispered Esau, motioning with his eyes toward Areef and signaling to the captain to come closer.

The frowning captain glanced at his soldiers and approached. He stood a few steps back, clutching his sword.

Esau raised his hands and said, "Don't worry—no sand, no knife here."

As the commander kicked away Esau's weapon and warily leaned over, Esau swiped at his eyes with spread-out bent fingers, like a wild cat. The officer yelped and recoiled. In a heartbeat Esau wrestled the sword from his hand and slit his leg.

By the time the captain sunk to the ground, shrieking and trying to cushion the fall with his hands, Esau was on top of him, jamming the sword against his throat. The rest of the soldiers stood paralyzed.

Esau dragged the commander a few paces away and barked, "Tell your men to back down, or you're dead!"

The officer wavered, and Esau said, "You'll just bleed to death here if you waste time." The captain ordered his men to obey, and they did.

"Get your weapons," Esau told Areef and Anadil. Addressing the captain again, he hissed, "Now tell them all to dismount and drop theirs."

With reluctance, the soldiers followed their chief's orders, except for one man. While Areef and Anadil were collecting swords and spears, the soldier who had identified Esau rushed toward Areef's back and stuck a knife to his throat.

"Hey, that's my move!" Esau smirked.

"Looks like we have a stalemate," observed the captain, cringing with pain and pressing on his leg.

"Not really. If your man kills mine, you're dead. Is this trade worth it to you?"

"And so will you be . . . you and the girl—against nineteen of them," retorted the captain.

"We'll see about that—but *you* won't be able to!"

Nobody wanted to concede, and it seemed that Esau's leverage was slipping away. As the soldiers started to creep toward their weapons, Anadil grabbed her bow and aimed an arrow at the guard holding Areef.

"Pretty girl, you want to shoot your buddy?" scowled the guard.

But the soldiers gasped when Anadil's arrow hit him in the cheek and Areef pushed away the limp hand with the knife. Seeing Anadil pointing another arrow in their direction and Areef facing them with a sword, the soldiers halted. When their commander ordered them to lie down with their faces on the ground, they complied.

Anadil stood guard as Areef tied their hands. Only then she bandaged the captain's leg.

"Don't try to follow us," warned Esau. They left with the soldiers' camels and weapons.

"Shouldn't we kill them?" asked Areef. "So many witnesses."

"I'm done hiding," was the reply. Then a yell filled the desert air, scaring away a flock of desert doves, "Tell your king, my name is ESAU!"

Chapter 10

Anadil was getting used to outlaw life, protected under Esau's orders. She started cooking for the gang and introduced a refreshing diversity into their monotonous diet of stolen barley and stolen meat.

With a full month to prepare for the raid of his life, Esau was drilling the gang on various attack maneuvers, and when his scouts reported that a caravan matching Dershah's description was coming, they were ready. Esau did not flinch when he heard that sixty-four soldiers accompanied the procession. We just need to work harder and smarter, he told his men.

When the caravan turned off the road for the night, the Egyptians arranged the camp in a square. Seven tents surrounded the center where the donkeys rested; the kitchen was in the place of the eighth. The guards were unloading the animals and carrying the bags into the tents, watched over by the four sentinels that stood at the corners of the camp. Several people were tending the kitchen, where the evening meal was boiling in a huge copper pot that reflected the last rays of the sun.

Lying down on top of a nearby hill, Esau noticed that the Egyptians carried bows, spears, and the famed *khopesh* swords, which had the shape of a shallow sickle with a sharpened outer edge. Esau had never acquired one for himself, because he thought that these weapons were best suited for slashing from chariots and were too heavy for quick attacks he favored. He ran his fingers over his own short straight sword—this one was great for both slashing and stabbing.

He decided to get a closer look at the camp, taking Dekel with him. He left Ardon and Areef to keep an eye on the rest of his men whom he allowed to get some sleep.

Esau and Dekel were lying still, listening to the howls of jackals that echoed through the night. Esau reckoned that the dawn would come soon and sent Dekel to wake up the gang, giving them plenty of time to assume their positions. According to the plan, one man and Anadil would stay with the camels; Dekel and Areef would join Esau at his hiding spot.

The kitchen attendants arrived and started the fire for the morning meal, pouring water from large leather pouches into the copper pot and throwing some food in it. After they stepped away from the fire, Esau nudged Dekel and patted him on the back.

The young man crawled towards the pot without making a sound, stopping and glancing at the two nearest corner guards. When he was almost there, he pulled out a jar and removed the cork with utmost care. He looked around again, leaned over the pot, and emptied the jar.

Dekel lingered near the pot for a few seconds, covering his face with a sleeve of his cloak, and the empty jar slipped away from his hand. He tried to catch it, but the jar still dropped to the ground with a clink, and he sneezed.

The two sounds filled the nighttime quiet, and Esau stiffened. The sentinels and the cooks turned toward the noise. One guard rushed to the boiling pot; he shouted something and pointed to the shadows where Dekel had fled. The sentinel pulled out an animal-bone whistle and tried to sound an alarm, but a thwack of Esau's arrow stopped him.

An Areef's arrow pierced one of the cooks, but the second one let out a loud cry before he too was shot. The second sentry managed to blow his whistle before a thrown spear found his chest.

What a mess, thought Esau. Still, it was one of the scenarios for which he had trained his men. As he expected, two of them speared the remaining sentinels in the back, while the others rushed inside the camp and took their positions near the tents.

The attackers were swinging their swords and thrusting their spears at the sleepy Egyptians who were scampering out blinded by the camp fires. It was still too dark to properly aim the arrows, and Esau joined the hand-to-hand combat.

From the corner of his eye he noticed that Anadil disobeyed his orders and came out shooting. Could she see at night better than him?

The outlaws mowed down the first few disoriented Egyptians, but the guards emerging now seemed awake. With only one or two raiders for each tent of seven or eight better-trained soldiers bristling with spears, Esau recognized he could not win this battle. He sounded a signal to retreat.

The attackers escaped into the darkness. The stunned Egyptians did not pursue them.

***

The first rays of sunlight made the task of counting and examining the outlaws easier. Only twelve survived, plus Anadil, but three of them were wounded. The men still clutched their weapons, looking up at Esau in silence. He had to say something.

"We are not done, folks—this was just the first skirmish. We'll continue to attack them, and we'll get our gold, I promise! We will not give up until we avenge the lives of the brothers we've lost today. All of you were brave—we just had some trouble executing a good plan." He did not look at Dekel.

The men just stared at him. One of them asked, rubbing his bruised arm, "Do you mean we'll go there again—after we had to run? After we've lost the element of surprise?"

"Yeah, we'll go back. Not right now, of course. But we'll wear them down little by little. No matter how much they expect it, they'll be stunned by each attack and dread the next."

"So, how long do you see us doing this? Days? Weeks?" asked Areef, swatting a fly on his scratched leg.

"However long it takes—until we have won! Think about it: they are tied to the road, while we can move anywhere, day or night. They have to travel for at least a month to either return to Egypt or reach their destination. Either way, they can't get away from us," concluded Esau with a spark in his eye.

The bandits fell silent again, looking at each other. One of them took another swig from a leather pouch and asked, "Can't they get some help along the way?"

"Who's going to help them? There are no Egyptian outposts out here. The guards from other caravans? Remember, the gold ones like this one only travel once a month, so they'd have to wait that long to get any real help. The rest, with perhaps six guards in each of them, of what value would they be? They still need to deliver their own stuff!"

"But how about the local kings? Wouldn't they go after us?" asked another man with the arms folded across his chest.

"Do you think they would help their enemies? Haven't you heard of the Canaanite kings themselves robbing Egyptian caravans?"

"I guess you're right, Esau. It all makes sense, and the payoff is worth the trouble. We knew what we were getting into, right?" said Areef, watching the others. Seeing them nod, he added, "So let's do it!"

"Till the victory!" shouted Esau, raising his sword.

"Till the victory!" yelled the gang.

***

Esau was sitting outside his tent, deep in thought, when he noticed Anadil passing by. "Planning another attack?" she asked, giggling.

"Something like that."

"Mind if I join you for a minute?"

He invited her to sit down on the sand gleaming with the warmth of the setting sun. Her sleeve was touching his.

"It is a beautiful evening," she murmured. "Look at all the stars coming out. It is so peaceful—and here we are, killing people."

"But that's what you wanted, isn't it?"

"Yes, today was very exciting."

"I've seen you kill at least one of them. And that shot at the soldier from Ashdod was incredible! Maybe you can indeed hit a bird's head a hundred paces away."

She just smiled.

"Anadil, but I've told you to stay in the camp. You shouldn't have come out at all."

"Sorry, I wanted to help."

"And you did. But please listen to what I say in the future. I need to maintain discipline here."

"I will, I will."

He glanced at her. She is so lovely tonight, he thought. "Anadil, you've never told me why you wanted to join a gang."

Her smile disappeared. "I just needed to get away from them."

"But why?"

"They mistreated me."

Esau peered at her, expecting more.

She added, "I don't want to talk about it."

They sat still for a while, taking in the last rays of the sun.

All of a sudden she resumed, "They've always treated me like a little girl. They wouldn't look for a husband for me. They made me feel like a slave!"

"Slow down. How old are you?"

"I am almost sixteen!"

"You'll have lots of time to establish yourself, to marry, to make . . ."

"I don't want any of this now. I just want to be free. I feel free with you!"

Esau kept silent, waiting for her to continue.

"Esau, why aren't you married?"

"I don't know. Haven't met anybody suitable, I suppose. And this wild life is not for most women."

"So why do you lead this life then? You could've been a chief of your tribe! Your father is the richest and the most famous man around!"

That was unexpected, and Esau felt a sense of unease. "How do you know about my father?"

"I know all about the famous bandits, and you are the most famous of them all." She laughed, throwing her head back. "Everyone knows that Isaac, the wealthiest man in the land, has an outlaw son Esau with a ruddy face and red hair."

He cracked a smile, too, studying her dark long hair that blended with the gathering darkness and her delicate profile that the dying sun did not yet wish to leave.

"Esau, you've never answered my question: why do you need this gang?" She was trying to look into his eyes.

"I too chose to be free, to do as I please," he said, prolonging his words. "My father wished me to pursue religious studies, but all I desired was to hunt, to be alone with nature. To do what I wanted. Not having to wait for tomorrow or for any rewards in the afterlife. I can't wait!"

"And you think this outlaw life will make you happy?"

"I don't know, but I am happy now, and that's all that matters—this moment."

"Yes, this moment," she echoed.

She kept staring at him. He brought her closer and they kissed, tentatively at first and then with the passion that he never knew he had.

CHAPTER 11

Two days later, it was time for the next attack. While the Egyptians were setting up their camp, the outlaws hid behind the rocks and bushes to the west of them. The entire gang assembled for the assault, save for one wounded man guarding the animals. Biding his time, Esau counted forty-two remaining guards. He grinned when he saw them placing their giant pot away from the perimeter—he would never try the same trick twice.

Esau gave his signature attack sound—a call of the desert eagle—and arrows started to rain on the camp. Before the Egyptians realized what was happening, several more volleys fell upon them. When the shaken soldiers started their blind shooting into the sun, the attackers sent a parting salvo and retreated without taking any casualties.

***

Esau congratulated his band and let them rest for the night. He saw Anadil and smiled at her, as they sat down outside his tent.

"Anadil, I never thanked you for patching up my men yesterday."

She shrugged without saying a word.

"No, I mean it! It was a great job. And yet you say you don't want to continue your father's practice. Why not, if you are so good at it?"

"Esau, there's more to practicing medicine than bandaging up people. My father had learned this whole system of healing in Egypt. We lived there for years while he was studying. As for me, I don't like their system at all—I think much of it is fraud."

"But the Egyptian medics are supposed to be the best in the world!"

"I now think just the opposite. I've rarely seen a disease that we cured with our prescriptions."

"Oh?"

"Yes! Much of this is simply nonsense. My father would often send me to find some weird ingredients for him, and then he'd mutter some mysterious incantations while giving the 'cure' to the patient."

"How weird?"

"Well, do you know what he would prescribe if a patient came to us with indigestion?"

"No, what?"

"He'd give him a crushed hog's tooth placed into four sugar cakes and tell him to eat one cake a day."

"Hey, as long as it works . . ."

"You think it does? People would return in a few days and demand their money back!"

"And what would he do then?"

"He would insist that they didn't follow his instructions strictly enough."

"Sounds like something I could've said. Another example, perhaps?"

"How about our 'cure' for cataracts? We'd give them a mix of tortoise's brain and honey and administer it reciting a lengthy incantation. Esau, I've never seen this treatment remove cataracts!"

"Hmm. Maybe that's why I've never gone to a physician—and now probably never will."

"I sure wouldn't. Most of the problems clear up on their own, or people just learn to live with them."

"Or they die."

"Yes, or they die."

"Anadil, but the two of us will never die, right? We will cheat death and always be together." He was glad the night concealed the gathering tears.

"Yes, we will!"

They kissed and went inside his dark battered tent.

Later that night, Esau tore himself away from her gentle embrace to lead two of his archers back to the enemy camp. Groping through the rocky hillside, careful not to dislodge any stones, they arrived undetected. They shot a dozen arrows, targeting the sentinels and anybody else unfortunate enough to be near the camp fires, and retreated before the Egyptians sounded an alarm.

***

After shadowing the caravan the next day, Esau prepared for another assault. Three hours after the nightfall, four teams of two men crept behind the four Egyptian sentinels and lunged at them with spears. All four guards were killed; the attackers escaped unhurt.

The next morning Esau's scouts reported that only thirty-two soldiers remained, one-half of their original number, with five or six of them wounded. He addressed the gang again, "Good job, people." Seeing a question in their eyes, he continued, "Today we just follow them; the decisive attack should take place tomorrow night, before they could make it to Ashdod."

"But if we are doing so well, shouldn't we just continue to kill them one by one? Keep doing this, and soon there won't be any of them left," one man ventured.

"True, but we don't want to give them a chance to hide in the city for a month. There they could wait for another gold caravan to help them. It's a remote scenario, I know, but still . . ." replied Esau.

"Also, we don't want to be anywhere near Ashdod, right?" asked Areef with a crooked smile.

"That, too. So as I said, have patience—we're almost there. One more quick attack tonight, same as before."

"Patience? I thought you couldn't wait," laughed Anadil, tugging at his sleeve.

"This is different. This is war."

***

The gang followed the caravan to its overnight camp and assembled near the top of a stony hill. The outlaws were busy digging a large pit and making a fire in it under a pitch-filled vat procured from the traveling Ishmaelites. Esau explained that while they could not hope to conceal the smell, they could at least conceal the location.

The attack started around midnight. The raiders dipped their cloth-wrapped arrows in the boiling pitch and advanced toward the Egyptian camp, where they lit them. As Esau had commanded, the arrows flew into the tents, into the sleeping donkeys, into anyone who could be seen.

The tents were easy targets, and soon all seven caught fire, prompting the Egyptians to scamper out. The disoriented soldiers had to choose between trying to extinguish the fires, protecting themselves from the barrage of arrows, or shooting back. The donkeys, some of them also on fire, were still tethered to one another. Braying and trying to free themselves, they were knocking each other to the ground and bumping into people.

Esau took his best archers—Ardon and Anadil—and led them in darkness circling around the camp. Being the only one who could speak the Egyptian language, Anadil pointed out the commander screaming orders among the other shouts and cries. She shot him. The commander went down, and with him any remaining semblance of discipline among the soldiers.

With arrows flying, and the middle of the camp all but impassable because of the panicked donkeys, the Egyptians gave up on trying to put out the fires. They converged behind the three tents that were the farthest from the main point of attack and tried shooting back into the shadows.

"Should we hit them from here?" whispered Ardon.

"Yes, but we need more people, so go bring them all. Hope you remember how to walk in the dark. And tell them, we cannot attack from the rear with our own arrows flying," said Esau.

****

Esau detected a glint and saw four soldiers staggering towards them. He muttered, "They must be trying to outflank our archers.

Let's back out of here, quietly. Take cover—over there." He pointed to several large rocks behind them.

The soldiers passed by. As Esau and Anadil loaded their bows, they heard the muffled voices of Ardon and his group moving in their direction. Esau cursed to himself: the Egyptians must have heard that, too.

"Now!" he said and let his arrow loose; Anadil followed suit. Two of the soldiers fell, but the other two sent their arrows toward the approaching outlaws, and Esau heard a shout. "One of ours," he grumbled.

Ardon's men seemed to be shooting blind. A couple of arrows whizzed by.

"Hide!" yelled Esau, turning to Anadil, but it was too late: an arrow hit her in the chest.

He rushed to the girl and dragged her behind the rock. One glance at the wound was enough.

He brought his face to hers, and she twisted her lips into a smile, "Sorry." Then she breathed out, "Don't be so sad. We'll be together, remember? In the next life . . ."

Esau fought back the tears as he held her in his arms. But another arrow landed nearby, reminding Esau of the battle still raging around them.

He screeched, "Lie still. I'll be back!" and rushed to join the fight. He saw the two remaining Egyptians running back to their tents—toward him.

Grabbing an arrow, Esau shot one; reaching into his quiver for another, he realized he was fresh out. He grasped his sword and ran toward the soldier who was loading his own bow.

Esau plunged the blade deep into his chest, and the guard crumpled. More arrows flew by. "Esau is here!" he yelled at the top of his lungs. Soon he saw a glimpse of Ardon's face.

"Follow me!" shouted Esau and ran toward the remaining guards crouching behind the tents. Along the way he snatched a quiver from a soldier lying on the ground. He kept hocking and sending arrows until they too ran out.

The soldiers were shooting back, and one of their arrows nicked Esau on the head, enraging him even more. With Ardon and Areef behind him, Esau ran into the huddled mass of the Egyptians, swinging his sword without thinking, trusting his body to find the right position and distance. His thoughts were elsewhere.

He stopped only when he saw that the guards had dropped their weapons and kneeled together, bowing their shaved heads and muttering something in their incomprehensible language.

He told Ardon, "Tie them up and count them, both dead and alive. I want to know how many might still be lurking out there." Turning to Areef, he said, "And you, take some men and start putting out the fires—it's all ours now."

He ran back to Anadil. She lay motionless, clothed by thick black air. With tears streaming, he kneeled to kiss her still-warm face. Brushing the hair off her cheek, he laid his head on hers. He stayed there minutes, maybe hours, and he got up only when he heard Ardon calling his name.

Esau lifted Anadil's body and walked with her into the camp. He put her down and stood there, gazing at her face shrouded by darkness, reflecting the fleeting lights of the last fires. He snapped the arrow that had taken her life and proceeded to break it into small pieces.

Ardon came back with his report and interrupted Esau's stupor. All the burning tents had been extinguished and the Egyptians counted, he said; none escaped. The outlaws had suffered only two casualties: a wounded man and Anadil. "Esau, what now?" he asked.

"Sift through the stuff and pack anything valuable onto those donkeys that are unhurt."

"Now, in the dark?"

"Yeah. We are too close to the road to do it in the daytime. Don't want to take a chance being seen here in the morning. That's when the travelers start leaving Ashdod and the patrols go out." Sensing that Ardon was still unconvinced, Esau added, "Have them light the fires around the camp and carry torches— this should help."

By the time the caravan was reassembled and the boxes with gold and silver delivered into Ardon's care, the gang got used to the acrid smell of burning pitch and animal flesh. It was time to go, but there were still two more things to do.

Esau signaled to a pair of the strongest-looking Egyptian prisoners to dig a grave for Anadil, using the shovels they carried.

He took another shovel for himself and buried her, just like her father and brother had been buried.

As he was throwing the last few shovelfuls of desert sand on her body, he reflected that the two nights they had spent together were the two best nights of his life. He flared his nostrils and almost snapped the shovel handle. He kept thinking about who could have sent the fateful arrow, even though he recognized that nobody would ever know.

But he still lost her. What if she was the only true love he was ever destined to have? Somebody was going to pay!

The two Egyptian grave diggers were standing in front of him, awaiting his instructions and silently pleading for their lives. With all his might, he struck one of them on the head, then another. Both men collapsed, their blood trickling into Anadil's grave.

He was still pondering the unanswerable question, when Ardon asked him what to do with the rest of the captives. "Kill them," replied Esau, as he turned to look at Anadil's grave for the last time. "Kill them all."

He paused and added, "No, I'll do it." Returning to the kneeling and bound Egyptians, he took his sword and slashed the neck of the closest one, repeating this again and again on the others. He did not notice that the black eye paint of the men helplessly awaiting their execution ran down their cheeks. He did not hear their cries for mercy that needed no translation. He did not stop until all of them were dead.

Chapter 12

Esau was sitting with his men around the fire that refused to quit, tracing shooting sparks. He shoved a smoldering branch deeper into the flames and leaned over to Ardon, "What a silly way to die—a minor flesh wound, and you're gone."

"He was a good man; a bit rough maybe . . . Wasn't he the one who accosted you at the tavern where you first met Areef?"

"Oh, yes. He was with us for more than two decades and with his other gang for who knows how long." They sat in silence for a few minutes, and Esau added, "And what has he left in the world after all these years?"

"My friend, what are you trying to say?" Ardon wrinkled his forehead.

"I'm saying that for him it was all for naught, and I don't want to end up like him. Maybe I need to take a break from this life. I've got more than enough stuff, so perhaps it's time to do something else."

"Like what?"

Esau cleared his throat and replied, looking down, "I've been thinking about getting married."

"You—married?" Ardon chortled. "I don't quite see you in the house full of kids. And why now?"

"I am almost forty, Ardon. My father got married at this age. I know I'm not like him, but at least I could follow his footsteps in this . . . in starting a family."

"You love him so much, don't you?"

"Yeah," sighed Esau, biting his lip and sharply inhaling.

"And your brother is still single, right?"

"He is. One more reason to get married now, to show my father who loves him more."

"Have you discussed this with your parents? I bet they would be delighted!"

"Sure, they hope that I settle down—and maybe I will. Maybe not."

"So who's the lucky bride? Found her yet?"

"No, not yet. I suppose I'm still looking for another Anadil," Esau masked his choking by a cough, "but my parents have somebody in mind."

"What, a little matchmaking? And who's she? Tell me." Ardon turned his body toward Esau.

"Have you heard about the land of Charan? It's in the north. Laban, my mother's brother, lives there. He has twin daughters, Leah and Rachel. Believe it or not, I and Jacob were born on the same day, but many years apart, as those girls."

"Wow, that's something!" Ardon rubbed his hands. "You never told me that. So I presume as the older twin you'd marry the older sister Leah and Jacob would marry Rachel? Is this the plan?"

"Well, that's what people were always saying—a match made in heaven! In fact, my father and Laban had exchanged engagement letters decades ago."

"Esau, I can't believe that I'm hearing about it for the first time." Ardon's wide-open eyes reflected the glimmers. "So have you met Leah? Stayed in touch?"

"Never met her. It takes seventeen days just to get there, you know. Why should I bother?"

"Well, if she's waiting . . ."

"No, she isn't. Somebody told me that she was terrified when she learned about the sort of life I led. She was crying nonstop ever since, and her eyes have become swollen—for good. She might not look so hot now." Esau threw up his hands.

"I see . . ." Ardon stretched his lips in a crooked smile. "So now what?"

"I'd rather find my own wife from the local girls. A cute one."

"So you'll be leaving us for a while, I take it? Don't forget to visit me and Dekel when you become respectable."

"No, no, I am not dropping out. Don't go away; stay around until I return. And I'll tell Areef to take over while I'm gone."

*****

Esau began his bridal search in the lands surrounding Mount Seir, which was located south of the Salt Sea. He recalled from his prior exploits that the area, inhabited by the Horites, teemed with beautiful girls. He set up a tent in the wilderness and proceeded to visit local markets and villages.

One day he happened upon a Horite holiday—a boisterous festival to their deity, a must-be event for the local maidens. The young men and women filled the square dominated by a huge wooden idol with deep sand-filled cracks running down its body. The girls were dancing in a circle, holding hands with each other, their bodies shimmering, their heads adorned with fresh flowers. Esau had never seen so many young women in one place.

He watched the dancers, mingling with the other young men ogling the girls. Among the shouts and spilled beer, he examined one damsel after another, undressing them in his mind, when one young beauty caught his attention. Easily the most captivating of the lot, she was wearing a long flowing white dress without a plunging neckline like the dresses of all the others. Long black hair was swirling around her face, briefly covering and then uncovering it, not allowing her beauty to be admired for too long. Their eyes met, and he detected a faint smile—Anadil's smile.

Esau elbowed the locals to get to the front, his eyes fixed on the girl. When the dance was over and the exhausted maidens staggered to drink water and wine, he approached her with his warmest smile.

"Young lady, you've been dancing so well and for so long! And yet you don't seem to be out of breath! Can you share your secret with me?"

She tilted her head, gave him a sideways glance and smiled. "I walk a lot. All day long. I'm used to it." Seeing a question in his eyes, she added, "My family owns a lot of sheep, and I keep going from flock to flock to check on the shepherds."

A rich family! Even better, he thought. They went for a walk, wandering around town for hours, talking, laughing. His golden tongue was well versed in these light-hearted seductive conversations, but it was so hard fighting the urge to just take her right there by force. Esau offered to accompany her the next day.

The maiden agreed, staring into his eyes with a chuckle, "If your feet are strong enough for that!"

She was flirting now, he concluded, so why wait for tomorrow? He drew her towards him and kissed her with all the pent-up passion of the day. She joined in and told him about a good secluded spot where they could relax.

Her name was Oholivamah. She introduced herself as a daughter of Anah the Hivite, but after they met a few times, she confided her shameful pedigree. In truth, she was an illegitimate daughter of Anah's wife by Anah's own father Zibeon the Hivite. Zibeon was a son of Seir, the chief of the Horites, for whom the mountain was named.

This helped explain why such a beautiful girl was not yet married, Esau reasoned. He was glad that such foolish prejudices kept her available for him.

He offered to marry her, and she agreed on the spot. They discussed the logistics. She expected him to move in with her family and become a part of the dominant tribe on Mount Seir, but Esau was not so sure. Where would this leave his father who always called the Horites a despised tribe?

After much deliberation Esau decided to stay at his father's side rather than moving to Mount Seir, even though he anticipated big problems ahead.

"My parents might disapprove of our marriage. They abhor idol-worshippers. And we could never reveal to them the true story of your birth," he told Oholivamah.

"So what should we do about that?"

"Let's pretend that you are a convert to the faith of my grandfather Abraham."

"And how are we going to pull that off? I've heard of Abraham, of course—everybody has—but I don't know anything about his faith. What if your parents quiz me?"

"Don't worry," Esau assured her. "I will explain the basics to you, so we'd fool them for a little while. It's all we need."

"But I like my faith and my idols, and I want to continue burning incense to them. That's the way I was brought up! How am I going to do that in their house?"

"Oh, we only need to trick them for a short while. Once we are there, they won't kick you—us—out, whatever you do. But we need to put up a good act at first."

"What do you have in mind?"

"Let's give you a new image. Even better, let's change your name to . . . to . . . Judith. They would think you have converted to their faith."

"Judith?"

"It means, 'idolatry is false.'"

"I see. What else?"

"Let's tell them the name of your father is Beeri, which means 'my well.' They would assume he makes his living digging wells of water, something my father has done and could relate to. Also, let's tell them you are from the Hittites, not the Hivites or the Horites. It sounds better."

"But what if your father wants to meet mine?"

"Let me worry about that," Esau said with a tight-lipped smile.

***

An old Horite priest conducted a quiet, brief, and uneventful wedding ceremony outside Anah's home. Standing with his bride in the shade of leafy fig trees, Esau ignored the incantations and observed the guests out of the corner of his eye. All of them were Oholivamah's relatives wearing similar white tunics embellished with the threads of gold, as did his new wife. He wore his leather hunting clothes. Truth be told, he didn't care much for the wedding, even for the lavish dinner that followed; he couldn't wait for all that to end and be alone with his new wife.

The next day Esau sent a messenger to his parents, informing them that the marriage had been in the Hittite territory and that he had not invited them because he did not want his elderly father to travel that far. The message also advised that Esau would soon bring Judith home to Be'er Sheva.

For now, the newlyweds lived in the large and comfortable home of Anah who treated Oholivamah as a precious daughter. Anah and his family followed both the Hivite and Horite traditions; they did not push Esau to convert. He liked the surroundings, but he soon discovered that living with his new wife was not all bliss. Her character turned out to be not as sweet as it seemed at first, and there was a nasty streak in her. Worse, Esau caught her lying a few times and after a while started disbelieving everything that came out of her mouth.

He kept asking himself, why didn't I see it before? Was I, a pretty good trickster, trumped by a better liar in the marriage? How am I going to trust Oholivamah with my money and my future offspring? And there is something else, I have to admit. However ravishing she is, I miss a variety of women that I enjoyed in my single days. Why not find a second wife while I'm still living in the place where beautiful girls are plentiful?

*****

Esau revisited the same mountain villages, looking for somebody direct opposite from Oholivamah. But all the young women he met were just like her—outgoing and beautiful but shameless liars, as he was now able to tell. Where else could he look? Perhaps a girl who was a regular in a house of prayer would be more trustworthy? He went to the temples of idol worship, and in one of them he saw a maiden who was burning incense in front of a large frowning wooden idol painted in gold.

The sweet smell and the sight of a stunning slender girl caused him to linger in the temple and observe her. She was chanting a soothing melody in a soft yet beautiful voice that captivated him. He asked a boy helping around the temple about the young lady.

"Her name is Adah," the boy replied, "but people call her Basemath, 'the spice woman,' because she's always here doing this."

Esau approached the beauty with a ready smile. "Your incense is so sweet—just like you!" he exclaimed, tilting his head back.

The girl returned the smile and pointed to his hair. "There aren't too many people like us, are there?" she teased.

Esau immediately wanted her. He had to have her—wife or not. He let his golden tongue loose, and pretty soon he succeeded in sampling the goods. He liked them.

By now, the process of local courtship was familiar. Esau met with Adah's father, Elon the Hittite, to discuss a marriage proposal. Elon, a short but energetic and prosperous man not much older than the suitor, was happy to give away his daughter to someone from such a distinguished family as Esau's.

After suffering through another unremarkable ceremony at Elon's estate, Esau brought his new trophy to join Oholivamah. He used the same pretext of trying to save his parents from an arduous journey to explain why they had not been invited to the wedding. His message advised that Basemath was so named because her deeds were as pleasing as the smell of spices.

For now two wives should be enough, Esau decided. It was time to return to his parents' home in Be'er Sheva.

***

Isaac and Rebecca were resigned to their son's choice of wives. Just as Esau had anticipated, his parents knew that they had only two options: to accept his wives with all the problems they brought, or to ask them—and Esau—to leave. As expected, they did not want to take the second option.

But they were not the only ones unhappy. Despite their different hair color, Oholivamah and Adah proved to be similar in character, and Esau could not trust either one. Even worse, he had to assign someone to keep an eye on them at all times, because he was not convinced they would resist the advances of other men. Each time he reflected in sadness about this, he realized that he missed Anadil, whom he could not imagine ever being unfaithful. He did not even trust his wives with the safekeeping of his precious hunting clothes when he was not in the field, and so he kept the garments with his mother. Though she made no secret of loving Jacob more, at least she was trustworthy, he knew.

***

Adah was the first to bear a son, Eliphaz. Being the only grandson of Isaac, Eliphaz received much attention. He studied with Isaac and Jacob and grew attached to both. Esau did not approve, of course, but he did not care much about child-rearing chores, other than teaching his son the basics of hunting and fighting.

As he grew older, Eliphaz started to behave just as Esau had done at his age, despite the best efforts of Isaac and Jacob to improve the boy's character. Like young Esau, Eliphaz was drawn to the field rather than to his studies. More than once he was seen in the company of Canaanite girls, although he never brought any of them home. His grandparents shivered pondering his future—with good reason.

CHAPTER 13

Slouching on his bed, Esau endured Rebecca's unflinching stare. He knew that look well. For decades.

At last, she began: "Esau, it's time we talked about your wives. Their made-up names don't fool us. They've been in our home for two decades now, burning this acrid incense all the while. Everything now reeks of it. We cannot even invite the followers of your grandfather's faith any longer, or else we'd have to explain why the place smells like a temple of idol worship. But that's not the worst of it. The smoke keeps irritating your father's aging eyes—he's going blind, Esau! Because of them! Because of you!"

Esau glanced at her clenched fists and replied in a calm voice, "Mother, why do you say that? Yes, the women have reverted to the faith of their ancestors, despite my best efforts to the contrary. But how could I force them to stop? Umm? I am not a tyrant! I'm sorry about my father's losing his vision, but how is it their fault? His eyes had gotten weak well before my wives arrived here."

"How's that?"

"Well, did you forget that he was nearly killed—sacrificed by my grandfather on the Mount Moriah? I remember the story. The angels could not bear the sight of the righteous man being slain and wept. Their tears got into my father's eyes and weakened his eyesight."

"Yes, that's true, but it has gotten much worse since then."

"Because he's older now. Much older." Esau paused and continued, looking her straight in the eye, "Mother, we've all been exposed to the smoke, right? Yet neither my vision, nor yours, nor the vision of my wives has suffered. And my wives have been much closer to the source of smoke than my father and you! Or are you saying that your own eyes have dimmed, too?"

"I didn't say that . . ."

"Then you agree!"

Rebecca stood for a while without saying a word, puffing, her lips tightened, and stomped out.

***

Isaac was jolted when Rebecca stormed in. She told him about the conversation she just had and added, "I think I have figured out the problem with your eyes."

"You did? Pray tell."

"Isaac, you've often said that the attempted sacrifice at the hands of your father changed you. Since then Abraham started calling you a perfect sacrificial offering without blemish—as a real sacrifice should be."

"Right, that's how he used to call me. And?"

"This means that both your body and your soul are now exceptionally pure, yes?"

"That's right. And I've acted to preserve this purity in the past. Remember when we had the famine and my people wanted me to move to Egypt? I couldn't do that. Just as a real sacrificial offering would become unfit if it were moved outside the future Temple, so would I lose my holy status if I ever left the Promised Land."

"But this also means that your pure and holy eyes have become vulnerable to the visible effects of idol worship—the smoke . . ."

"Yes, it would stand to reason . . ."

". . . and because your eyes couldn't avoid that smoke, they had nearly shut themselves down to at least avoid seeing it!" Rebecca concluded, her face gleaming.

"You are right, my dear wife, as usual. I suspected as much. Come here."

They sat for a few minutes without uttering a word, holding hands. Then Isaac coughed and resumed speaking, "Rebecca, I am 123 years old. I feel old and frail, I can't see much, and I don't know when I'm going to die. By my reckoning, this day might be very close, and I wish to bless my firstborn son while I still can."

"Don't say that," Rebecca started, tugging at his sleeve, but she halted after looking at his anguished face. "What would this blessing do?"

"It would show that the spiritual leadership of our family is passed to the next generation."

"But it's more than that, isn't it? I know that the blessing of a holy man can positively transform the life of the person being blessed. I also know that you received the power to bless others from your father, who obtained it from God Himself. Are you trying to change Esau with this blessing?"

"I do. He's not a saint, and I detest his lifestyle. Yet I still hope that his great potential will be realized one day. Perhaps with proper blessing and Divine guidance he could turn his life around."

"Isaac, do you truly think that his slippery nature—like of that snake he saved you from—is capable of changing?"

"I hope so. And I hope that Esau would become a fearless, mighty, and righteous warrior who would tear down the gates of his enemies."

Rebecca sighed and looked sideways. "Well, if that's your will . . ."

"It is. But to be able to bless him, my soul needs inspiration. Esau could provide it by a physical deed that requires some effort," Isaac said.

"Like what?"

"I have something in mind. Bring him here, please."

When Esau came in, Isaac said to him, "Look, I am old now, and I do not know the day of my death. So please sharpen your weapons and go out to the field and trap me some game. It must be an ownerless wild game like deer, nothing stolen."

"Yes, father. But why sharpen my weapons?"

"Because I want you to slaughter the animal in accordance with the ritual traditions of our faith. You need an extremely sharp knife for that, as you should know. Then prepare and bring me the savory food that I like, so that I may eat and grant you the blessing of my soul before I die."

Esau grinned from ear to ear, grabbed his sword and his bow and ran out. All he could think was, at last I would be named my father's successor! By the time he realized that he had left his hunting clothes behind, he was far away.

Fine, so I'll hunt without the garments this time, he decided. The game is plentiful here, and this should be a short errand. If by some chance I don't find anything soon, I could always steal some animal. Who's going to know? And my weapons are sharp enough already.

Rebecca rushed into Jacob's room and pulled him away from his studies. "I just heard your father speaking to Esau, saying, 'Bring me the savory food that I like, so that I may eat and bless you before God before I die.' So now, my son, listen to what I'm telling you. We need to outwit Esau, so that he is NOT elevated above you. I cannot let it happen!"

Stunned Jacob extended his hands towards her. "But mother, maybe it's for the best? Maybe it's supposed to happen this way?"

"No, Jacob, no!" Rebecca cried out, her eyes shooting arrows. "Listen, I've never told you or my husband about this. Before you and Esau were born, I went to see Shem and asked him about my future children. He revealed to me that the older son will serve the younger. It's his destiny!"

"Mother, I didn't know. But he has sold his birthright to me decades ago, so he is no longer a firstborn."

"What? And you've kept this from us? But never mind—it is even clearer now that the blessing must go to you. We need to hurry!" She pointed to the door.

"And do what, mother? Plead with my father to reconsider?"

"No, no," she waved her palm at him. "He won't listen. Instead, I'll make a savory stew he's expecting and you'll give it to him before Esau could. Then *you* will receive the blessing and keep your father from making a grave error."

"Are you telling me to act contrary to my father's wishes?"

"Yes! There is no other way. Trust me on this one, son." She gave him a forceful glare.

"But . . . how? I am not a hunter," muttered Jacob.

"Everybody knows that. I have something else in mind. The taste of kid goat's meat can be made to resemble the taste of deer, right?"

"True, but where are we going to get a goat? Steal it from my father?"

"Not steal. My marriage contract allows me to take two kid goats for myself from his flock every day. Now is the time to make use of this allowance," Rebecca cracked a smile.

"Actually, tonight we are preparing to celebrate Passover, and we need a goat kid for the Passover offering in any case," Jacob said.

"Yes, so run to the flock and bring me two kid goats without blemish. We will use one of them as a Passover offering, and I will make a savory stew that your father likes so much out of the other. Bring them to your father, and he will bless you before his death."

Jacob locked his ankles together and said, "But my brother Esau is a hairy man, while my skin is smooth. If my father touches me, he will call me an impostor, and I will bring a curse upon myself rather than a blessing!"

His mother said to him, "Then your curse would be mine, my son. Just listen to me and bring me the goats!" She pulled him up and pushed him out the door. Jacob staggered out with tears in his eyes.

Once the meal was cooked, Rebecca took Esau's hunting clothes that she kept and put them on Jacob. She then placed the kid-goat skins on her son's hands and the smooth part of his neck. With the dish in hand, Jacob went to Isaac's room and greeted his father.

Isaac stirred when the door opened. He replied to the visitor's greeting and asked who it was.

"It is I, Esau, your firstborn," Jacob said, straining to keep his voice from breaking. "I've done what you said. Please get up and taste my food—and give me the blessing of your soul."

"But how did you catch the game so fast, my son?"

"Because God, your God, made it happen." Jacob looked down.

"My son, I'm overwhelmed. The pleasant aroma that entered with you is like the scent of the Garden of Eden! I've never experienced such sweetness before. Only a righteous man's clothes could smell like this. Have you finally mended your ways, Esau? Wasn't I right in deciding to bless you?"

As no answer followed, Isaac rubbed his forehead and said, "But you've rarely mentioned God in conversations. Come closer and let me touch you. Are you truly my son Esau?"

When Jacob approached, Isaac touched him and pronounced, "The voice is the voice of Jacob, but the hands are the hands of Esau."

The patriarch asked his son once more whether he was indeed Esau and received the same answer. After eating Jacob's meal, along with bread and wine, Isaac said, "My son, please come here and kiss me."

Isaac then blessed him: "May God give you the dew of the havens, the fat of the land, and much grain and wine. Nations will serve you and kingdoms bow down to you. May you be the master over your brothers, and may your mother's sons prostrate themselves before you. Those who curse you shall be cursed, and those who bless you shall be blessed."

***

Meanwhile, Esau puzzled over why it was taking so long to trap a game. Everything that moved ran away from him. When he would at last trap an animal and tie it up, somehow it would manage to set itself free, however strong Esau's knots were.

Was it because he missed his hunting clothes? It must have been, he thought, as nothing like this had ever happened to him. In fact, he had no such bad luck even before he got Adam's garments. Was somebody—or something—trying to delay him?

After many attempts, Esau was able to catch a stray dog and cook it. Better this than coming back empty-handed, he reasoned.

***

Having received the blessing, Jacob turned around to leave. As he was walking out of his father's room, Esau was just coming in with his own food. Jacob halted, his eyes widened. The house had a double set of doors, and while Esau was opening the outer doors, Jacob hid behind the inner ones. With trembling hands, he slipped away.

Esau called out, "Arise, my father, and taste my game, so that you may give me the blessing of your soul."

Bewildered Isaac asked who he was.

"Your firstborn, Esau!"

Violent trembling overcame Isaac's body, and he uttered, "What is this terrible smell of burning flesh—as if the Purgatory had opened up underneath you . . ." He wondered out loud who brought him the savory dish that he had eaten minutes ago and who was it that had received his blessings.

"It must have been Jacob, who else? Father, how did his dish taste like?"

"Impossible to describe. I could taste everything I desired at once . . . A heavenly meal! This could only mean one thing: Even though he received my blessings by trickery, I see now that he is the one who deserved them. And he will remain blessed!"

Esau let out a howling cry, as that of a dying beast, "Father, bless me too!"

"But your cunning brother took away your blessing . . ."

"Isn't this why I call him Jacob the trickster, so that he would ensnare me twice?"

"Twice?"

"Well, he stole my birthright—tricked me into selling it for some food, for a plate of red lentils—and now he stole my blessing, too!"

"Oh, then I've blessed the rightful firstborn son."

"Father, but what about me? Bless me also!"

"But what can I bless you with?" Isaac asked. "I have made him a master over you and all that is yours—even your children— now and forever. I have blessed him with abundant grain and wine. What's left, my son?"

Esau cried even more loudly, shedding three tears, "So, you only have one blessing? Father, bless me too!"

Isaac said, "Fine, I will bless you as well. Whether you will deserve it in the future or not, your home will be blessed with the fat of the land and with the dew of the heavens. You shall live by your sword, and you shall serve your brother. Yet if his heirs sin in the future, you would be allowed to break his yoke off your neck."

***

Rebecca called for Jacob and told him, "My son, I have learned—don't ask how—that Esau now hates you because of the blessing. Even worse, he has vowed to kill you when your father passes away and the days of mourning for him are over. You are in mortal danger! In fact, Esau regrets even being your brother; to him, you're dead already."

Jacob just stared at her, as she continued, "Don't try to confront him. Even if you manage to kill him somehow, his descendants might kill *you*. Why should I lose both of you on the same day?"

"So what then, mother?"

"You need to disappear for a while. Flee to my brother Laban in Charan and remain there—up to seven years, perhaps—until Esau's anger subsides and he forgets about what you've done to him. I will let you know when that happens."

"But how can I abandon my father like that? I cannot flee in the middle of the night like a thief without his permission."

"True, you need a purpose. I have an idea: What if you venture out to find a wife? It's time for you to marry, isn't it? That's another reason to go to Charan, where your bride awaits you."

Rebecca approached her husband and reminded him that Esau's Hittite wives made her life miserable. She said that if Jacob, too, married a Hittite girl, her life would be over.

Isaac agreed and sent Jacob to Charan, giving him additional blessings and bidding him not to marry Canaanite girls. He gave him many gifts, gold and silver, to find favor in the eyes of Laban and his daughters. He did not foresee too many complications on this journey.

CHAPTER 14

Esau was furious when he learned that his brother had left. Jacob has slipped away, and I cannot go after him myself, not while my father is still alive, he thought. But someone else could do the job.

"Eliphaz, we need to get rid of someone. Someone you know. Will you do this for me?" Esau whispered, as his eyes drilled into his son's.

"Of course, father! Who is it? Uncle Jacob, perhaps?"

Esau beamed with delight. "Very good! Yes, him. He has just left for Charan, trying to run away from me, under the pretext of looking for a wife. You could catch up with him if you hurry. I don't think he's a fast rider."

"But father, why should I kill my uncle? He was always good to me!" Eliphaz crossed his hands behind his back, gripping the wrist of his arm.

"Lower your voice," Esau hissed. "Because he stole my birthright and my blessings, that's why. Also, he has no children of his own. If you kill him now, *you* would gain the status of the firstborn in this family after my demise. Think about that!"

Eliphaz agreed to do the job but did not leave right away. He went to seek the advice of the only other person he trusted—his mother Adah.

Putting her cooking aside, Adah told him, "Don't listen to your father. Jacob is a righteous man, and he is blessed and protected from above. He is also a very strong man—too strong for you, my son. If you try to kill him, he'd kill you instead. Don't even think of going after him!"

"But my father . . ."

"If your father could, he'd slay his brother himself. Why do you think he is sending you?"

"Because I am younger and stronger?"

"No, because you are younger and more stupid!"

"I am not stupid, mother! I am just young and strong . . ." He hugged her and kissed her on the lips. She pushed him away and smacked him with a spoon.

"I'm still going, mother!"

***

Eliphaz kept urging his horse through heat and dust. Ten of his mother's brothers, the sons of Elon the Hittite, followed behind. They caught up with Jacob between Be'er Sheva and Hebron and drew their swords, trying to look menacing.

Jacob stopped his camel and greeted them with a smile. "Good day, my nephew! Is everything well? Do you need my help? And what's with the swords?"

"Everything's fine, but not for you! You must pay for what you've done to my father!" Eliphaz yelled a bit too loud.

"Pay? How? Did he send you to kill me?" Jacob kept smiling, as wrinkles spread across his forehead.

"Yes, he did!"

"But why you? You and I have spent a lot of time together, and you've learned so much with my father, too! Why didn't my brother come to kill me himself?"

Eliphaz fiddled with his sash, coughed, and glanced at his posse. All the men were looking down. He blurted out, "Uncle, I adore my father and cannot disobey him. But my mother is also right. She told me you're a holy man. What should I do? Tell me!"

"You're asking me?" Jacob swallowed hard. "But I understand your predicament." He thought for a second and added, "Here is what we could do. I could just give you everything I own—gold, silver, even my camel and the clothes I wear. As we have studied together with you, a pauper is considered like a dead man. Take it all, and then you could tell your father that I was dead."

Eliphaz and his companions took all the Jacob's possessions but did not touch him.

****

As the dust under the hooves of his nephew's horses settled down, Jacob stood in place, his lips moving, his eyes raised to the sky. He walked toward a distant river, immersed himself in it like in a ritual bath, and lifted his hands in prayer.

Less than a minute later a loud sound startled him: a horseman was galloping toward the water. Jacob stared in astonishment as the rider charged right in.

The horse stumbled in the soft silty riverbed and fell over, throwing the man off. He thrashed about but could not free his leg caught in the stirrup. Jacob hurried to help, but it was too late.

He carried the body ashore, horse's reins in hand, and tried to revive the man—in vain. Jacob buried the body in the sand and sat down, holding his head in his hands.

When he got up, he examined the man's clothes, horse, food, and money, shaking his head. He turned the horse towards the Academy of Shem's grandson Eber—the same place his mother had visited to seek Shem's advice. Shem himself had since passed away, and Eber was running the academy alone.

Jacob ended up studying there for the next fourteen years.

****

Eliphaz returned to his father with the loot, including Jacob's clothes, but admitted that he had left their owner alive. He stood in front of Esau with hunched shoulders rising up to his cheeks.

Esau overturned a heavy bench and yelled, "You've disobeyed me, Eliphaz! Explain!"

"Father, I couldn't bring myself to kill my uncle. Instead, I robbed him of everything he had. As I've studied—with him, by the way—a man without any possessions is like a dead man, so technically I have fulfilled your order."

"Technically? This is the kind of a slick tale *I* could've spun, and I don't need you to give me this sort of an explanation! Go now. I suspect I'll have to deal with this unfinished business again, soon."

Eliphaz staggered out. Esau hid Jacob's possessions in his room, away from his parents' eyes.

***

Ever since Eliphaz chanced upon Oholivamah dressing up in her room, he started to drop by her home, ostensibly to check on her two sons, Jeush and Jaalam. She smiled but avoided his persistent stares.

One day Eliphaz followed Oholivamah to her bathing spot in the nearby brook. On Esau's orders, his wives were always accompanied by two of his servants when venturing outside. The servants stood more than a bowshot away behind a small hill—far enough not to see, but close enough to be summoned if needed.

As Oholivamah was coming out of the water in all her naked beauty, which had not been diminished by pregnancy and childbirth, Eliphaz got up from his hiding spot and strolled toward her. She stopped with a puzzled look and attempted to cover her body.

Eliphaz came up to her and gazed into her eyes. She did not stir. He embraced and kissed her, as she tried to push him away in silence under the cloak of her black hair. He continued to kiss her with passion, and at last she responded, feeling his face with her delicate lips. He led her to a nearby verdant bush, and they slumped to the ground.

Eliphaz has not been with Oholivamah after that day, but the next year she had a baby—the third son. When Eliphaz dropped by to congratulate, she whispered, "This one is yours. I named him Korach. Don't let your father suspect anything."

CHAPTER 15

With Jacob gone, Esau had nobody to argue with, save for his two wives, and he felt restless. Awash in possessions, he kept thinking about having accomplished so little in his life. He missed military exploits, yet without an army of his own, he could not fight kings and conquer kingdoms. He asked his trusted friend for advice.

"Ardon, I'm sick of raiding and pillaging. Nobody wants to challenge me anymore. What else can I do for fun?"

"Hmm . . . I know you like fighting more than being a common bandit—I feel the same way. Robbing people of their last possessions eventually loses its novelty."

"So what then?"

"I think you'll enjoy finding someone who is impossible to defeat—and defeating him."

"Who do you have in mind?"

"Well, if you want to fight the strongest, fight the Anakim."

"The great giants? The offspring of the antediluvian fallen angels? Are they still around? I thought Nimrod and the other kings had finished them off long ago."

"No, a few are still with us. Some of them live right here near Hebron, don't you know? I've also heard that one of them lives in Arad and a few others dwell along the seacoast in Gaza, Gath, and Ashdod. And of course there is the famous king Og in the land of Bashan."

"Great! I could start with the locals then," said Esau, rubbing his hands.

"Maybe not. The king of Hebron has made a pact with three of those: Sheshai, Ahiman, and Talmai. But the others are fair game, if you think you could somehow defeat one of them."

"I sure do. So let's see . . . Hebron is off-limits, you say. I cannot show my face anywhere near Ashdod without battling the whole king's army after what we've done there. How about the one in Arad then? It's only a day's walk from here. Let's go there tomorrow."

***

In the morning, Esau and Ardon rode their camels without saying a word. Esau was thinking through various battle scenarios. The face of his companion was limp, and his lips moved in silence.

At last, Ardon uttered, "Esau, you said something about these giants being the progeny of the fallen angels. Do you think it's true?"

"Who knows? But I remember learning about them when I was young."

"So tell me what you know. Otherwise, I'm worried out of my mind," grunted Ardon.

"I think it all started with the generation that lived before the Flood. They angered God to the point that He regretted having created humans. Seeing this, two angels named Shamchazai and Azael asked God to send them into our world in flesh to supplant us. They promised to take care of the land, even if the sons of man were to disappear from it."

"So did God agree?"

"He told them that if they descended into our world, they would succumb to its evil desires—and become worse than us. But the two angels were certain that, being pure and holy in Heaven, they'd remain so in our world as well, despite all its temptations. They kept asking to be allowed to go. Eventually, God acceded."

"And then?"

"They came down looking like enormous giants, and our beautiful girls were fascinated with them. The two angels couldn't resist their flirtations and immediately went astray."

"And their children were giants, too, like the Anakim?"

"Right."

"Esau, that's a nice story!" Ardon's lips loosened into a tight smile.

"Yes, it's cute, but I don't believe in these religious legends."

"I know you don't, although I've never understood why. How else would you explain a presence of these giants here? And how could they have survived the Flood unless they were superhuman?"

"Not sure, but there has to be another explanation. It's my brother Jacob who sees the hand of God in everything that's going on. I'm not like him! Please stop saying that I should think like that bookworm."

"Esau, I wasn't!"

They arrived in Arad, and the conversation ended. They found a roadside inn and chatted up the innkeeper, who turned out to be quite familiar with the local giant.

"How many of these monsters live here?" asked Esau.

"As far as I know, there's only one," answered the innkeeper, looking sideways at Ardon, who stayed out of the conversation.

"Doesn't he have a family?"

"I don't believe so. At least, nobody has ever seen it."

"And what do the locals think of him?"

"Huh! We hate him. He steals our animals and ruins our sheepfolds. We pray somebody would rid us of this menace. After each of his raids we spend much time and money gathering the flocks and fixing the enclosures." The innkeeper sighed and continued to wipe the same dish over and over.

"So why don't you ask your king to send his soldiers after him?"

"We tried. He did send the soldiers—a score of warriors in full battle armor. None returned. Since then the king keeps finding one excuse or another not to get involved here."

"And I figure you can't afford to hire mercenaries on your own, right?"

"Of course not, my lord. We are poor, as you can see." The man put down the dish.

Esau glanced at the cracked wall plaster and nodded. "Then maybe I'm your man—I'll do it for free!" he grinned.

"Just you? The two of you?"

"Sure!"

The innkeeper gave them a crooked smile and said, "Well, he lives on a mountain. I'll ask somebody to show you the way there, if I could find anyone brave enough. After that, you're on your own. But remember: nobody who wished to fight him has ever made it back."

***

The two visitors and a few curious locals left early next morning. Esau asked Ardon to stay behind and be ready to help if needed—or to collect his remains if it came to that. The townsfolk stayed even farther away. Esau was wearing Adam's leather garments underneath his shawl. He had never worn them in battle and wasn't sure if they'd help, but decided they couldn't hurt. He carried a spear, two swords, a bow, and several knives.

The giant's home looked like a regular house from a distance, but was overwhelming up close. Two towering stone columns supported a large entrance portico. With a deep grunt, Esau strained to push the hefty front door open.

The interior looked like that of a regular house, but scaled up many times over. The roof was so high up that Esau had to crane his neck to have a good look at its framing made of huge tree trunks laid side by side on top of enormous hewn timbers. As he gaped at the dinner table, which was at least twice as high as he was, Esau heard rumbling footsteps and felt the ground shake.

The giant who waddled in had immense hands and feet; each of his arms was longer than Esau's whole body. His shaved head seemed too large; his face had protruding chin and forehead, prominent eyebrow ridges, and thick lips. He came closer and asked in a voice that rattled the clay pots stacked on the floor, "Who are you? What do you want?"

Esau swallowed hard and scowled, his eyes narrowed. "I am Esau. And what's your name?"

"Darimai. Why are you here, uninvited? Did you come to fight me and die?" The sound of his voice, echoed in close quarters, was hurting human ears.

"Yes, Darimai, I came to fight. But you can save your life if you surrender and give me all the gold and silver that you've stashed away!"

The giant blinked twice and started to laugh. Shards of clay rained down from the table.

Esau turned pale but did not move. "I'm not joking," he howled, bracing himself against a chair leg, "Give me the gold, or I'll kill you!"

Esau ducked and barely escaped a huge fist that passed over his head. He ran out of the house and faced the entrance. My leather is useless here, he thought in passing.

The giant staggered out, carrying a huge spear that made the one Esau was holding look like straw. But that was not Darimai's weapon of choice. He opened his mouth and took a deep breath.

The deafening sound of his yell, louder than the roar of a hundred lions, swept Esau off his feet. He covered his ears with his hands, but his head was still ready to split apart.

Esau pushed himself up and glanced at his weapons. Nothing was broken, even his bow and arrows were intact.

Darimai's jaw slackened when Esau picked up his spear. The giant took another deep breath that sucked the sand off the ground, and right then Esau threw his spear into the open mouth. It was a perfect hit. Instead of making another roaring cry, Darimai was choking. He bit on Esau's spear and pulled its remnants from his mouth and from the back of his neck.

The monster took a few thundering steps toward the man, trying to jab him with his own spear, but Esau evaded the strike. Darimai tried again, with the same result.

He then swung the spear as a club with a forehand strike aimed at the man's legs. Esau jumped high off the ground and then fell back on the sand, avoiding the return backhand sweep as well. The giant halted, coughing up blood, and almost fell forward, but caught the ground with his massive hands.

Wasting no time, Esau rushed toward him and jammed the sword into his ear, forcing it in. Darimai tried to get up but collapsed, his face buried deep into the ground.

Ardon and the townsfolk started cheering in jubilation, but their shouts soon turned to screams, "Look! LOOK!"

Two other giants emerged from the house and stomped toward Esau, holding enormous clubs made of uprooted trees. They looked just like Darimai, with the same big bellies, barely covered by the short shawls worn over crudely stitched tunics.

Were they all brothers? The giants halted in front of the house, standing side by side, peering at Darimai's body.

Esau raced into the narrow space between them, where they could not swing their clubs without hurting one another. He managed to strike both of them on the legs with a sword and drew blood, although this seemed to inflict little damage.

The hulking creatures stepped apart and in a rage tried to whack Esau with their clubs. They missed and hit the ground instead, kicking up dust.

Trying to protect his eyes, his ears still ringing, Esau took cover behind one of the stone columns. He waited for the brothers' next move, bow and arrow at the ready.

The giants approached, trying to outflank Esau from both sides. When one of them bent down and tried to grab the man with his enormous hand, Esau shot him in the eye. The giant roared, sprung back, and remained in place for a few seconds, shaking his head. The second giant turned towards his brother and received an arrow in the ear.

As the first giant struggled to remove the arrow with his huge fingers, his other eye was also hit. The monster roared yet again and tried to swipe the man with his arm but smote the column instead, knocking out a stone that barely missed Esau. The column buckled and collapsed; the portico roof creaked but remained in place in a precarious balance.

Esau ran out in the open, skipped behind the second giant, and struck the back of his ankle. Blood started pouring on the colossal leather sandals.

After another deafening roar, the second giant turned around and tried to smack Esau, who again evaded the strike. After a quick glance at the roof, Esau ran behind the still-standing stone column.   The giant tried to reach him with his club but missed. Infuriated, the monster kept swinging, until he miscalculated and knocked out the remaining column.

The portico roof groaned and sagged, and the enormous tree trunks came crashing down. Esau sprinted away for his life, but the injured giants were not as agile, and the huge timbers struck them both.

Esau gazed at the carnage, unable to take his eyes off the three hulking corpses. The excited cries of Ardon and the town people shook him back to his senses. He did it!

The inhabitants of Arad celebrated for days. The news of Esau's great victory spread throughout the land of Canaan and beyond. People started to call him the mighty man.

Chapter 16

A few months later, Esau watched his children play outside from the window of his parents' home. Although Isaac's servants had built separate houses for both his wives, Esau still preferred to sleep in his old room. Rebecca was passing by, and he saw her cringing as she glanced over her grandsons throwing rocks at one another.

Esau locked his jaw. It's obvious that my parents abhor my Canaanite wives, he sighed. Is it possible that I didn't receive the blessing I desired because of these women? If that's true, could I improve my lot by getting yet another wife from my father's extended family? But who could that be? Surely not Leah with her tired eyes. What about the daughter of my uncle Ishmael? Perhaps when my father sees all my efforts to please him, he might find another blessing for me.

Besides, Ishmael might be useful not only for supplying me with a wife, but also for getting rid of my bothersome brother, once and for all. Ishmael would understand my feelings, having been in my shoes, because Abraham blessed not him—the firstborn— but his younger brother Isaac. If I could entice my uncle to kill Jacob, my hands would be clean. Not only that, but I would then be entitled to kill Ishmael to avenge my poor brother—and become the ruler of both tribes! He rubbed his hands.

Esau told his parents about his interest in marrying an Ishmaelite woman, and they liked the idea. He informed his wives about the trip to Ishmael but did not reveal its purpose. They will know in due time.

He went alone. He was not afraid of any trouble along the way: *he* was the trouble. He knew most of the way to Paran Desert, where Ishmael lived, and there was only a single path that extended through the mountains. Getting lost would be difficult.

***

Traveling along the rocky mountain road, Esau caught himself snoozing more than a few times, but he was jolted awake when his camel stopped on a narrow passage. An arrow just landed in front of him!

He scanned the gentle slopes but could not see anyone. He wiped his hands and jumped off the camel. The next arrow could be in my chest, he worried, and I would die like Anadil.

He turned the animal across the road to shield him. Still no sign of the attackers. This is unnerving, he thought—usually I'm the one doing the ambushing. Should have taken some of my men with me. Being robbed of the engagement ring and the presents would be bad enough, but to die like this . . .

An archer stepped out from behind a jagged rock. He was dressed in the typical nomadic garb—a sun-bleached *simlah* shawl with a *sudra* head covering extending over his shoulders. Pointing an arrow at Esau, he yelled, "Who are you? What is your business here?"

"I am Esau, the son of Isaac and the grandson of Abraham. I am on my way to see my uncle Ishmael."

The archer lowered his bow and came closer, soon joined by the others. "I am Nebaioth, Ishmael's firstborn," the archer said without smiling. "Welcome, my cousin!"

The men embraced. Seeing Nebaioth's craggy and open face, Esau was relieved. Perhaps he won't sink a knife in my back, he hoped. Not right away, at least. But why does he look so fidgety?

"Are you traveling alone?" Nebaioth asked, fiddling with his sash.

"Yes. I have nothing to fear," answered Esau.

***

Ishmael's camp had forty or fifty tents arranged in a circle—the same black goat tents Esau knew all too well. To relieve the midday heat, the bottom covers of the tents were raised up. Ishmael's tent, made of white goat skins, was larger and taller than the others.

Esau stepped inside, where his uncle sat on a plush embroidered cushion wearing a ceremonial white and red robe with gold accents. A bushy white beard rimmed his dark wrinkled face. Nebaioth and his other children also had a dark complexion, no doubt because Ishmael's mother was Hagar, Abraham's Egyptian concubine. Every Egyptian Esau had ever met was swarthy. Ishmael looked rather old for his age. Being only 137 by Esau's reckoning, he appeared much frailer than Abraham was at 175.

The host gave Esau water to drink and to wash off the dirt from his feet. They exchanged pleasantries and waited for the food to arrive.

"My nephew, we are so similar, you and I," said Ishmael. "Like you, I was a bit of a wild savage in my youth, preferring to hunt in the fields to my religious studies." Esau nodded, and Ishmael continued, "My father didn't like that. He sent me away, so I wouldn't threaten Isaac, his chosen heir."

"Yes, we are so similar," agreed Esau. "As you, I am an older son passed over the family leadership in favor of a younger brother. And both you and I have been blessed to live by the sword! I see that you are prospering doing just that."

Ishmael glanced at the servants swaying ostrich feathers behind them and chuckled, "I wish. Yes, for a while we were on top of the world, unbeatable, and everyone was afraid of us."

Ishmael's face turned limp and the corners of his mouth dropped. "But look at us now. Since my father's death, things changed. Nobody is scared of us anymore. People are eager to fight us, and sometimes they are winning! Perhaps my short-lived glory was owed to my father's merits, not my own . . . We are spread out in the lands of our relatives, from Egypt all the way to Assyria, without a single strong homeland."

He bowed his head, as if apologizing for something, and continued, "I am not at all certain this is the life I wanted. Had I known then what I know now, I would've taken a different path."

"You would?" asked Esau.

"Oh, yes. And I tried to change, I did. As you know, when Abraham died and I came to bury him together with your father, I allowed Isaac to lead the funeral procession. I let him be the successor. But maybe that was too late." He paused again and looked up at Esau. "And what do you expect out of *your* life, my nephew?"

"My life should be long and fulfilling," answered Esau without hesitation. "What's out there other than a long and happy life?"

Ishmael gave him a long and intent stare. Esau did not quite understand what that stare meant. But if my uncle thinks himself a reformed sinner, he thought, talking about killing Jacob would be out of place. Too bad.

The dinner was served. It was the food Esau loved from his childhood—fish, cheese, mutton, vegetables, but with some added local spices. Each dish was served in an exquisite gold plate of a unique shape. Esau was particularly fond of the condiments, such as a mixture of Egyptian garlic, olive oil, and some lemon juice, as Ishmael explained.

After the meal Esau put down his silver wine goblet and announced, "My uncle, perhaps I could help you regain your former glory. This is the reason I'm here."

"You want to join us?"

"No, no. I want to marry your daughter, my cousin."

Ishmael's face broke out in a broad smile, and he replied, "I am honored by your request, my nephew. I should have thought of this myself. Let me call her."

A young woman came in, wearing a simple white dress; she could have been mistaken for a maid. Unlike most Canaanite girls, she was not skinny, but her soft round face radiated warmth, and her complexion was lighter than her brothers'. Esau would not call her beautiful, but she looked like someone he knew all his life—like his sister.

"I have twelve sons but only one daughter," said Ishmael. "My cherished Basemath, please meet my dear nephew Esau."

Esau had to restrain himself from bursting out laughing. Basemath? Why didn't I ask about her name in advance? But it makes no difference—I know what to do.

Basemath was quite pleasant in conversation and seemed to appreciate a golden tongue. Esau told her that he had two Canaanite wives but wanted to marry someone from his own family. She didn't seem surprised. They talked for hours, with Ishmael obliged to listen.

At last, he stepped in, fighting a yawn, "My nephew, I have a room prepared for you in the tent next to mine. Let's retire for the night."

Esau thanked his host and walked Basemath to her tent. After they said good-night, he tried to kiss her.

She demurred with a smile, "I am not that kind of a girl, my lord."

Esau felt relieved. Perhaps she would indeed be different. Perhaps Anadil would be buried at last. As he turned around, he noticed a man standing in the shadow. Nebaioth.

"Are you your sister's protector?" Esau inquired, smiling his best. Nebaioth did not smile back and did not answer; he stepped away and disappeared.

Esau made a marriage proposal in the morning, and Basemath accepted. He gave her a golden nose ring and two gold bracelets, the kind his mother received from Abraham's servant when he traveled to engage her to Isaac.

"How long before the marriage ceremony?" Esau asked.

"Please give us ten months to a year," replied Ishmael.

"Why wait so long?" I could barely wait one night, he thought.

"It is a custom in these lands. The time allows the bride to acquire proper clothes and other items she'd need in marriage. Such things are not easy to come by in the mountains and the desert."

"No need to wait!" exclaimed Esau. "I have everything she might need!"

"Even so, let's do it the traditional way," concluded Ishmael with a polite grin. There was no use arguing.

Nebaioth and his brothers accompanied their guest part of the way back without saying a word, and Esau was on guard the entire time. They arrived at the narrow passage where they first met, at which point Nebaioth and his brothers turned around and left. Esau was not sure whether his life was in danger or not until he arrived home. But what about the next time?

Chapter 17

Esau shared the news with his parents, and they were pleased. His other wives would have to wait to be told, though—the less time they had to plot anything the better, he reasoned.

Meanwhile, he had a home built for his future wife. Like the houses of his parents and wives, it was of a typical Canaanite construction: single story, flat roof, four rooms. The rooms were small, limited by the length of the trimmed tree trunks spanning the distance between the walls made of unburned bricks. The bedrooms had built-in elevated platforms for sleeping.

In a couple of months, a messenger arrived. Ishmael was dead.

This changed things, Esau realized. *Now I'll have to deal with Nebaioth and his uncertain sympathies. Why weren't my father and I invited to the funeral? Was Nebaioth plotting something? At least it's clear now why Ishmael had given me such an intent look upon hearing what I expected out of my life.*

***

At the appointed day Esau, accompanied this time by Eliphaz, Ardon, and Dekel, returned to marry Nebaioth's sister. After the marriage ceremony, which to Esau looked the same as the previous two, the Ishmaelites assembled for a lavish feast. The tables, covered with white linen tablecloths, groaned under an abundance of delicacies and wine. The servants refilled the glasses without delay.

Sitting at the center, Esau announced to his new wife, "My dear, I wish to call you Machalat from now on."

"Are you joking? Why?" She shoved the dish away from her.

"Because I already have a wife called Basemath."

"You do? But why 'Machalat'?"

"It means 'the forgiven one.' Our family has a tradition that if you repent from all your sins on the wedding day, they are forgiven. You would become a righteous and innocent woman, as if you were just born. Don't you know that?"

Basemath replied with a twinkle in her eye, "So you care about righteousness? Perhaps all the bad things I've heard about you were untrue!"

"Perhaps. But I have to ask you something else," said Esau with a serious look.

"Ask."

"What's the story with Nebaioth? I don't think he likes me."

"Hmm . . . Why do you think that?"

"I don't know, but he hasn't said much to me since we have met. It's not about you, is it? You two were not . . ."

"No, no, no!" Her eyes were glaring.

"Then why?"

"I don't have a clue. Maybe not everybody likes you. Why don't you ask my other brother Kedar? He's having a good time."

Indeed, her brother was wobbling in his chair. Esau sidled closer to him and asked, "How's your day going so far, my brother Kedar?"

"Great! I love this wine . . . over here. My father . . . never allowed us to have it, saving it for some special oc-casion," Kedar replied, head swinging on his neck.

"I am sorry about your father," said Esau, grabbing Kedar by the sleeve. "But he's gone, and we cannot bring him back . . . So what's next for you boys?"

Kedar mumbled, trying to string words together, "I don't . . . know. Nebaioth is in charge now. Ask him-mmm."

"I'm not sure he wants to talk to me. Why do you think that is?" Esau peered into Kedar's murky eyes.

"Oh, I know why!" Kedar leaned to the side. "He's afraid of you. He thinks you'll take over . . . once you are married into us. Don't tell him I told you . . ." He tumbled to the floor.

Esau felt relieved. That's all it was? After more wine was consumed, Esau plunked down near Nebaioth and said in his sweetest voice, "My cousin, I am grateful for your hospitality. The dinner is fabulous!"

"Thank you, Esau! With this marriage, you have bestowed a great honor upon our family," Nebaioth replied without smiling, rubbing his thighs under the table.

"No, it's I who is honored to be in your company. Perhaps we could collaborate in our endeavors . . ." Seeing that Nebaioth's ears perked up, Esau added, "Under your leadership, of course. Let's enjoy the dinner and discuss our plans tomorrow."

***

Around mid-day, after the newlyweds had a chance to sleep off their bliss in Machalat's tent decorated with fresh desert flowers, Nebaioth invited them for another festive meal. This time he was seated next to Esau.

"So Nebaioth, what do you plan to do now?" Esau asked.

"First, we need to build a secure home. A base where we could regrow our strength in peace."

"Any particular location in mind?"

"We have a few, but it's too early to discuss. What about your plans?"

"I'd like to do the same," replied Esau. "Now that I have a family and am sixty-three, I need a place of my own, a place where my future clan, the Edomites, will grow and prosper. I need to make a mark in the world while I still have the time."

"And where might that place be?"

Esau got to the point. "Some of my relatives live near Mount Seir—such a fantastic location. It's so beautiful up there."

"A fine area," agreed Nebaioth. "But it's occupied by the Horites. Those people are vicious. We've had some dealings with them."

"Perhaps we could deal with them together. How about paying them a visit while I'm still here?"

Nebaioth looked down. "We could fight them together, if it ever comes to that, but I wouldn't want to just go to look around there. They know my face all too well."

"No problem. But I might need your help later."

And so it was agreed.

Chapter 18

Esau introduced Machalat to his family. To avoid confusion, he told everyone to stop using the name Basemath. He no longer cared to keep up the pretense of having married a proselyte, thus he dropped the name Judith as well. He now called his wives Oholivamah, Adah, and Machalat.

Oholivamah and Adah resented that Esau was spending much more time with Machalat than with both of them combined and gave the young newcomer a cold shoulder. Machalat tried to find a common ground with the older wives but could not engage them in any conversation beyond pleasantries. She could only speak with her husband and his parents.

Esau suspected that his three wives did not get along and was unconcerned at first. After all, he did not want all three of them to conspire against him, did he? But then things worsened.

Early one morning he heard a loud scream. He recognized Machalat's voice and rushed to her house. She sat in bed, wailing in pain.

"What happened?" he cried out, barging through the door.

"I've been stung in my sleep!"

"By what?"

"By these!"

Esau lit a lamp and saw two squished scorpions lying on the bed. His heart sunk when he recognized them as deathstalkers—the most dangerous type of yellow desert scorpion.

How could this happen? Yes, snakes and scorpions were common in the desert, but they rarely stung people in elevated beds; they usually went for people's feet on the ground. And two scorpions attacking a person in bed at the same time? Esau had never heard of such a thing, yet Machalat showed him the sting marks on her body.

He poured some water over the wounds and said, "Machalat, we all get stung once in a while. I know it hurts, but it's not that serious. At worst, you'd get a rash and a painful couple of days." Or you wouldn't make it at all, he thought.

"I know what they are," she squealed, "I've lived in the desert all my life, remember? I cannot believe it occurred in bed! And the two of them! Things like that just don't happen!"

"Are you saying someone planted them? Hmm . . . " He considered that possibility for a while. "By the way, have you been locking the door at night?"

"Of course."

"I'll check it out."

He turned around to leave, but Machalat grabbed his cloak. "Don't go! Sit with me for a while."

Esau sat down on the corner of the bed and looked at her.

She was still sobbing. "Esau, I know your wives hate me. It's them, I know it, or maybe they asked one of their children to do it. I'm afraid what they'll do next—*if* I survive this."

"You will, you will! You're a strong woman, and you must have been stung before, right?"

"Yes."

"See? You'll get better in no time, believe me."

She quieted down a bit and asked, "What are you going to do about it?"

He shifted his body and purred, "Don't know yet. I told you, I'll check it out. But I can't just punish my two wives without any evidence. After all, it could have been a rare unfortunate event."

She sighed. "Just stay here for a little bit and talk to me."

"Of course, my dear! And I'll find out if my wives or anyone else was involved in this—I promise!" He sat there for a while, watching the sides of her body swell around the red marks.

"Esau, do you love them?" she asked all of a sudden.

"Well, they are my wives . . ." Wrinkles spread across Esau's forehead.

"I know that. But do you love them?"

"Not as much as you," Esau's golden tongue retorted.

"Then tell me, what did you find in them?"

"I just wanted to get married at the age of forty, like my father. Remember, I didn't know you then."

"And now? Why do you need them now?"

"They are still my wives of twenty-three years, and they have given me children. As you know, I have Eliphaz from Adah; I have Jeush, Jaalam, and now little Korach from Oholivamah."

"But children aside, do you feel close to them?"

"Not as close as . . . " Esau started saying but bit his tongue. "Look, Machalat, I don't know what you're asking."

"A simple question. Do you share thoughts and desires with them that you keep from others? Can you unburden yourself with them when things go wrong?"

"No."

"I thought so. But you can share things with me—I hope you know that."

"I do. But I need to go now." He left without stopping to look at her disappointed face. He was happy to get out of there.

In the morning he asked Oholivamah and Adah about their role in the attack. They both denied having anything to do with it, as expected. He then went to see Ardon and Dekel and asked for their help.

***

Ardon and Dekel alternated watching Machalat's house over three uneventful nights, with only an occasional fox or jackal passing by. But on the fourth night Ardon saw somebody crossing the courtyard. He followed, moving stealthily in the darkness, as Esau had taught him.

A human figure was hunched over Machalat's front door, holding a sack. In a few quick steps Ardon was over the intruder, jamming the sword against his back and grabbing him by the throat. It was a young boy, one of Esau's.

"What are you doing here?" Ardon demanded in a gruff voice. The boy didn't answer, trying to free his head.

"What's in the sack?"

"You don't want to find out!"

"Oh, we surely will!" Ardon dragged the child, still clutching the sack, to the house where Esau slept and knocked on the door.

Esau came out, holding an oil lamp and a sword. Seeing him, the boy dropped the sack and tried to flee, but Ardon's grip was firm. Esau brought the lamp closer to the boy's face—it was Jaalam!

Esau poked the sack with his sword. Something was moving inside.

"What's there?" Esau growled. The boy was silent, and Ardon squeezed his throat harder.

"Find out yourself!" Jaalam hissed.

Esau struck the sack several times and emptied it. The remains of three large snakes were twisting on the ground. "Great. Did you put the scorpions there earlier?" he barked. The boy kept quiet, and Esau scooped what was left of the snakes back into the bag, being careful not to get his hands too close to the severed heads. "They could still bite, you know," he muttered.

He started dragging the boy to his mother, but before they could reach Oholivamah's door, Machalat's scream stopped him. He rushed to her house.

His young wife was sitting on her bed in sheer horror, screaming at the top of her lungs. A large snake was biting her cheek.

After checking the bed for any other creatures and finding none, Esau put down the lamp and drew his sword. He grabbed the snake and tried to pull it off her, but it would not budge. He sliced through its body, yet the head remained attached to Machalat's face.

He lifted the lamp to observe the snake up close. It was a familiar desert viper with a thick brown zigzag stripe running along its back. Esau grasped its neck, trying to stick a knife between its fangs and pry the head off, but the fangs were sunk so deep that he couldn't do it without cutting off a piece of his wife's cheek. It was as if the snake's head had become a part of her face.

Esau tried again, with the same result, so he abandoned the effort and ran out. He sifted through Anadil's medicine containers stashed in his room. Here! Esau grabbed a jar full of brown liquid—a strong drink that Anadil's father used to give his patients to dull their pain—and pulled out the cork.

He ran back and poured some of the liquid on the viper's head. It promptly loosened its grip, and Esau pulled it off the screaming woman. He dabbed a bit of the medicine onto the wound and hugged Machalat, trying to console her.

Ardon and Dekel came inside, hauling a young man along with them. Shining a light on his face, Esau recognized Jeush, Oholivamah's oldest.

"Caught him running away from the house," said Dekel.

"Bring him closer!" commanded Esau. Looking at his son's face, he screeched, "Is this your doing?"

Jeush did not answer, and Ardon grabbed him by the hair and pulled on it until Jeush confessed, "Yes, we did it! Jaalam and I."

"Why such a fancy operation, with the two of you involved?" raged Esau.

"We've discovered them hiding in the bushes. We needed a distraction."

One part of Esau was glad that his sons could come up with such an elaborate plan, but the other part was burning with hot anger. "Did your mother put you up to this?" he demanded, but Jeush just lowered his gaze.

"He doesn't have to say anything—who else would think of such a nasty treat? Let him go. I'll have a talk with my wives in the morning." He sat down on Machalat's bed, comforting her through the night.

***

When the sun came out, Esau called his two Canaanite wives and their children into the courtyard and announced, "Machalat is badly hurt. I don't know if she'll make it."

He then addressed Oholivamah, "Whether you confess to sending your children to kill her or not, I know you did it. Here is what I'm going to say, and I'm going to say it only once: If she dies, so will you! You'd better pray she lives."

"Esau, what are you saying? You cannot kill me! I am your wife, too! A law of the land protects me. If you kill me, you'll have to deal with my relatives, the avengers."

Esau detected a hint of smugness in Oholivamah's voice, but she did have a point. "I didn't say I'd kill you. I said you would die one way or another. By drowning or by fire or by a wild beast—justice will find you!"

"So you believe in Divine retribution now?" asked Eliphaz. "I thought you didn't."

"This is none of your business!" Esau huffed with flared nostrils and clenched fists. "Oholivamah, for now your punishment will be taking care of Machalat. You'll stay with her, clean after her, help her with anything she needs, until she either recovers or . . . or . . ." He coughed. "You better pray to your gods that she does."

He then looked at Jeush and Jaalam. "And you, despicable young men, will be helping your mother. I'll think of a punishment for you later."

He dismissed everyone with a flick of a wrist and returned to Machalat. She was terrified but somehow lethargic. Her face was now red, swollen, and full of fear. With a feeble grip, she grasped his hand and brought it to her chest, letting him feel how fast her heart was beating. She had vomited all over the bed. When Oholivamah came in, Machalat looked at her with a panicked grimace.

"Machalat, don't worry." Esau said, "I've asked her to stay with you at all times and watch over you until you recover from this horrible accident." He gave Oholivamah a stern look and left.

He stood in the courtyard, gazing at the mundane goings-on without focusing on anything in particular. He needed to talk to someone about all that had happened—someone whose opinion mattered. Esau called for Ardon and Dekel and asked them to prepare for a trip. He told Eliphaz to keep an eye on Oholivamah and Machalat in his absence. Who else could be trusted?

Chapter 19

Nebaioth flung open his arms, welcoming the three visitors inside his white tent. After the meal he and Esau went for a stroll, enjoying a pleasant sunny day and invigorating mountain air.

The host asked, "How are things really going with you, my dear cousin? Is my sister well? I know you've just told me that everything was fine, but I doubt you'd make this long trip without a good reason."

"Nebaioth, you are a discerning man, and that's why I came. Yes, I have a problem." Esau related what happened with Machalat.

"Then why are you here with me and not with my sister?"

"I am not very good at nurturing. Somebody else is watching her in my absence."

"So you've come here just to get out of town because you didn't want to stay glued to her?"

"Well, maybe some of that, but mostly to ask for advice. I don't know anybody as wise as you, other than my father, and I don't want to involve him in my problems."

"Esau, aren't we all like that? We would rather seek advice from our friends than from our parents. But how can I help?"

"Nebaioth, this might surprise you, but for once I'm stumped. What should I do to my wives, or at least to the one who was surely involved, and to the youths who've helped her? I cannot kill them, for then I would be a hunted man, yet I cannot pretend that nothing happened either. I have upbraided them already, so now what?"

After a long pause, Nebaioth answered, "Esau, I don't see an easy solution here. If you love Machalat more than your Hittite wives—and if she survives—then perhaps you should think about divorcing them. I don't know what you'd do with the children."

"I was thinking more about punishing them without getting in trouble with their vengeful relatives."

"*That* you have to be careful about. It might be easier to divorce them in peace than to flog them or anything like that. I know these Hittites and Horites—two vindictive tribes!" Nebaioth kept silent for a few minutes. "On the other hand, you've lived with them for so long . . . A divorce would be painful, too."

"That's my problem."

"Let me consider your question a bit longer. Please stay the night with us, and I might think of something. Of course, please join us for the evening meal."

Esau and his friends enjoyed the Ishmaelite food. Esau recalled how much he liked it the first time he visited. Spiced mutton with garlic was even better now. With wine in abundance, conversation flowed, too.

"So what happened with your plans regarding Mount Seir?" asked Nebaioth. "Last we spoke you wanted a place of your own, and you wanted to make a mark in the world."

"Glad you remember. I still plan to explore Mount Seir and spend more time there."

"Esau, but you never explained why you couldn't just stay where you are now—in Be'er Sheva with your father—and make your mark there. Everyone already knows you in that land."

"Be'er Sheva belongs to my father. He is the wealthiest and the most famous man in the region. I want a place known after me!"

"But is this not true of any notable family? A son succeeds his great father and struggles to make a name for himself. He usually does in the end."

"Nebaioth, it might be true, but my father and I just don't lead the same kind of life. He is a holy man, restricted by his knowledge and tradition—and I am a free man, totally free! I don't want to be like him, even though I love him."

"Nobody is truly free. Are we free of our fears? Our desires? Our bad memories? Are we free not to work and earn a living? Are we free to marry any woman we want—or do we have to respect the fact that the woman of our dreams might already be married, or just doesn't love us back?"

Or dead.

***

Eliphaz went to check on Oholivamah and Machalat, as his father had commanded. Machalat was asleep; her face was so swollen, it was barely recognizable. Oholivamah was sitting at the foot of Machalat's bed, eyes closed. Soft light from the entrance bathed her face, and Eliphaz stood and watched.

He wrapped his arms around her, caressing her long dark hair. She stirred and turned her head. With a crooked smile she tried to push his arms away, but he didn't let her. The smile disappeared. She glanced at Machalat and then at Eliphaz.

"Please, no," she whispered.

"Why not?" he whispered back.

"It's not right. Please leave," she said with more conviction, trying to get up.

"I won't leave. I don't care if it's right or not."

"Yes you will!" Her lips closed tight and turned down at the ends. She overcame his resistance and got up.

He tried to embrace her again but froze in place.

"Get away from my mother!" a child's voice demanded. Jaalam was standing at the entrance, extending a knife toward him. "Leave her alone!" he ordered.

Oholivamah freed herself and said, "It is fine, my son. Thank you for trying to protect me, but Eliphaz meant no harm."

"Yeah, we were just wrestling a bit to stretch," mumbled Eliphaz and left.

CHAPTER 20

Nebaioth had something to say in the morning: "I've thought about your problem a bit more. Forget about divorce and punishment. The best you could do is to make your other wives feel guilty for what they've done. If they repent from their ugly deed, you might find a new peace among your women—assuming Machalat survives, of course."

"Thank you, cousin," replied Esau. "Wise words. I was thinking about the same thing. Do you know who's watching over your sister while I'm away? The same woman who offended her."

"Excellent!" exclaimed Nebaioth. He gave Esau a steady stare and continued, "I have a favor to ask of you."

"Anything!"

"We . . . we have a caravan departing this morning, going in the same direction as you are. Robbers have been active along that road, yet we cannot spare any more guards."

"So you want us to accompany the caravan?"

"Yes, at least until it clears that same treacherous pass where we've first met."

Esau exchanged looks with Ardon and Dekel and nodded. "It would be an honor to help."

"We would be forever in your debt," Nebaioth concluded, beaming.

***

The caravan was carrying the usual Ishmaelite fare: the barrels of tar and oil. Esau did not appreciate the pungent smell and wondered why this merchandise needed any protection at all. He rode up to the caravan leader, who had only two guards with him.

"Have you ever been robbed of this stuff?" Esau asked.

"No, of course not. But the bandits might rob us of our food and money—and even of our freedom! Some of my traders have been kidnapped and sold into slavery."

"Sorry to hear about that . . . Where did these attacks occur? Always at the same place or anywhere throughout the route?"

"As I understand, always at that treacherous mountain pass Nebaioth told you about."

"Does this caravan travel on the same schedule?"

"Yes, it does."

"Then let's prepare for a possible ambush. Halt before you approach the pass and wait until we send an all-clear signal before moving on."

With the pass in sight, Esau, Ardon, and Dekel left their camels with the traders and continued on foot. Esau reasoned that since the sun was shining from the right side of the road, any attackers would be waiting there.

The three of them moved up the mountain with great care, watching for any signs of people below. Halfway up, Esau noticed several large rocks clustered together along the road, and the group started descending towards them. "Step sideways, slowly. These rocks are loose," cautioned Esau.

As he had suspected, there were people hiding behind the rocks, looking at the road. At least eight of them. Esau pointed at the probable gang leader, who had a commanding view, and started to creep down toward him. Ardon and Dekel were advancing toward the others, when Dekel's foot slipped and a couple of dislodged pebbles tumbled down.

One of the bandits looked back and shrieked. The gang leader turned around and froze in place, having noticed an arrow pointed at him. It was Areef, their former comrade!

As Areef raised his hands, Ardon and Dekel aimed their arrows at two other bandits. In turn, the outlaws targeted the three of them. The archers on both sides recognized their former buddies but did not lower their bows, even though their hands were starting to shake. It was time for quick negotiations, and Esau hoped that his golden tongue would allow everybody to come out of this stalemate alive.

"Areef, my brother, I am so glad to see you," he grinned, still pointing an arrow at him. "I am a little surprised to see you guys here. Didn't know you were working this road."

"That's what we do, my brother Esau. You have disappeared, and we haven't seen you in what . . . two decades? We need to eat, man. But what are *you* doing here? Robbing caravans on your own now?"

"No, no, Areef. I'm not competing with you at all. I have married, and I've been occupied by the family life. Sorry I haven't let you know."

"Congratulations, Esau! Still, what are you doing here and why are the three of you pointing arrows at us with those shaky hands?"

"Tell your people to put away their bows and I'll explain."

"Not until your band does so. You are outnumbered anyway. I hope you don't expect to survive if the arrows start flying."

"And neither would you, my brother Areef. I have a much better chance of getting you from this distance than your people do, shaky hands or not."

Areef repeated, "So again, what are you doing here?"

"I've married an Ishmaelite woman, and her relatives asked me to accompany this caravan."

"So you are in the business of guarding caravans now, Esau? That's a nice change!"

"No, just this one." Seeing that Areef still dithered, Esau added, "Look, we've done great work together. You know how good a shot I am. There is no need to hurt each other over this silly caravan."

"But we need the money!"

"I will make it up to you in the next score we take down together. As for today, I will give a piece of gold to each man in your crew—and two for you. A deal?"

Areef bobbed his head, and at last everyone could exhale and lower their weapons. Esau and Areef embraced, and the rest of the men followed with hugs and backslaps. Areef dug Esau in the ribs and said, "There are nine of us here, including the one with the camels. So I expect ten gold pieces from you, right?"

"Correct. Our things are still with the caravan, so let's wait for it to pass through. Then we'll celebrate the reunion in some roadside tavern. Meanwhile, let's get off this wretched mountain."

Areef gave him a sideways stare and said, "Sounds good. Meet you at the next turnoff going north."

Areef's men left. Esau and his friends waited for the caravan, with plenty of time to discuss the trouble they have gotten themselves into.

"Are you really going to pay them off with gold? Your own gang?" asked Dekel.

"Perhaps not. But even if I was, wouldn't it be better to let go of some money than risk being killed in a place where we were badly outnumbered?"

"You're right, as usual," conceded Dekel.

"You'd better remember that. Now stay alert and follow my lead whatever happens. We might have to . . . I hope they don't insist that I follow through on my promise. I don't carry so much gold, as you know."

When the caravan arrived, Esau told the leader to continue on. The leader thanked Esau, returned his camels, and looked at the hills ahead with suspicion.

***

Esau soon met up with Areef and his gang. Since the closest tavern was far away, he rode next to Areef for hours, feeding him a diet of stories to forestall the inevitable request for money. When the request came nevertheless, Esau said that he would distribute the gold at the celebration table. Having bought himself some time, Esau needed to satisfy his curiosity.

"By the way, Areef, were you expecting this particular caravan?"

"No, we were waiting for anything to pass by."

"But have you robbed any Ishmaelite caravans earlier?"

"No, we haven't. What's the point? We know what they carry."

"Areef, there is a reason the prince of the Ishmaelites asked me to accompany this one. Some of his traders had been attacked at the pass where we've met today. They were kidnapped and sold into slavery."

"Esau, we don't do that. Too much risk. These Ishmaelites—they are ferocious! If they see us in the market trying to sell their men . . ." Areef rolled his eyes.

"But you've used this spot for an ambush before, right?"

"Yeah, it's such a great place for that."

Esau fell silent, unsettled. So there are some other gangs preying on the Ishmaelite caravans, using the same ambush spot. We were fortunate coming upon our own people. It could have turned out much, much worse.

***

It was already dark when the band arrived at the inn, the only building around with the lights on. Boisterous songs beckoned the travelers. But once inside, they halted at the door, startled at the sight of a large group of men—outlaws like them—filling the room.

Everyone who entered looked around with hope in their eyes, but the hope quickly changed to despair. Every table was taken. The latecomers' hungry eyes revealed a desire to eat, not to fight over a place to eat. With nowhere to go, the men crowded around the entrance, waiting for their leaders to do something.

"Esau, what do you think?" whispered Areef.

"We might have to camp outside," said Esau, stroking his beard, "but let's talk to them first."

Esau and Areef approached the diners, who sized them up with lazy confident looks. Judging by the empty jugs, they had already consumed quite a bit of wine and beer. Esau knew his local competition rather well but did not recognize anyone among the revelers. These folks must have been from somewhere far away. He nudged Areef toward a rough-looking heavyset man, who did not reply to their greetings and did not take his feet off the table.

The chieftain raised his bloodshot eyes, exuding quiet aggression, which alcohol had not diminished in the least. Pushing back his torn and greasy *sudra*, he bellowed, "What do we have here? More people! The place is taken, my friends. You'll have to go next door." He scowled, revealing many missing teeth. The brigands chortled, pointing outside.

Esau counted the bandits. Twenty-four, compared with twelve in his group. *The odds are not very good,* he thought. *I could probably win a fight with these drunks all by myself, but it's risky. Funny, at a younger age I would have taken the chance without hesitation. Now I worry that some of Areef's men might get hurt in the melee. But on the other hand, the fewer of them remain, the fewer I'd have to pay off—or fight—later. An interesting dilemma.*

"Can't we just share this large table? I see there's some space left for us at the end," asked Areef.

"No, boy, there ain't. Not for you! You need to go get some milk from your mama! They don't serve it here."

"That's too bad," muttered Areef.

Esau did not participate in the conversation; he was still thinking. He and Areef left, hearing wild laughter behind them.

"Let's camp out in the desert for a while. Don't drink any wine or beer," Esau told the men, who covered themselves with their heavy *simlah* clothes and sat down around the fire.

***

Two hours passed. The twelve outlaws have eaten from their supplies of dried fish and pork, and Esau was concerned that they might fall asleep if he did not act soon. He sent Dekel to peek inside a small tavern window. Dekel reported that he could not see well through the window, but that at least some bandits were still sitting around the table, either drunk or asleep.

"It's time," announced Esau. "Get ready, people. I'll start with the sentry." He pointed to a young man who was guarding the bandits' camels and belongings, shivering in the frigid desert night.

Soon Esau appeared behind the guard, grabbing his forehead with one hand and holding the knife in the other. But he dropped the knife when he felt two sharp points digging into his back. *An ambush? How?*

Esau glanced at his men—they were surrounded. And four swords were poking at him from all sides. Stay still, he told himself.

The chieftain looked even larger walking out of the tavern than he was sitting inside. He came up to Esau, smirked, and ordered, jabbing the air with his finger, "Your sword on the ground or your gang dies!"

Esau dropped his sword on the sand next to the knife and said in a cheerful voice, "Fine. And you can keep your table, too. We won't bother you anymore!"

"A joker, eh?" The chieftain came closer, and the four ruffians backed away. A huge hand grabbed Esau by the throat, trying to lift him in the air.

"Leave us alone, and I'll give you all the money we have. Here! Here!" Esau choked out, reaching inside his clothes.

The chieftain grinned wider but soon lost his smile and stiffened, as he stared at the dagger jammed into his chest. He tried to squeeze Esau harder, but instead his grip was getting weaker and weaker. Soon his mouth cracked open and he sank to the ground, his hand still extended toward the joker.

The four thugs surrounding Esau seemed unsure about what just happened in the dark, until one of them pointed to the glinting dagger. As they hesitated, shuffling from foot to foot, he bent down to pick up his sword.

Still crouching, he held it like a spear and rushed forward between the two bandits in front of him. Having ripped into the thigh of one of them along the way, he slashed the back of the other. Both men sagged, screaming.

The two remaining bandits charged, but Esau moved to the side and struck the closest one on the shoulder. The man yelped and dropped his weapon. The last brigand tried to run, but the sword of Esau found his back. It's for such maneuvers that he preferred his straight double-edged swords over anything else.

As the screams filled the air, the bandits surrounding the campfire kept peering into the night. When Esau appeared near them, unharmed and with a glistening sword in hand, they glanced in the direction of their camels and stepped back. One of them grabbed Dekel and put a knife to his throat, shrieking, "Let us go—or say good-bye to him!"

"Fine! Go! All of you! Just let him be," Esau screamed back.

The bandits raced toward the camels, pulling Dekel along with them.

"Put out the fire! Quick!" Esau barked. His men hastened to do so, and everything went dark, save for the glimmering old moon and a faint glow in the tavern window. Esau followed the Dekel's kidnapper and soon caught up with him, plunging a sword into his back.

"Drop on the ground! And stay there!" Esau shouted, and Dekel complied.

Esau was running around the camels, striking the bandits who tried to find and mount them, ensuring that none could escape. He did not stop until all of them were down.

Wiping away sweat and blood from his face, Esau hollered, "Light the fire!" and his gang struggled to resurrect the flames they had put out only minutes ago.

"Finish them all and bring them inside!" ordered Esau. "And count them! Should be twenty-five."

As Areef's people executed the wounded, the night was filled with anguished screams that drowned out the calls of the jackals. They dragged the bodies into the tavern, leaving a red carpet at the entrance. The dining table was now theirs.

The victors stripped the slain of any valuables and weapons, and piled them up behind the building. To the surprise of the living, the dead had a lot of money on them. The chieftain alone carried more than fifty gold pieces.

"They must have robbed someone rich and were celebrating," said Ardon.

Esau gave Areef and his men twice the agreed-upon amount of gold, as well as all the other plunder, keeping only the remainder of the gold for himself, Ardon, and Dekel.

The terrified old innkeeper and his sons needed not be threatened to keep mum about the night's events. The innkeeper approached Esau and said, "Many, many thanks for ridding us of these vermin. They kept coming here, not paying for food and drink, trashing the place, and abusing us. They even . . . they even . . ." He started sobbing and could not finish.

Esau put a hand on his back. "We are not like them."

"Thank you, thank you, my lord Esau," the innkeeper bowed.

"You know my name? How?"

"I've heard your people call you that. And everyone knows about you and your family. I see that the rumors are true! You killed all those thugs by yourself, didn't you? I wouldn't be surprised, after what you've done to the giants. I know about that, too!"

"Yeah, not bad for a man over sixty!" Esau grinned. "You can take their animals and sell them. There are at least two dozen camels outside. Should be enough to pay for the damage. But you'd have to bury the men yourselves. I'm tired."

"Thank you, thank you, my lord," beamed the innkeeper. "Please feel free to stay here tonight and eat and drink to your heart's desire." He bowed and backed away. His sons were smiling.

CHAPTER 21

Nebaioth's advice proved useful, and within a year the wives reconciled with one another and healed their rivalries. Machalat recovered after a long struggle with venom. Each woman has now given Esau at least one son, the latest addition being Machalat's Reuel.

Esau kept the family by his father's side in Be'er Sheva but was spending more and more time in the lands surrounding Mount Seir, often bringing along Eliphaz. As hazy outlines of the Edomite clan were emerging, it was time to start building his own country within the Horite kingdom.

For now Esau stayed with prince Zibeon, Oholivamah's nominal grandfather, through whom he befriended Zibeon's father Seir, the chief of the Horites. The chief's palace was in the capital city located on a high plateau, a trip of couple of hours from Zibeon's estate.

One day, Chief Seir invited Esau to a feast at his palace, and Eliphaz, who had never met the chief, tagged along. Passing by the royal guard, the father and son kept nudging one another, marveling at the sights of carved wood columns, polished stone floors, and colorful hanging fabrics.

When they entered the dining room, Seir was seated at the center of a long table, flanked by his family. The chief smiled and gestured to Esau and Eliphaz to sit across from him. The introductions followed.

"Here is my wife Nureen, whom I believe you've never met."

Both Esau and Eliphaz gazed with interest at the slender and very attractive woman, but she gave them but the briefest of glances. As befitted the wife of a tribal chief, Nureen was wearing an exquisite blue dress, a well-arranged long black hair, and finely woven gold chains on her neck. A shiny gold nose-ring, gold earrings, and gold bracelets on each arm added even more sparkle.

Esau could not tell how old she was behind the makeup, but her dark eyes showed unusual depth, probably concealing a very intelligent mind and a passionate soul, he guessed. Having noticed that Eliphaz could not take his eyes off her, Esau gave him a discreet but sharp elbow under the table.

"Next to my dear wife is my firstborn Lotan, and on my other side are my sons Shoval and Zibeon, whom you know." While Seir proceeded to introduce his four remaining sons and the other guests, Esau sized up the potential enemies.

Both Lotan and Shoval appeared like princes accustomed to giving orders, but their soft faces suggested a pampered lifestyle, and their satisfied eyes lacked harshness. His host Zibeon looked like an average guy, a bit plump, on the softer side as well. None of the other people around the table seemed like trouble.

"I am happy to receive such distinguished visitors," said the chief. "A grandson and a great-grandson of holy Abraham are always welcome in my land."

"We are greatly honored that our master has chosen to extend his hospitality toward his servants," replied Esau, as expected.

"The honor is mine," smiled the host. "The great victory of your grandfather over our enemies shall forever live in our minds."

Esau and Eliphaz remembered that story well, as it was often recited in Isaac's household. A combined army of four kings—King Chedarlaomer of Elam, King Tidal of Goyim, King Amraphel of Babylon, and King Arioch of Ellasar—fought against the alliance of five kings from the cities of Sodom, Gomorrah, Admah, Zeboyim, and Bela.

The invading army of the four kings, known as the kings of Elam after their leader Chedarlaomer, defeated the five kings in the valley of Siddim. They also crushed a number of other mighty forces on their way to Siddim, including a Horite army. After their victory the kings of Elam took many captives and with them Abraham's nephew Lot, who lived in Sodom.

When Abraham heard about Lot's capture, he took 318 of his servants and pursued the vast army of the victorious kings. His meager contingent attacked in the middle of the night, taking the huge force by surprise, utterly routing it, and bringing back the captives. This miraculous feat earned Abraham an eternal glory throughout the world, making him into a legendary figure.

Esau was alarmed that Chief Seir brought up the story, because one of the participants in it was King Amraphel, that is, Nimrod. Did Seir know how Nimrod died? Was this meeting a trap? He glanced at the guards standing around the room and detected none of the nervous clutching of weapons or shallow breathing that would indicate an impending attack. The guards stood motionless, staring straight ahead, and Esau allowed himself to loosen up a little.

The food was served, and with it an abundance of old-vintage royal wine. As the goblets emptied, the bodies loosened. Some guests started dancing with their wives, including the chief himself, which Esau thought odd. They swirled for a few minutes until Seir stopped and braced himself against the edge of the table, cradling his belly.

One of his sons muttered, "Not again! If he cannot drink, he shouldn't!"

Esau and Eliphaz rose and, holding their host from both sides with the lightest of touches, asked if they could be of help.

He mumbled, "I'm fine, I'm fine . . . just need to sit down. Somebody please dance with Nureen for me—she likes that."

Still standing, Nureen observed all this playing with her necklace. After her husband made it back to his purple seat, Eliphaz invited her to dance. Esau sharply inhaled but decided not to make a scene. Nureen hesitated for a short while, with a quick glance at her sons, and accepted.

Following every movement of the whirling couple, Esau noticed that Eliphaz kept his eyes fixed on her, yet she did not look at him even once. When they got to a slow part of the dance, with their faces almost touching, Nureen said something, still looking away, and Eliphaz lowered his eyes.

Esau waited until his son escorted Nureen to her seat and tugged at his sleeve, motioning with his eyes to step away from the table. With a polite smile, he looked around and hissed, "What's going on? Are you flirting with her? And what did she say to cause you to blush? I haven't seen you blushing like that in years."

"Oh, she said that I should stop staring at her, or people might notice. She said she saw me doing it since we walked in here."

"And?"

"I said, 'I apologize, my lady. Your beauty is breathtaking, that's why I couldn't take my eyes off you.' Something like that."

"Good. She's beyond your reach, my son, so don't even try."

"Maybe not. She said that if I really wanted her to be 'my lady,' I could come see her tonight. Then she turned to me with that delicate smile, and I was speechless."

"Are you insane, my son? You are not a boy anymore. Do I need to explain what might happen if the two of you are caught? Say goodbye to the dreams of building our home on Mount Seir! Are you going to risk our future for this?" He stopped, lowered his voice, and continued, "Hey, we wouldn't make it back to Be'er Sheva alive!"

"Father, I'll be fine! Why do you worry so much about everything? Maybe she just needs some company—this Seir doesn't look like much of a stud."

"You are still talking like a hot-blooded youth," Esau screeched through his teeth, but Eliphaz did not back down—it was clear that his stubbornness was inherited. Esau took a deep breath and did not argue any more. Having realized that he would have done exactly the same, he asked in a calm voice, "How are you going to find your way around here? Ask the guards?"

"She said to stick around until she sends one of her handmaidens for me."

"This should be interesting . . . idiot!"

They remained at the table, drinking, even after Seir and his sons excused themselves and left one by one. Nobody approached Eliphaz. Just as Esau started to sneer, a young servant girl carrying a bulging leather pouch stumbled next to them, spilling small perfume jars all over the floor.

As she was picking them up, she whispered, "Follow me, my lord, at a distance."

Eliphaz glanced at his father and left. They had agreed that Esau would wait for an hour, and if nothing was amiss by then, return home.

Eliphaz followed the girl around the sprawling palace, dodging the guards, until she brought him to a room in the rear of the second floor. He knocked on the door—Jacob had taught him to always knock before entering someone's dwelling, something the Canaanites did not do—and entered upon hearing Nureen's voice. The elegant furniture and fabrics in her quarters rivaled the beauty of the jewelry she was wearing. O, the life of luxury.

With a delicate smile that captivated him, Nureen pointed to a large red embroidered pillow on the floor next to her bed. After Eliphaz sunk deep into the pillow, she looked at his bewildered face and extended her hand toward him.

She said in a soft voice, chuckling, "Wondering how you'll be able to get up after all this wine you had to consume while waiting for me? Don't worry!" She pulled him up and pushed him onto the bed.

Before dawn, Eliphaz had to confront the last challenge of the night: evading the guards milling inside and around the palace. The handmaiden helped by opening the back door, but then Eliphaz was on his own. He waited for the first rays of the sun to find his way home.

Neither of the two lovers suspected how important this night would be in their lives.

CHAPTER 22

Years later, Esau was still dividing his time between the family home and the getaway at Mount Seir, except that the family home was now in Hebron. Esau did not care why Isaac and Rebecca wished to move there—perhaps Isaac wanted to be closer to Abraham's grave—but he followed his parents all the same.

Someone told him that Jacob had surfaced in Charan, in his uncle Laban's house, where he had married both Leah and Rachel. But Esau stopped being obsessed with his brother and the stolen blessing, or so he kept telling himself. And now he did not have to worry about Leah anymore.

One day some travelers showed up on his doorstep at Mount Seir. Their leader introduced himself as Beor, a son of Laban, and said, "My master Esau, I have a message for you from my father."

"Speak."

"My master, do you know that your brother has lived with us for twenty years and fathered eleven sons?"

"I know," answered Esau.

"He misused the hospitality of my father and amassed a great fortune at his expense . . ."

"Sounds like him."

". . . But now he has departed our land and is returning home carrying everything he owns."

Esau's ears perked up, as Beor continued, "My father is a prophet, and he is well aware of how Jacob has deceived you. Should my master desire it, now would be a great time to exact vengeance from your brother, while he is on the road, exposed . . ." He caught his breath and added, " . . . with all his wealth."

"Hmm. Why did he decide to return now?"

"My father asked him the same question."

"And?"

"He said that with the birth of Joseph he at last had a son who could overcome your might, my master."

"Is that so? Huh. And why did your father send you to tell me all this?"

"Because he is powerless to stop your brother and exact revenge, but you would have no trouble."

"And where is Jacob now?"

"We parted ways at Mount Gilead—that's nineteen days' travel from here."

"Beor, stay here for a while and enjoy the food, while I decide what should be done about this. Won't take long."

Esau stared at the trees outside for a few minutes and made a decision. He assembled his sons and servants, sixty men in all. Chief Seir provided another 340 Horite warriors, the relatives of Oholivamah and Zibeon, for a total of 400 men under Esau's command.

The last to join was a youth called Nymeer. He was way too young, Esau thought at first, but the boy's desire to fight was commendable, and he got accepted. The warriors were told to be ready to leave right after securing provisions for the trip.

Esau debated whether to take horses or camels. Ever since his first caravan job he preferred horses for raids of plunder and for battles, where moving fast was a matter of life and death. But for this round-trip adventure that should take four to five weeks? High endurance in the desert was more important than speed.

***

While Esau left Mount Seir for a rendezvous with his brother, Beor traveled to Hebron to inform his aunt Rebecca about Esau's plans for revenge.

Without delay, Rebecca sent seventy-two armed servants to join Jacob's party to warn her favorite son of the impending attack and to help him ward it off.

***

After traveling for days, Esau's troops met a group of camel riders who said they were Jacob's messengers. They confirmed that Jacob was returning to Hebron with his family and all that he owned.

"Why did you come to tell me this?" Esau asked.

The messengers bowed and replied, "Your servant Jacob wishes to announce his arrival to his beloved brother and assure him of his good intentions. He is asking our master Esau to forget the old grudges."

"And why would I do that?" Esau asked with a one-sided grin, his fingers tapping on the sword's handle.

"Because your father's blessings are not working. Instead of the promised great success, your servant Jacob had to toil as a shepherd in Laban's house for twenty years. Meanwhile, our master Esau has acquired a great fame, and he commands a great army that's in front of us."

Esau stared at the messengers in silence. These people are puzzling. Their bearing is too dignified for household help; they are polite but a bit too self-assured. Yes, they keep calling me 'our master' but do not act as servants at all, and they seem not to be afraid of me and my warriors. Are they assassins? Magicians?

He asked, "You say my father's blessings have not been working for Jacob. And yet you also say he has acquired much wealth? Explain!"

"Your father has blessed Jacob with the dew of the heavens and the fat of the earth, but your servant's possessions did not come from these sources. Yes, he has servants, oxen, donkeys, and sheep, but none of those are from either heaven or earth. So there is nothing to hate him for!"

That's cute, reflected Esau. But none of this matters now. The unfinished business ends soon.

He pushed further, "I've heard from reliable sources that Jacob decided to return only after a son was born to him—a son who was supposed to help him overcome me in battle. So he thinks he can defeat me now?"

"Your servant Jacob seeks only peace, but if you want war, he is ready for that, too. His camp is strong!" The messengers were standing upright with their heads held high, looking Esau straight in the eye.

"Oh? But how does he hope to prevail over me in battle, son or no son? Over me, who was blessed to live by the sword? Is Jacob relying on some Divine protection? If so, go remind him that he had abandoned our father for thirty-four years, while I've stayed with him all this time. And, I've been living in his Promised Land and he hasn't!" He congratulated himself on another clever argument.

The messengers did not offer a rebuttal. They glanced at Esau's 400 warriors and left.

***

Wary of being ambushed, Esau rode in the middle of his troops. One morning he noticed that his vanguard warriors had stopped. Some people were standing in front of them. He hastened to investigate.

"These men are saying they are Jacob's servants. They've brought a gift," explained Eliphaz, who was the vanguard commander. He pointed to a large wooden chest sitting on the ground. Inside was a treasure of gold, silver, and precious jewels.

"What's the meaning of this?" demanded Esau.

"This is a present from your servant Jacob to you, our master Esau, and Jacob himself is following behind us," said one of the servants.

Esau grinned. So this is how he is planning to save his life— with gold and jewels! We'll see if this helps him or not.

"Eliphaz, take the chest and carry it with you at all times. Stay close," he ordered.

"Yes, father," replied Eliphaz in a loud voice. Then he whispered, "This treasure alone is worth the trip, isn't it?"

Jacob's servants turned around and left Esau's presence, and his camel train continued on. He stayed with Eliphaz, anticipating seeing his brother soon.

The next day Esau spotted a herd of goats blocking the road, and the troops had to stop.

The shepherds approached Esau, bowed and introduced themselves, "We belong to your servant Jacob. This herd of 200 she-goats and twenty he-goats is his gift to our master Esau. Jacob himself is following behind us."

Esau was not sure what to do with the herd. It was an expensive gift, but was it a ploy to slow him down? He decided to keep the animals for now—at least his men won't lack for food during the journey to kill the giver.

"Follow behind us with the herd until we meet your master," he told the shepherds.

He then said under his breath, "Eliphaz, have them checked for any weapons."

The next day, a flock of sheep met the caravan. As before, the herders came forward and announced that the flock of 200 ewes and twenty rams was Jacob's gift to Esau and that Jacob himself was following them. Esau again told the shepherds to follow behind with the herd for the time being.

The day after that, Esau was surprised to see a herd of camels coming toward his procession. Another gift? Yes, these thirty male and thirty nursing female camels with their young were a gift from Jacob.

The next day, yet another gift of forty cows and ten bulls met Esau on the road. And the day after, a drove of twenty she-donkeys and ten he-donkeys appeared, with the same explanation.

By this time, Esau resigned himself to seeing droves of animals dragging behind his convoy. He could not wait to be done with his mission and with all this shepherding, although he saw that the animals were of great quality and could be sold for good price.

Out of the blue, Esau heard the unmistakable sounds of the approaching horsemen. Is it Jacob's ambush at last? Surely the gifts were but a trick to slow me down. Now comes the attack!

He soon saw a troop of mounted warriors galloping toward them. There must be 2,000 horsemen in all, he reckoned. The riders, divided into four camps, carried all kinds of weapons, even whips. They were clad in some unusual armor.

The first camp slammed into Esau's vanguard. The Edomites tried to defend themselves as best they could—in vain. The attackers were so fierce and well-trained, and their fighting form was so flawless, that they seemed invincible. For all his battle prowess, Esau could not land a single blow on any of them, and his people did no better.

The mysterious horsemen did not aim to kill but to hurt, to beat up, using their whips as if they wanted to teach Esau and his companions a lesson. While the Edomites were drenched in sweat, there was not a drop on the warriors' stone faces. Their armor looked pristine despite them having traveled through clouds of dust.

One of the attackers threw Esau off his camel. The rest of the Edomites retreated, trying to avoid the onslaught, and he was left all alone.

The rider yelled at Esau, "Who are you?"

"I am Esau," he gulped.

The attacker continued to beat him. Other horsemen were whipping his men, who were throwing down their weapons and pleading for mercy. With hundreds of men crying in pain, the desert had to close its ears.

Esau shrieked, "Leave me alone! I am Abraham's grandson!" This did not stop the attack.

"I am Isaac's son!" he yelled. The hitting and whipping continued.

"I am Jacob's brother!" Esau exclaimed, and the humiliation came to an abrupt halt.

His attacker roared, "If so, you are one of ours," and left with the other horsemen.

Esau glanced back on his men, who seemed as confused and alarmed as he was. Myriad thoughts swirled in his head. What was going on? 'One of ours?' Where did Jacob get these perfect warriors? No human could fight like that! Are they angels in a human form? But I've never believed that angels existed. I thought my grandfather's stories were just tales . . .

An attack of the second camp of fierce warriors interrupted his thoughts. They acted in the same manner as the first group. Then the third and the fourth camp attacked in an identical fashion, stopping their assault and moving away once Esau told them he was Jacob's brother.

When it was over, Esau commanded his men in a stern voice to clean themselves up and resume their travel. He saw that they were bruised, shaken up, and intimidated, but this game had to be played to the end.

That night Esau could not sleep, which was very unusual for him; typically, he'd be snoring the moment his head touched the pillow. He was tossing and turning, and when at long last he dozed off, a nightmare pursued him. He saw a ferocious-looking man with a dim halo above his head wrestle with Jacob—and his brother was winning!

Bewildered, Esau woke up. He was feeling helpless, abandoned, scared. His heart was racing. He could not breathe. He was dizzy. He felt that his strength was sapped and his self-confidence drained away. He was exposed to all the dangers of the world at once. It was as if the mantle of invincibility was torn off him. He fell into fitful darkness.

***

When the sun rose, Esau pulled himself together and ordered his men to get going. At mid-day, the Edomites encountered two large groups of people, all of them dressed in white, as if prepared to die and be buried on the spot. Enormous droves of animals, which covered the landscape as far as the eye could see, accompanied them.

Esau and his troops tried to look tough but were terrified to move a step forward, vividly remembering the beat-down of yesterday. Was more of it in store? Surrounded by his warriors, Esau approached the first group.

"Who are you?" he demanded in a harsh voice.

"We belong to your servant Jacob," answered a dignified white-haired man, whose clothes did not have a speck of dust on them.

Esau had never seen him before, but he recognized some of the others in the group as his father's help. How could they possibly be here with Jacob? Was Isaac here as well? Or am I being deceived somehow—again?

"Where is my brother?" he asked the servant.

"He and his family are behind us," answered the man, pointing to the second group farther back.

Esau glanced around. There are a bit too many of them here, but they look like scared servants, not warriors. No need to kill them.

He ordered the rear guard to keep an eye on the servants and be ready for any sneak attack from behind. Esau and his vanguard continued toward the second group, scanning the horizon over and over. No sign of those fierce horsemen.

An old man with a flowing white beard was coming toward Esau, limping. Jacob!

Coming forward, Jacob prostrated himself on the ground seven times. Esau's eyes moistened: his brother was asking for mercy!

For some reason, Esau could not control himself. His fear and anger have turned into kindness—white kindness, the color of his brother's clothes. With a swelling in his chest, he dismounted and ran toward Jacob.

The brothers embraced, and Esau threw himself on Jacob's shoulders. At that instant he was truly happy to see him. He kissed Jacob, and the brothers wept together with joy.

Esau's companions were also overcome with kindness. Each of them, even Eliphaz and his four brothers, hugged and kissed Jacob and wept with him.

Pointing to a small crowd of women and children standing at a distance, Esau asked, wiping away tears, "Who are these children with you, my brother? Your family? Your servants?"

Jacob answered, "These are my children that God has graciously given to your servant."

As Jacob called for each member of the group, they approached and prostrated themselves on the ground. Bilhah, Rachel's handmaid, came up first with her sons Dan and Naphtali. Zilpah, Leah's handmaid, and her sons Gad and Asher followed.

Then it was the turn of Leah and her children, Reuben, Simeon, Levi, Judah, Issachar, and Zebulun. Seeing his intended bride for the first time, Esau noted that her eyes lacked any eyelashes. He was glad he had not married this one.

Rachel approached last, with her son Joseph standing in front of her. It seemed the boy—he could not have been older than six or seven—was trying to shield his mother with his small body.

Esau's mouth slackened, but he forced himself to look away and change the subject.

He asked, "Jacob, why do you own so many animals and servants? I thought you were concerned only with religious studies and with the World to Come?"

"I need all these possessions in this world in the service of God," replied Jacob. "That's why they were given to me."

"I see. And what is the meaning of all these gifts of animals that greeted us on the way here? And who were the fierce warriors that attacked us?"

"The gifts were intended to gain favor in my master's eyes," Jacob said, answering only the first question.

"Oh, I have plenty—more than I need," said Esau with a broad grin. "Keep what's yours, my brother." He paused and added, "And keep the birthright, too. After all, I did sell it to you."

Jacob implored, "Please, my master, accept the gifts. Don't worry about their cost. I have all that I need."

In the end, Esau relented and accepted the gifts. He divided the animals into two droves, one for the Horites and the other for his sons. He let Eliphaz keep the chest.

"Well, let's go then," he said. "I will travel at a slower pace, so that I could walk together with you."

Jacob demurred, "I am caring not only for young children, but also for nursing animals. If they are driven hard for even a day, they will die." He kept asking Esau to continue at his normal pace, with a goal of meeting up at Mount Seir at some point. He was vague about when that point might be.

Esau offered to leave some of his people with Jacob, who again demurred and explained that he did not want such a favor from his brother. He would rather be the one offering gifts. With nothing more to accomplish, Esau departed.

As he was getting farther and farther away from his brother, Esau's feelings of brotherly love kept getting weaker and weaker. It was if a spell of some sort was gradually lifting.

He was wondering in amazement: What happened out there? Why didn't I kill Jacob as planned? Did he use some magic on me?

But the job could still be finished, just in a different way, he thought. I cannot turn around and attack him now. All these herds of animals that I have foolishly accepted are trudging behind.

Perhaps I could divide my forces and send some of my men to attack him, while the rest of us continue on. Or, I could return to Mount Seir and ask the Horites to go after him, promising them his great riches. I would only ask to bring me Rachel.

Esau was immersed in his schemes when he realized that the sun was already kissing the horizon. They needed to stop. But why didn't anyone remind him of that? His men should be following behind, because he heard the sounds of camels' paws even while deep in thought. He turned around.

There was nobody behind him. The herds were gone, too. He was alone.

The 400 men must have disappeared one by one, not to arouse my suspicion, he figured. Were they so afraid of Jacob's fierce warriors that they did not want any more dealings with my brother?

Fine. I'll think of something else. Too tired to get angry.

Chapter 23

After the encounter with his brother, Esau went back to his getaway at Mount Seir and waited there for a few weeks. When it became clear that Jacob was not coming, Esau returned to his family in Hebron, where he later learned that his brother was spotted first in Sukkot and then in Shechem.

The thoughts of revenge receded from Esau's mind, and he immersed himself into taking care of his growing family. Among his progeny, for the reason he could not name, he felt the closest to Korach, even more so than to Eliphaz. Grandkids started to follow, too, but not from Eliphaz—his firstborn was still single.

One day a messenger arrived with the news: Simeon and Levi, two young sons of Jacob, had killed 24,000 Hivite men in Shechem. Esau did not believe that at first.

"How did they manage that feat? I couldn't have done it myself!" he exclaimed with a furrowed forehead. "And to what end?"

"The son of a local Hivite chief had abducted and raped Jacob's daughter Dinah and then asked Jacob for her hand in marriage. Her brothers didn't like that."

"Wait, wait. My brother has a daughter named Dinah? I've checked out every female in his family when I met him. There was no Dinah."

Unless Jacob hid her in one of those large chests his men were carrying, he thought. But why? Was he afraid I would take her? Well, maybe I would . . . But then again, perhaps she could have been my fourth—and best—wife! How can I find my soulmate if all the good women are hidden from me? Or die?

He sniffled and continued, "Fine, so Jacob had a daughter. What came upon her? How could the daughter of a pious man be raped? She must have been flirting with the prince."

"No, people say it was a chance encounter, after which the prince was smitten with Dinah and wanted to marry her. His father was ready to pay anything to make his son happy, but Jacob's family did not want money. They told the Hivite chief that they would only give Dinah away if the whole town was circumcised beforehand, just as they were circumcised."

"What?"

"Yes, that's what they demanded. And the Hivites agreed! The prince and his father had all the males in the city submit to the knife in haste."

"Again, to what end? They wanted to convert the Hivites, or something?"

"No, no. It was just a tactical ploy. Jacob's sons knew that a circumcised person is in pain, which crests on the third day after the procedure. So on the third day, when the males in Shechem lay in their beds, Simeon and Levi took their swords and killed them all."

"The women, too?"

"No, they took them, the children, and all the possessions as booty."

"Ha! I should try this!" Esau chuckled, as his face brightened. "But why didn't their neighbors, some other Hivites, retaliate? They were not in pain."

"I've heard that everybody was terrified of Jacob after the incident. The local Canaanite kings assembled their troops to wage a war against him but did not dare to attack, because the dread of him fell upon them."

Esau tightened his lips until his cheeks hurt. If two of Jacob's sons could kill 24,000 men, what could his whole family do? My might alone might not be enough to overcome them. I must outsmart Jacob if I ever hope to wipe him out, although so far he has outsmarted me. Maybe the local Hivites could help avenge their relatives? I should speak with Oholivamah about that. Or just wait until my brother gets himself in some sort of trouble.

***

Two years after these events the brothers came face to face in Hebron, where Jacob and his family had arrived to join their father. The meeting of the two centenarians was cordial enough. Jacob told Esau that during his travels back to Hebron God had given him another name—Israel.

As his brother was introducing his family again, Esau was looking for Rachel, but she was not there. With tears in his eyes Jacob explained that his favorite wife had died during the trip.

The brothers had accumulated so much livestock that there was not enough pasture land around rocky Hebron for all their herds. They knew they had to separate, but who would be the one to stay? Both wanted to be near their father.

Seeing how wealthy Jacob had become and how much more livestock he owned, with heavy heart Esau recognized that he should be the one to leave. In any case, it was time to move to Mount Seir permanently, he told himself. Staying in Hebron just kept bringing up daily reminders of his now-inferior status in the family.

***

The caravan going to Mount Seir stretched as far as an eye could see. Esau and his wives rode in front, followed by the wagons, donkeys, and camels laden with their possessions. Esau wanted his wives near him, so that he could keep an eye on them during the day and call upon them at night whenever he desired.

***

The Edomites took a temporary residence all over Zibeon's sprawling estate. Oholivamah and her sons chose to be with Zibeon's son Anah, who still believed her to be his daughter. As guests of honor, Esau and Eliphaz were staying in Zibeon's own home. One day after dinner, two father-and-son couples were sitting around the fireplace on plush upholstered benches.

"My friend Zibeon, what's the word on Mount Seir about us, now that we've been here for almost two weeks?" asked Esau, putting his hand into a large bowl of dried figs and dates.

"The Horites are buzzing with the news of your arrival," answered Zibeon, his feet twitching.

"But what do they say? Come on, you can be frank with us," prodded Esau.

Zibeon took a deep breath and said, without looking at Esau, "There is a lot of debate going on."

"About what? Do we have a problem?" Eliphaz interjected, and Esau gave him a stern glare.

"If you really want to know—yes, there might be a slight problem." Zibeon took another breath. "Some people are alarmed by a mighty family with so much livestock moving in . . ."

" . . . and invading their pasture land?" This time, Esau himself jumped in.

"Well, yes. There've been some arguments between the local shepherds and your people. A few have ripened into minor skirmishes." Zibeon was looking at his feet. "I am sorry, Esau, some of us have a warped sense of hospitality."

"My dear friend, then we must resolve this. Amicably," said Esau. "There's no going back for us. This is our home now." He fell silent. "Can you arrange a meeting with Chief Seir?"

"Of course," said Zibeon, his face glowing. "You've attended many of his parties in the past. Shouldn't be a problem."

"True, but having a good time with him many years ago is one thing, and showing up in his land now with a family and countless animals is quite another," Esau said.

"We'll see," said Zibeon, losing his smile. "By the way, let's take my camels going up there—they know this road well. If you ever have to go up the mountain on your own, just walk. Your camels wouldn't know where to step on the rocky path and just rip their paws to shreds. You'd have to put them down then."

***

Esau, Eliphaz, and Zibeon arrived at Seir's palace at the appointed time. Everybody had to leave their weapons at the door, as was the rule of the land. They entered the dark throne room—Esau remembered its narrow windows—and bowed to the chief.

Esau noticed that Seir had aged a lot since the last time they met. He was frail, shrunken and stooped now, swallowed by the throne. His dark face was furrowed, and his long white hair looked unkempt.

Excellent, thought Esau. Unless someone else is running the show behind the scenes. He glanced around. Seir was flanked by Nureen, who looked almost the same as the last time, and four men. Three of them were Seir's sons whom Esau had met.

The fourth man was wearing the regalia of Seir's army chief. A strong and rugged man in his prime, he was dressed in full battle attire even for this gathering. Radiating sheer confidence, he had the most commanding presence of the group. Esau remembered where he had seen him: he was a young officer in charge of gathering Horite mercenaries for Esau's confrontation with Jacob. His name was Geelahon.

After the initial welcome and pleasantries Seir coughed and asked, looking at Esau, "Is there anything I can do for you, my dear Esau, to make your stay with us more enjoyable?" He flicked away a youth who was serving water and wine but no food.

"We are fortunate to have much cattle, sheep, and goats," replied Esau, weighing every word. "We don't want to inconvenience our lord with taking up too much of his land. We would like to reach an understanding as to where exactly our animals may pasture." Esau was hoping to receive a magnanimous answer that any of the pasture land at Mount Seir was at his disposal.

Indeed, Seir started to say, "Esau, you are blessed with many possessions, but why are you even asking about this trivial matter? I haven't heard of any problems between your people and mine. Has anyone? So there is really . . ."

"I have," Geelahon interrupted. "I understand that there have been arguments and even fights between the Edomites and our shepherds."

Geelahon paused and glared at Esau. "As our dear guest Esau must realize, here on the mountain a good pasture land is scarce. It's difficult even to build houses in this hilly terrain, and many of us live in caves; others live in tents. The lushest grass is way down in the foothills, where my master prince Zibeon dwells."

Geelahon looked at Zibeon, then at Seir, and continued, "If our guest Esau is seeking our guidance on where he may pasture his herds, I have an idea."

"Your servants are grateful for your consideration," answered Esau, nodding.

All throughout the exchange Seir and his sons remained quiet, shifting in their seats.

Geelahon went on, "It's simple. As we've said, Prince Zibeon is blessed with much meadow grass. Why don't you confine your herds to his property?" He shifted his eyes from Esau to Zibeon and back, without as much as a glance at the chief.

Esau did not reply and stared directly at Seir, who said, looking away and fiddling with his goblet, "If this is acceptable to my guests, so be it."

Esau bowed his head without saying anything more. They all sat in awkward silence for a couple of minutes.

"Would my esteemed guests care to join us for dinner? It will be served in about an hour," asked Seir, straightening his clothes.

"No, thank you, my lord. We need to get back to deal with the cattle and the herds, as you have commanded," said Esau. Seir did not insist, and the visitors left.

***

They rode back to Zibeon's estate saying nothing. At last, the prince uttered, stroking his neck, "I have to apologize for what happened. I don't know how to explain my father's behavior."

Esau replied, "Neither can I. This was about the chilliest reception I've ever received. Are they afraid of us and trying to look tough? I didn't feel welcome there at all."

Zibeon said, "Yes, that's what it looked like, although I hope my father didn't mean that. And he must recognize that my land is not vast enough to sustain both your flocks and mine."

"Then why would neither your father nor your brothers say anything other than to agree with the army chief? Is Geelahon running the show now?" Esau did not ask about Zibeon's own silence.

"Yes, he is. We have no choice but to obey, even if our flocks die as a result."

"Nothing's going to die," objected Esau. "We'll deal with Geelahon."

"Deal how? His army is powerful! Do you want to ask for help from Jacob's sons Simeon and Levy? I've heard what they did in Shechem!"

Esau grinned, "We can take care of him ourselves. Maybe with some local help . . . Are any of Seir's sons or others close to him unhappy with Geelahon? I don't mean you, of course."

"Not that I know of."

"What about your mother Nureen? Seir seems to be too old to be of much help to her. Is she involved with Geelahon?"

"I really don't know. Please don't ask me these things," Zibeon squirmed in his saddle.

"Sorry. By the way, Zibeon . . . don't worry about the flocks yet. Let's just move a few droves into your territory for now."

"But Geelahon . . ."

"We can always move more droves later if he insists."

They arrived at Zibeon's home, and the conversation ended. It was time to start scheming.

Chapter 24

The next morning Esau and Eliphaz moved a flock of sheep onto Zibeon's pasture. With many more flocks to go, it was clear there would not be enough space for all the animals. They glanced at each other and grunted.

"Father, how are we going to deal with these Horites?" Eliphaz asked.

"With the help from someone close to Seir. I don't see any other way to get them off our backs," said Esau.

"Forget Zibeon, right?"

"Yeah, with his divided loyalties he is either unwilling or unable to help. Or he might be waiting for a chance to turn on us," Esau frowned.

That afternoon, Eliphaz was alone in the house, staring at the fireplace. A doorbell rang. He opened the door and saw a teenage girl holding the reins of a well-groomed camel with a fancy red saddle.

"My lord, I am looking for my master Esau."

"He is not home, my child. Perhaps I could be of assistance?"

"Perhaps you could. I am a maidservant of Princess Timna. My mistress asked me to invite your father to a dinner tonight. Perhaps you'd want to come instead?"

Eliphaz blinked hard. "What, either one of us would be acceptable?"

"Yes, my lord. But I'd rather it be you." Her face turned the color of her saddle.

"I'll be there," said Eliphaz.

Hearing about this, Esau scratched his head. "Smacks of an ambush. I wouldn't risk going there, but you are more reckless than I am. On a positive note, this could be an opportunity we've been waiting for. Let's see who this princess is."

***

Eliphaz knocked on the door of Timna's house, which was located next to the chief's palace. Esau and three armed servants concealed themselves in the trees.

The attractive woman in her thirties who opened the door wore an elegant deep-purple linen dress, which went well with her gold necklace, and a matching pair of shoes. Surprisingly, she had reddish hair. She greeted him and invited him to a table filled with food.

Eliphaz smiled his best at the princess and at the maids who served the local lamb and beef delicacies. Discussing the weather, he kept taking small bites of beef tongue spiced with mustard. The wine was excellent, too.

At last, the princess sent her maidens away and moved closer. Looking at him with tilted head, she murmured, "My lord, I am so happy that you and your family have moved here."

Eliphaz cleared his throat and answered, "I am also happy we did, seeing such a beautiful princess welcoming us. In turn, you are always welcome in our company."

Timna giggled, "Thanks! Too bad that your extended family has not been as welcoming as you are."

"How could it be with a woman as lovely as you?"

"And yet that's what happened. You see, I wanted to convert to the faith of Abraham, your great-grandfather, and asked your uncle Jacob and his sons to accept me into their tribe. They refused."

"On what grounds?"

"They didn't believe my motives were pure enough. They thought I was insincere, wishing to convert only to become a part of the chosen people."

"I'm sorry that happened. Do you want me to speak on your behalf with my uncle?"

"No, it's too late for that."

"Then what can I do for you?"

"I . . . I want to become your concubine, if you take me, my lord." She lowered her gaze and dropped her head, covering her eyes with well-nourished bony fingers.

"You . . . what?"

"Your concubine. I know you cannot take a mongrel like me as a wife."

"Young lady, this is not a kind of request that I receive often. I am honored but, umm . . . why? Do your kinsmen mistreat you? You are a princess in their midst! And what do you mean by 'mongrel'?" His eyes were bulging.

"They treat me well, my lord. But I want to be a part of the Abrahamic family, even if it means being a concubine to you or to your father!"

"But what's so special about their . . . er, our family?"

"Because I am already a part of it. Chief Seir thinks I am his offspring, but I am really your daughter from Nureen."

"What?"

When Eliphaz regained the ability to speak, he puffed, "This must be the first such request ever. Actually, no. Something like this had happened in our family before." He crossed his legs.

"I know—it was the Egyptian princess called Hagar. Her mother gave her to your grandmother Sarah for the same reason: she thought it was better for Hagar to be a servant to Abraham's wife than a princess in Egypt. Ishmael was her son." Timna's eyes were smiling, surrounded by creases and crinkles.

They sat staring at one another, until Eliphaz said, "It would be a privilege to keep your company. But now I have to go, because I've promised my father a speedy return. He was worried about an ambush." Eliphaz did not add that his father was waiting outside.

"There is no ambush, my lord," chuckled Timna, "except maybe by these . . ." She pulled him in.

He did not need to be persuaded for long, and they consummated their new relationship on the spot.

"Timna, I need your help in something," Eliphaz said afterwards, straightening his tunic.

"Anything, my lord!" Timna's eyes were glowing with joy.

He leaned forward and said, "If you want to be a part of our family, you are welcome to move in with us . . . eventually. But not now, because we don't yet have a place of our own. For now, my father and I are staying in your brother Zibeon's house. We need your help in getting settled here."

"Of course, I'd be happy to help."

"Let's meet again tomorrow at this time, and I'll tell you what we need. But I do have to go now—my father is indeed waiting."

They kissed good-bye, and he left.

Esau was not amused. He grumbled, "You surely took your time! How about if *I* go inside next time and you wait here?"

But after he heard about Timna, his mood changed. "Good job, my son! This arrangement is a tad unusual, but hey .. . Let's see if she knows somebody who could help us."

***

The next evening Eliphaz and Timna met again—this time, without an escort—and he explained what trouble awaited the Edomites.

"I'm not the person who lives by the gossip, but my mother is. She knows everything about everybody. I'll arrange a meeting. You've met her!" Timna said with a twinkle in her eye.

After a few joyful hours, Eliphaz left in the middle of the night, figuring that by this time he could find his way back in the dark. They decided to keep it quiet for now.

***

"Eliphaz, I have to apologize for the rude behavior of both Geelahon and my husband," Nureen said. "I presume that's why you are here."

"Yes, my lady. They demand the impossible. All our flocks must be squeezed into your son Zibeon's property, which barely sustains his own animals."

"Yes, I remember that conversation. What can I do?"

"Would appealing to your husband on our behalf help?"

"Of course not! The old fool is under Geelahon's thumb. Seir won't go against him."

"And why is that? Your husband is the chief! Does Geelahon hold something over him?"

"Just a threat to kill all of us."

"Oh. Perhaps you'd want our help in getting rid of this menace?"

"Of course! I have heard so much about the Edomite military prowess. If anybody can help us, it's you."

Eliphaz then asked where Geelahon lived, how his home was guarded, and who could be trusted in Seir's entourage. They agreed to meet again the next day.

***

Eliphaz took his father for a walk to make his report.

"Father, I cannot believe how far our plans have progressed in the last two days."

"True, but remember—we haven't done anything yet."

"I'm a bit concerned about Nureen. She was helpful but kept her distance. Do you think it's her refined bearing—or is there someone else in her life besides Seir? That could be a problem."

"Or perhaps she doesn't want to compete with her daughter?"

"Perhaps. In any case, keeping our relationship with her business-like suites me just fine."

***

"Nureen, is there anyone among the military commanders who could be of help? How about Geelahon's second-in-command?" Eliphaz asked.

"Jaarib seems like a quiet and unassuming man, doing Geelahon's bidding. Don't know much about him. Hard to tell where his loyalties lie, but I suspect in his heart he hates Geelahon."

"Why? Have they been rivals before?"

"No, it's because of what Geelahon has done to Jaarib's sister when they were young. She has moved away to the Hittites, since her life here was nothing but shame."

"Jaarib is worth a shot then. We'd like to meet with him—discreetly."

"I can arrange that."

With nothing more substantive to discuss, Eliphaz and Nureen just sat in her room, watching one another, fidgeting, adjusting their clothes.

Eliphaz took the plunge. "Nureen, our daughter Timna is all grown up now . . ."

"Yes she is, isn't she?" said Nureen, looking at a far corner of her room.

"She is beautiful and smart and engaging . . ."

"But?"

"But I wasn't aware she existed before this week. I wish you'd let me know."

"Eliphaz, she and I were the only two people who knew who her father was. Why drag you into her life when you were living in Hebron? Who would have known you'd come here?"

"I'm glad we came then."

"She always wanted to become a part of your family, and from the looks of her the other day, she might have succeeded already."

"Yes, she did." Eliphaz did not elaborate.

"Good luck to both of you," she said. Her body was still turned away, but her feet were facing him.

Chapter 25

After a loud bang on the door of Zibeon's home, a gruff voice announced, "This is General Jaarib, General Geelahon's deputy. Open up!"

When Esau opened the door, the visitor boomed, "We have just observed your animals well beyond the borders of Prince Zibeon's property. You are in violation of a royal edict!"

Esau replied, "There must be some mistake, my lord. We meant no disrespect. Perhaps we did not know where the property of my master Zibeon's ends. Please come in to discuss this."

Jaarib motioned to his four Horite guards to stay outside, walked in, and closed the door. Wearing well-worn leather armor and muddy sandals, he seemed to fit Nureen's description of a serious, quiet, and unassuming man. Yet there was something odd about him. Was it his sunken eyes? Stony face?

The two of them sat down, and Esau began, "My lord, we are privileged to reside here with your people. Yet, as you know, my family has been put in an impossible position. We were told to crowd all our animals into my master Zibeon's land. But we could move only a few droves before the place got almost filled up. Perhaps something could be done about this situation."

Jaarib sat up straight. "What do you mean? This order of General Geelahon has been approved by Chief Seir himself!"

"That's true, my lord. But, as perhaps you'll agree, the order is very hard on us. If we do as we are told, most of our animals—and those of Prince Zibeon—would die."

"It does not matter whether I agree or not. An order is an order, and I must uphold it." Jaarib locked his ankles and spoke in a softer voice, which Esau noted with satisfaction.

He asked, "My lord, have you always upheld unjust orders? Have you not ever felt that the people who commanded you could be wrong?"

"Whatever I might have felt, soldiers do not discuss orders. That's what makes us soldiers."

"General, but you are not a mere soldier. You are a second-in-command in the chief's army. Surely General Geelahon seeks your opinion in the matters like these?"

"Not always. He likes to make such decisions by himself."

"But all of us are occasionally wrong, aren't we? And such a wise man as you surely must know the difference between right and wrong. I have learned about that on the knee of my grandfather Abraham. What do you think he would have done if a man commanded him to carry out an order that he felt was wrong and unjust?"

Jaarib leaned back and stared at the fireplace, rubbing his hands against his thighs.

Esau continued, "I understand Geelahon has made some bad decisions in the past, with which you've disagreed? Sorry about your sister."

Jaarib shuddered and held Esau's gaze. "What do you want from me? I am powerless against him—is this what you want to hear?"

"But *I* am not powerless against him. How would you like to become the new army commander, my lord?"

Esau held his breath and felt the handle of his sword lying behind him under a thin carpet cover. This is it!

"You are talking treason now!" hissed Jaarib in a near-whisper. "What exactly do you have in mind?"

"Leave the details to me, my lord. All I want you to do is to be ready to assume the command. And to be friendly toward us, if and when some unfortunate accident befalls somebody in the future."

The two of them said nothing more and did not shake hands. Esau exhaled.

"You have forty-eight hours to move all the cattle!" proclaimed Jaarib from the doorstep as he was leaving.

***

With a soft touch, Esau and Eliphaz closed the door and inhaled the cool breezy air. They both wore black hooded cloaks, which Esau now favored over the traditional while *simlah* shawls. They lit the torches after they passed the border of Zibeon's land, and Eliphaz pointed to a glimmer of light way up the mountain.

"It's Korach," explained Esau. "He needs to learn."

Walking uphill toward the light, they heard a faint roar at a distance and halted.

"Father, are there lions here?"

"Not sure."

Another roar echoed through the night, louder and closer this time, and then everything went quiet. Definitely a lion, maybe several, Esau thought.

The men exchanged glances and pulled out their swords, peering into the blackness around them.

"Father, have you ever fought a lion?"

"Never had a chance. But with two of us here, this shouldn't be a problem."

If there is only one lion, we might have a small chance of survival, he thought. Why have I stopped wearing Nimrod's clothes? They could have saved the day.

Eliphaz pointed at the two faint glistening dots that lit up on the road ahead. They were getting brighter and brighter—and then the head of a male lion appeared. The shadows concealed the true size of his body, but the head was massive.

"Son, when he charges, don't go for the kill. Try to cripple his legs first. Or the back. Stay away from the neck—you won't cut through the mane," Esau pushed out the instructions through gritted teeth.

The lion moved closer, still carrying the two shining dots with him.

"Maybe he has lost a fight and was expelled from his pride. And now he is a solitary nomad. That would be good news," Esau tried to cheer them up. "And son, move away a few paces. As he pounces on one of us, the other should strike him."

Now the lion was right in front of them, baring his canines. Yes, his roar is mighty, but I've heard much worse, reflected Esau, tightening up his abdomen. Where are you now, Darimai the giant? But a lion moves much faster than that slowpoke ever did—and faster than me.

With quick and shallow breathing, Esau laid the torch down on the ground in front of him. He needed to grasp the sword with both hands to have any hope of inflicting damage. Eliphaz, however, was still holding both the torch and the sword. They waited.

The lion bypassed the torch and pounced on Esau. In the nick of time, Esau moved to the side and rotated his hips, minimizing the exposed area of the body. The outstretched paws brushed past him, and Esau hit the predator's side with a glancing blow. He knew it would not cause serious damage, but it was the best he could do.

The beast reversed direction and tried to pounce on Esau again—and received another flesh wound. The lion changed course again and growled, creeping closer this time, shortening the distance for the final leap.

Spying his son lunging at the beast, Esau shouted, "Hit the back!"

But Eliphaz did not have a chance to use his weapon. The lion swiveled toward him, and his mighty paw knocked the sword out of the man's hand in a blink of an eye, as if the animal sensed where the danger was coming from.

Eliphaz shrieked and backed away, trying to stop the assault by waving the torch in front of the advancing menace, but another swift swipe knocked it out also. The beast crouched and prepared to jump at the new target as if forgetting about the old one.

With the lion's back now exposed, Esau hastened to strike it with all his might. He felt the impact of his sword against the spine and heard the thunderous sound of the backbone snapping.

The predator blared and turned his head toward Esau, but his body was left coiled on the ground. Esau held his sword at the ready, glancing at Eliphaz staggering and moaning behind the beast.

Using only the front legs, the lion swung his body around and began to crawl toward Esau, dragging his back legs behind.

Esau stepped aside and tried to deliver the decisive blow but stumbled and almost fell.

He caught the ground with his hand, staring into the bared teeth. He rolled away as fast as he could, narrowly missing a huge paw that hit the packed sand instead.

Esau was safe, but his sword was left lying near the predator's snarling head. Now the only weapon he had was his knife. The man and the beast gazed at one another in semi-darkness.

Esau circled around the lion's back, expecting the brute's head to follow him. When it did, Esau plunged the knife deep into a glistening eye.

The lion violently jerked but could not dislodge the blade, and swiping it with his paw only worsened the damage. As the beast howled in pain and rage, Esau picked up the torch from the ground and shoved it deep into the open jaws.

The smell of burning flesh and fur caused Esau to recoil. The lion rolled to the side, struggling with the torch and the knife, which gave Esau a chance to snatch his sword.

As the injured predator was violently tossing on the ground, he plunged the blade deep into his gut. The lion attempted to make one last roar but could only wheeze. Esau ripped into the white belly again and stepped back.

The two men slumped to the ground, panting and rubbing their eyes. Esau tore off the bottom of his tunic and bandaged his son's bleeding arm as best he could. *I'm getting too old for this,* he thought.

"A change of plans?" he asked, pointing at the bandage. "We can do it later."

"No way," smirked Eliphaz. He nodded toward the twitching body in front of them and asked, "Shouldn't we make a necklace of his claws, or something?"

"That's what savages do. Remember who we are, son. We are royalty."

***

Eliphaz slinked inside the palace through the unlocked back door, leaving Esau and Korach in the darkness. Nureen was up and waiting. She looked at his torn clothes and the bandage.

"We had an encounter with a lion on the way here," explained Eliphaz.

Her eyes opened wide showing their whites, but the deep scratch marks on his arm were certainly not from a sword. She cleaned and rewrapped the wound.

"What now?" she asked.

"Send one of your servants to fetch Geelahon. Instruct him to say that Chief Seir urgently needs his presence. Then go downstairs and wait. When you hear the news, hurry to your husband."

"And?"

"Tell him about the general's demise. Urge him to appoint Jaarib the new army commander and to stay calm. We'd rely on both you and Jaarib to keep things under control. The last thing we need is your husband sending a search party trying to find the offenders."

***

The three Edomites crept along the path toward Geelahon's house, which was separated from Seir's palace by a forest of acacia trees. It was a massive two-story structure, not quite as imposing as the chief's palace, but far larger than any other home in the area. They concealed themselves near the path.

Their plan was simple. They placed a few large rocks and tree branches along the darkest stretches of the path, hoping that Geelahon and his guards would come running. Esau was not sure about Eliphaz's sword arm, and he was ready to fight alone if it came to that.

He told Korach, "Observe from a distance. If we fail and are captured in the process, go find Ardon. Tell him to round up all our people and mount a rescue. Go!"

They waited until a young attendant from the palace ran into Geelahon's home and the commander came out. He was strolling in his battle attire, not running, and he was accompanied by two guards carrying torches. One was walking ten paces ahead of him and one ten paces behind. Esau cursed to himself: the general was no novice to night-time maneuvers.

His sandals wrapped in rags, Esau tiptoed behind the rear guard and soon caught up with him. Having synchronized their footsteps, he waited for Eliphaz to begin the assault.

He saw his son's figure emerging from behind a tree, rushing toward the front guard and striking him. It was Esau's prompt to attack the rear guard with his favorite throat-cutting motion. The two guards flailed their arms and dropped to the ground.

Now Geelahon was standing alone on the dark path. He started towards Eliphaz, a sword in hand, seemingly oblivious to Esau creeping behind—until a blade impaled him.

The Edomites hurried toward Seir's palace, with Korach following a bowshot away. They knew it would be about a half-hour walk in the dark.

They had expected everyone other than the palace guards to be asleep so late at night and were surprised to see bright lights all around the building. They hesitated to come any closer, trying to understand what was happening. To their relief, they saw Jaarib walking toward them with a group of soldiers.

"Please follow me inside," the new commander said. They walked into the palace courtyard illuminated by the guard-held torches.

"We are going to see Chief Seir," said Jaarib. "Please leave your weapons at the door, as usual."

Remembering the protocol from their last visit to the palace, Esau and Eliphaz complied. They exchanged glances and smiled. So far, things have progressed very well. The two Edomites approached the chief, surrounded by a multitude of guards, and bowed.

"I understand you've just killed my army commander," Seir said with a stern face. Esau and Eliphaz stiffened and gave each other a side-glance. How could he possibly know that?

"We have accepted you as brothers, but you have betrayed and attacked us. You are my prisoners now. You will be hanged in the morning, for all to see."

Esau and Eliphaz turned their heads. The guards bristling with spears surrounded them. Without weapons, there was no chance of winning this one. Handcuffed behind their backs, the father and son were taken to the holding cell located in a corner of the main palace floor.

Chapter 26

A narrow wooden bench along the exterior wall was the only furnishing of the cell. Esau stared at a bright spot on the floor, a reflection of the moonlight that seeped through a single narrow window above. Esau estimated that the massive wall was at least one cubit thick—the distance between the tip of a man's middle finger and his elbow.

"Father, we have killed a mighty beast and a powerful man tonight. And here we are," observed Eliphaz in a quavering voice.

"Hey, look on a positive side. At least this isn't a real prison, more like converted servants' quarters. We are not chained to the wall, and we are not in a dungeon!"

"Oh, what difference does it make? We're finished. Betrayed!"

"Yeah, looks like Jaarib has sold us out. Used us to dispatch his main rival. Smart! I thought there was something odd about him . . . How could I've been so gullible?" He shook his head.

"And Seir must be happy that Geelahon is no more. And soon he'll get rid of us, too!"

"Son, don't say that. We'll figure out something."

They mulled over their options. Either breaking out or fighting their way out with their hands fettered with bronze shackles was hardly possible. No other options came to mind.

"Father, should we pray for deliverance?"

"Pray? To whom? To God of Abraham? That's what my brother does, not me. To Horite gods? You know I don't believe in those either."

"But what do we have to lose? And do you really think there is no Creator who runs everything in our lives? Who holds the power over life and death? Don't you remember that believing in one God is the main lesson that both Adam and Noah have taught us?"

"Yeah, yeah. It's the first among the seven Noahide laws, as my father calls them. They are supposed to be the universal rules for all mankind to live by."

"Exactly—the Noahide Code. The first two of those rules are to believe in God and not to blaspheme Him."

"You've learned well, my son. Remember the rest?"

"I hope so . . . let me think. Yes! Don't murder. Don't steal. Don't cheat on your spouse. Don't tear off a limb of a living animal. And also, be just and establish the courts of law."

"Good job, Eliphaz! But I don't think I've observed any of those laws. Violated them all, though."

"But maybe now is the time to remember at least the first one?"

"You can do anything you want—just leave me alone. You start to sound like my brother."

"Well, he taught me a lot! Why do you hate him so much, anyway?"

"Eliphaz, I've always hated him since he stole my birthright and then my blessing."

"But wait. You sold him the birthright, haven't you? And the blessing belongs to the firstborn, right? So why are you so upset about not getting it?"

"Spare me your clever arguments! All this might be true, but I still hate him for tricking me—twice!"

"But father, after all these years, isn't it time to let go? Are you going to carry this hatred through the rest of your life? We might have only a few hours left."

"Yes, I will! I will never forgive him!"

"Father, my uncle taught me something about this, too."

"You're annoying me now, son. What?"

"About the nature of hate. He said hate is much more powerful than love."

"Is it?"

"Yes, he said that the feelings of a man who hates somebody are much more powerful than the feelings of a man who loves."

"Hmm . . . And why is that?"

"He said that hatred exists only so that its tremendous power could one day be changed into love. And when this happens, the resulting power of goodness becomes much greater than it was before the change, when it was still hatred."

"Son, that's a nice theory. But you can be sure that nobody is going to change my hatred for Jacob into love. Nobody! And I think you've spent way too much time studying with him!" He turned away.

***

Esau awoke from his halting slumber at the sound of gentle scraping. He nudged his son and squinted. To his amazement, he saw two metal keys hanging at the end of a rope, which somebody on the outside was yanking up and down.

"Korach, is it you?" whispered Esau. Who else could have scrambled up there?

"Yes, father," Korach whispered back. "We'll try to rescue you soon."

Esau took the smaller key in his mouth and opened his shackles; he then freed Eliphaz. The second key must have been from the cell door.

Having retrieved the rope, Korach whispered again, "Grab this!" and lowered something long and heavy.

The object turned out to be one of Esau's straight swords wrapped in sheep's wool. Another sword followed.

"Be ready." Korach was barely audible now. And then he was gone.

***

Jaarib was deliberating with Seir and his sons how to deal with the Edomites. He argued for an immediate preemptive strike, while it was still dark outside, but Seir and his sons were not convinced.

A guard walked in and reported, "My lords, I have two male relatives of Esau at the front door. They've heard that he was arrested and brought some food for him and his son. What should we do about that?"

"Oh, let them deliver the food," replied Seir. "As you know, we don't feed the prisoners here—their relatives do it for us. Esau and his son have a right to be fed before the execution. Just make sure you thoroughly check those relatives, as well as their food, for any weapons and contraband."

"Yes, my lord." The guard left.

"You see, Jaarib, they already know. I wonder how. Your element of surprise is lost," said Lotan, Seir's oldest son.

"Yeah, I see it. But what would you suggest we do now?"

The guard returned and announced, "My lords, the Edomites have gathered outside the front door. Many of them! They demand the release of Esau and Eliphaz."

"Are they armed?" asked Seir.

"I don't know, my lord. If they are, they don't brandish their weapons."

"Stall them. Tell them to come back tomorrow after Esau's fate is decided. Make them think we are still debating that," replied Jaarib. "Gather all the palace guards in front for a show of force. Leave only the guards at the cell and a roaming patrol inside. If the mob refuses to leave, start clearing the area by force. I will join you soon, but first we need to make some decisions here."

***

The sounds of squabble outside the cell door stirred the prisoners. Two familiar voices were arguing with the guards.

The voice of Dekel was crying, "Why did you need to ruin the food? Look at it!"

"Commander's orders. Making sure you scum don't smuggle anything."

"Then why don't you just eat the whole thing, while you are at it?" chimed in the voice of Jeush, Oholivamah's son.

"Quiet! Be thankful we don't throw you inside to join your relatives!"

With bated breath, Esau and Eliphaz stood at each side of the door holding their swords. Why were Dekel and Jeush arguing with the guards?

More sounds of commotion outside the door. People running. Clanging of weapons. Shouts.

"Give me the key to the door!" Dekel's voice demanded.

"We don't have it," was a faint reply.

"Search them!"

Esau yelled through the door, "Dekel, we have the key. Catch!"

The bottom of the door had a horizontal slot for food deliveries, and he pushed the key through it. Soon the door opened to the sight of Jeush, Dekel, and two other Edomites standing in the corridor. Two palace guards were quivering on the floor.

"How did you manage to get in?" asked Eliphaz.

Jeush replied, "The back door. But hurry—we must go!"

"No way! We are already inside, so let's finish it! Follow me!" Esau rushed to the throne room. He stopped to look back at his men and waited until they reluctantly caught up with him.

A group of palace guards emerged from a side corridor and dashed toward them. As swords clashed, Dekel shrieked, "Esau, watch out!"

From a corner of his eye Esau noticed an incoming arrow. Time stood still as he saw it flying closer and closer toward him, powerless to do anything about it.

In a flash somebody pushed him out of the way. When time resumed its normal speed, he saw Dekel wriggling on the floor next to him with an arrow in his back.

Seeing the shooter load another arrow, Esau sprinted toward him. The guard dropped the bow and tried to escape but could not run fast enough. Returning to his men and swinging his sword without mercy, Esau killed the rest of the Horites.

He bent over his fallen friend and looked into Dekel's drowsy eyes, shedding tears onto his face. He held and kissed his head, but there was no time to waste.

With flared nostrils, Esau looked up and yelled, "Let's go!"

The Edomites rushed into the throne room, where Jaarib, accompanied by four soldiers, was still speaking with Seir and his sons. Zibeon was not in the room.

Everybody turned toward the intruders. Jaarib's men moved in front of him, nervously brandishing their spears. Esau motioned to his men to engage Jaarib and his guards—four against five—while he hurried to Seir.

"You are protecting the wrong man!" the chief bleated, but it was too late. In an instant, Esau was behind him, holding a sword to his throat. The princes sunk deep into their chairs, eyes bulging.

"Stop, you morons!" cried Seir. "Lay down your weapons!"

The Horite soldiers turned toward their chief and, after some wavering, surrendered. They kneeled, looking up at Esau, their eyes pleading for mercy.

Jaarib stood alone, sword in hand, with his usual stony face. Then he placed the sword on the floor and straightened his shoulders, as if daring for anyone to touch him—until Eliphaz pushed him to his knees. Esau nodded to his son, and Jaarib's head joined his muddy sandals. Esau exhaled and let go of Seir.

He faced the chief and his sons, incinerating them with his eyes, and said, "My lord Seir and the princes! Both of your army commanders did not hold your interests in mind when they conspired to do us harm. But as you can see from today's events, your army is not very good. This is why it was overcome by a small team of my men. But I do not wish you ill. I want both our tribes to work together and succeed in making Mount Seir a great place to live."

The room was silent.

Esau continued, boring into the chief's eyes, "Here is what I propose. You, my lords, shall continue to reign over your people, but with me as your new army commander. I will reorganize your troops and make them into an army worthy of your name. I will reside in the former home of Geelahon, who has been terrorizing you, and my people will live here, too. We will intermarry and become one family, living in peace. What do you say, my lords?"

Seir and his sons exchanged glances. Esau knew they didn't have much of a choice. Everybody went outside, where Horite troops were in a standoff with the Edomites.

With Esau standing next to him on the front steps, Seir pushed back a wispy strand of his white hair and announced: "My fellow Horites! I command you to refrain from any hostilities toward Esau's family! Esau is my relative, my esteemed confidant—and now my new army commander. Plead your loyalty to him in my presence! From now on, the Horites and the Edomites will live in peace, as one people!"

Stunned, Horite guards kneeled before Seir and Esau. One by one they came up to the steps and pleaded their loyalty to Esau. The battle for Mount Seir was over. Or so he thought.

CHAPTER 27

The Edomites started to arrive at the capital even before sunrise, throwing the city into chaos. Having buried Dekel in haste, Esau tried to restore a semblance of order. His first act was to appoint Ardon the chief of security in the royal palace, to keep an eye on Seir and his sons. The new commander dispatched Eliphaz to the army headquarters to snuff out any unrest that might be brewing there.

All this done, Esau set out to examine his new home, taking four of his men with him. To his surprise, no armed guards met them at the door, only a frail and unassuming old man wearing a gray linen robe, who introduced himself as the chief servant. The man shuddered when he heard about the fate of his former master and pledged his allegiance to the new one.

Peering into his obedient eyes, Esau decided to keep him in charge, at least for the time being. He ordered him to rouse Geelahon's family and servants and gather them all in the courtyard. Some were already there, awakened by the tumult, murmuring.

Esau stood on the second-floor interior balcony, looking at the mass of people below, as his men watched the crowd from the four corners of the courtyard. The sun was still low, and the assembled Horites stood in the shadows. The face of Esau was already lit, and the contrast was magnificent.

The new master addressed his bleary-eyed audience in a firm voice. "I am Esau, the son of holy Isaac and the grandson of holy Abraham," he began. The people nodded.

Esau continued, "I am now in charge of our lord Seir's army. This house is now mine, and all of you are my servants. My family will move here soon. I am a fair master, and those of you who will faithfully serve me and my family have nothing to fear. But those who plot against me or steal from me will regret the day they were born."

Esau's new subjects trembled from fear even more than they shivered from the early-morning chill. Nobody said a word.

"Questions?"

An attractive dignified woman, her body and head tightly wrapped in black, stepped forward. "My lord, I am Geelahon's widow. What is your will toward me and my children?" She pointed to a group of boys and girls huddled in the corner.

Esau had not thought about that, but he replied without missing a beat, "I have no enmity toward you. But if you want to live, you and your children must pledge allegiance to me. If you do, you will be given a choice to either remain here as my servants, or leave as free men and women. If you don't, all of you die."

He paused and added, "If you decide to leave, and some of your former servants wish to go with you, they would be allowed to do so. But in any event, your former possessions are now mine. You would only leave with the clothes on your backs and the food you could carry."

The expressions on the widow's face and on the faces of her children alternated between relief and despair. The older children were hugging the younger ones.

The widow bowed and said, "If it pleases my lord, let me give our humble reply in a few minutes."

Esau bobbed his head. There was nothing more to discuss for now, and he dismissed the crowd.

He went to explore his new home, turning into every room and deciding where he would place each member of his family. The more he saw, the more he fell in love with this magnificent structure. It had so much space, and its construction . . . he had never seen anything like it.

The two-story home contained dozens of rooms arranged around a courtyard, unlike the houses of Hebron, which had only three or four. The walls were of plastered stone, not the familiar unburned brick. The beams used for the floor and roof framing were of cedar, not pine. These majestic timbers were able to span a long distance, allowing the rooms below to be spacious—he had only seen the rooms of this size in two kings' palaces. Heavy wood planks ran between the beams, making for a much stronger floor than the usual mix of woven branches and clay.

He wondered how the builders could get all these materials up here and who they were. Definitely not the local cave dwellers.

Esau ascended to the flat roof. Bracing himself against the parapet, he enjoyed the view of the capital, now bathed in sunlight and teeming with people. He grinned with delight—he could get used to this. Looking down into the courtyard, he saw Geelahon's family still standing there, looking up. Let them wait.

He climbed down the steps to the second floor and continued his tour. The sleeping quarters used by the master of the house should be somewhere on this level. How about this room? He opened a set of doors and stepped in.

Without a doubt, it was Geelahon's bedroom. Frescoes depicting battle scenes adorned the plastered walls, which held mounted weapons, armor, and trophies. Heavy blue-wool curtains covered small windows and the adjacent wall areas.

While Esau admired the beauty of the room, a corner of his eye caught some movement. Somebody was rushing toward him. Where did he come from? No matter—he had a knife!

Esau was able to parry the strike and rotate his body out of the way, so the blade only sliced the top of his sleeve. He caught the assailant's arm on the rebound and twisted it, prompting a shriek.

It was a young boy! Esau grabbed him by the throat and pinned him against the wall.

"Who are you?" he demanded.

"You killed my father," the boy choke out, trying to frown. Esau slapped him on the face a few times and dragged him down into the courtyard.

"One of yours?" he asked Geelahon's widow, holding the sobbing youth by his hair.

"Yes, my lord."

"He must be punished. But first, what have you decided?"

"We plead allegiance to you, our lord. And if it meets with your approval, we would rather leave this place. Some servants would also like to go with us. But please, don't hurt the boy. I'll do anything to save him and the rest of us!"

Esau released his grip and pushed the boy toward his mother. He stared at her for a short while.

"You can show me where you keep the valuables."

"Of course, my lord."

He followed her upstairs. Her oldest son tried to come along, but one of Esau's people restrained him.

They returned half an hour later to her family and servants. She did not look them in the eye.

Esau grabbed the boy and dragged him toward a long table standing in the middle of the courtyard.

The widow shrieked, "Please, my lord! You've said you'd spare him! What else can I do for you?"

"No, I only said he had to be punished."

Esau brushed away the jugs of water from the table, grasped the boy's right arm, and laid it across the top.

"Hold it!" he ordered one of his men. Then he took out his sword and raised it. Everybody gasped. Geelahon's family was speechless, both their eyes and their mouths wide open.

But Esau waited a few seconds and sheathed his weapon.

Shoving the terrified boy into his mother's arms, he said, "Be thankful that this did not occur twenty or thirty years ago."

Seeing that the family did not stir, he swore and bellowed, "Go! Leave now, before I change my mind!" The family and their servants staggered out.

Having left two of his men to watch over the house, Esau headed to the army headquarters with the other two.

***

Esau invited each of the senior officers for a one-on-one talk. Looking them in the eye, he said: "I know I am not a Horite. If you are uncomfortable obeying my commands for whatever reason, you may leave now. No harm will come to you. Just swear not to take up arms against us in the future."

All the officers but one wanted to stay. Esau ordered them to assemble the troops in front of the headquarters. He told the sole dissenter to wait in the room, leaving one of his men with him.

Observing the ragged lines of the Horites, Esau began, "My brothers! Let me speak with you for the first time as your new commander. Most of you have heard of me and what I've done. You'll be proud of my command, as I'll be proud of you. But I only want to fight with those who truly want to fight with me. All those who don't—you may leave now, assuming that you have joined the army as volunteers. Those who are indentured into service cannot leave, of course."

Esau glanced at the ranks again. Nobody stirred. He continued, "I can assure all those who stay that I will make this army the best-organized, best-equipped, and most lethal force in the region. As you know, my holy grandfather Abraham had only 318 people with him when he defeated the kings of Elam who had harmed your ancestors. My holy father Isaac blessed me to live by the sword. I have always triumphed over my enemies. Triumph with me!"

An old soldier in a tattered uniform started to bang his spear on the ground and chant "Esau! Esau! Esau!" The rest of the soldiers joined in, and the entire mountain heard their cheers. Esau smiled and dismissed his new troops.

Returning to the sole officer who wanted to leave, he told him, "You are free to go, but once you step out this door, you are no longer in the army. So leave your uniform here and pledge to never pick up weapons against us."

The officer did so, and two Edomites escorted him outside the borders of the Horite kingdom. Once he was out in a wilderness, they bid him good-bye. When he turned away, both of them drew their swords and struck him in the back, as their master had commanded.

***

Esau looked with satisfaction at his family and friends assembled to celebrate his first night in the new home. With everyone buzzing about the improbable turn of events, Esau asked who had come up with the winning plan.

Korach started off, "Father, after you two went inside the palace with Jaarib, I kept waiting and waiting. Then I overheard the soldiers talking about your capture, so I crept away from my hiding spot. I found my way to Ardon, as you've said."

"You've made it alone—in darkness?" Esau's eyes opened wide.

"I did. Wasn't that bad. I explained to Ardon what you wanted him to do."

"And?"

Ardon answered, "At first, I couldn't believe it. Then I marveled at your foresight. Then I trudged around the sleeping camp to rouse your family and servants. Then we all marched up to rescue you. We didn't yet have a plan of how to do it."

Timna continued the story from there. "I was awakened by the commotion in the palace and all the lights in the courtyard. I went outside just as you and Eliphaz were coming in with Jaarib. I later learned that you've been taken into custody."

"And what then?" Esau tilted his head.

"I saw a crowd of the Edomites making their way toward the palace," said Timna. "I ran up to them and found the man in charge—Ardon. I explained who I was and offered to help. The four-step rescue plan just popped into my head right then. Glad Ardon listened to me."

"A four-step plan? Nice!" Esau grinned.

"Yes! The first step was getting the keys. I knew where the holding cell was and where the spare keys were. So I retrieved the keys and asked Korach to scale the wall and bring them to you. And the swords, too."

"And that was only the first step?"

"Yes. The second step was to somehow bring a pair of unarmed men inside the palace. I told Ardon that the Horites did not feed their prisoners, so a visit from the relatives carrying a meal would be seen as perfectly normal. Jeush and Dekel volunteered, and I supplied the food."

"Timna, now I'm really impressed. And then?"

"The third step was to create a diversion, so I could open the back door. Ardon brought the Edomites to the palace entrance. With most of the guards watching the shouting crowd, I let two of your armed men inside. And the fourth step was to get you out of the cell. Since Jeush and Dekel distracted the guards outside by arguing with them, the attackers were able to get close. And here you are!"

"This was a gutsy plan," said Esau. "Could have gone wrong at any number of turns, but somehow everything worked out. Except for Dekel." He coughed and went on, "I'm glad you are on our side, Timna."

***

The next evening Esau made a formal party for his family and the Horite nobles. Chief Seir supplied the wine. Esau was watching the princes to determine which of them could be easily intimidated—and which could become a thorn in his side.

The party continued into the night, with Seir's wine flowing in abundance. Somebody compared Esau killing both Geelahon and Jaarib to Abraham's triumph over the kings of Elam.

Ardon asked, "Esau, why are the Horites so fond of your grandfather's victory? I know that he routed a great army with his 318 men, but still . . ."

"This does not amaze you?"

"Not sure. Abraham attacked at night, when the vast army was probably drunk from celebrating their conquest of the five kings. They were easy prey, just as perhaps we are here right now."

"We do have sober guards posted outside," retorted Esau. "But you don't appreciate what my grandfather was up against. Do you realize that the army of King Chedarlaomer and his allies was 800,000 strong?"

"What? So many?" Ardon's brows shot upward. "That would make it one of the largest armies ever!"

"And not only that, those were the best warriors in the world!" exclaimed Esau with an unexpected pride. "Do you know that Chedarlaomer was a famous war hero himself? He used to be one of the princes of King Nimrod. Then he rebelled against the king and defeated his great army—numbering about 700,000 men—with only 5,000 warriors of his own."

"I didn't know that," admitted Ardon. "So that's why Chedarlaomer rather than Nimrod was in charge of the coalition of the four kings? And why they were called the kings of Elam, the name of his kingdom?"

"That's right. So my grandfather managed to defeat an enormous army of elite soldiers with only a few of his untrained servants! Get it? Events like these are simply impossible, yet this one did happen." He paused. "But I'll outshine my grandfather's military glory. Just wait."

After Ardon ambled away, Esau fell deep in thought. Indeed, how *was* my grandfather's victory possible? How *could* Timna come up with her brilliant plan? Was it Divine intervention in both cases? I don't believe in this sort of stuff. But how else to explain it? Am I turning into my brother at this age?

No, it can't be, it just can't. My own genius made it all possible. After all, Korach, Ardon, and Jeush are my people. Dekel was, too. I have made them into whom they've become. Even Timna is of my seed.

Still, what about Abraham's victory? What about Jacob's fierce warriors?

If I could only banish these nagging thoughts once and for all . . . He sighed and reached for his goblet.

Chapter 28

Having made a promise to restructure the Horite army, Esau immersed himself into the task. Upon questioning the officers, he learned that new recruits received very little training—at best, a few days of practicing archery and fighting with sword and spear. Most soldiers served only part-time; they were peasants, artisans, and shepherds, called under arms only when needed.

Esau sat down with Eliphaz and Ardon. He said, "I've been meeting with Seir, telling him that the army badly needs new weapons and uniforms. I also told him that the troops must go through a good training program. He agreed to provide some funds, but not enough to do everything. Let's discuss what's most important."

"We should start with training, with whatever weapons they have," volunteered Eliphaz.

"Agreed. For how long?"

Ardon said, "How about one month right away and then two days every month after that?"

"Fine," said Esau. "Ardon, you'll supervise the training. Weapons and uniforms? You know I've always been impressed with an army dressed in good uniforms, rather than looking like an angry mob."

"What kind of uniforms are you thinking of?"

"Red, Ardon, red. My color! I'll design them myself," pledged Esau.

"Can't argue with that," said Eliphaz. "But weapons? I presume you won't be designing those?"

"Hold on. What do they have now?" interjected Ardon.

Esau replied, "I've checked the arsenal. They have a lot of weapons that look scary but are not very effective in the type of battle I envision. Mostly bows and arrows, bronze-tipped spears, maces, Egyptian sickle swords. Very few straight double-edged swords that I like."

"We used to carry those sickle swords ourselves, remember?"

"Yeah, Ardon, but I don't see one on you now," said Esau. "As you well know, the swords we carry are good for both slashing and stabbing. Those single-edged sickle swords are best for slashing from chariots. Do we have chariots here?"

The men smiled.

"So the straight double-edged ones, but which kind? The most expensive—with the center thicker than the edges?" wondered Eliphaz.

"If the price permits, sure."

"Getting them from the Philistines, like everybody else does?" asked Ardon.

"No, let's try getting the best—the swords from Ubulla. I know, I know, it's far away; we'll have to travel all the way to Tigris River."

"Who'll go there?" asked Eliphaz.

"You will. Ardon will be doing the training and be in charge of guarding the palace, remember?"

"Yes, father. How many do we need? And what are we going to do with the swords they have?"

"Let's start with a fully-equipped army of 4,000. We'll expand that number later if need be. As for the existing sickle swords— let's keep them for now and start training with them."

"Father, what about their other weapons? Bows, spears, shields, slings? It would be nice to get the Egyptian composite bows."

"All those should suffice for now. The composite bows— maybe later. It would take too long to train the Horites to use them. Anything else?"

"Armor?" asked Ardon.

"Yeah, we need some armor. Not for everyone, of course—that would break Seir's treasury. The Canaanites always provide armor for their generals and officers of high rank . . ."

" . . . the natural targets of the archers and the infantry. Killing them would render the army rudderless—even on land," smiled Ardon.

"Well, let's equip the army first, and then we'll think about the navy . . . on this mountain," scowled Esau in return.

"Father, which type of armor are you thinking of?"

"Remember the fierce warriors who attacked us? Many of them wore this fantastic armor. That's what I'd love to have."

"They wore scale armor—small metal scales sown to leather or some fabric, right, father?"

"True. If a coat of this armor extends from shoulders to thighs, it's great against arrows. Assuming it has no missing pieces, of course."

"Helmets?" asked Ardon.

"Yes, we should get bronze helmets for all the officers and for some foot soldiers," said Esau. "I think that's all Seir can afford."

CHAPTER 29

Timna moved in with Eliphaz, who had never lived with any wives or concubines before. Chief Seir still invited her to the family gatherings, and she often went there—alone, as Eliphaz always found an excuse not to go. She knew he did not feel comfortable among the Horites.

Arriving at one of such gatherings, Timna was surprised to see that everyone crowded around her nephew Anah.

"What's going on?" she asked Zibeon.

"Looks like my son lost all the donkeys I had entrusted into his care, and he's trying to explain it away. He also got wounded somehow."

Coming closer, she saw a blood on Anah's face. The wound was long and deep, as if somebody had slashed him with a sword or a knife. It was difficult to dress without wrapping up the entire head, and Anah didn't want that. In the end some cloth was wrapped around Anah's face, and he told his story.

"I was pasturing my father's donkeys in the wilderness. Sometimes I go all the way to the Salt Sea, and today I went into the wilderness near the seashore." He stopped and bit his lip.

"So?" his brothers prodded him.

"All of a sudden, a violent storm arrived from the opposite side of the Salt Sea. It seemed to target just me and my donkeys; the rest of the shore was quiet. The wind was whirling and howling and blowing sand just over us—nowhere else! My donkeys stood still. It looked like they couldn't move at all. I know I couldn't!"

"And what then? You were cut by a piece of flying debris and ran away—is that it?" Lotan smirked.

"No, no. Then I saw 120 strange animals that were coming our way from the other side of the sea. I had the time to count them, because I was frozen in place."

"How strange?"

"They were monsters! They looked like people, but only from their feet up to their waist. And above that . . ." He panted, as everyone waited.

" . . . and above their waist they were all different. Some looked like bears. Others looked like *keephas*, with tails extending from their shoulders all the way down to the ground. Those tails were like the tails of the *ducheephath*."

"Hmm. What did they do?" asked Lotan.

"These animals came and mounted my donkeys and rode them away."

"And you didn't try to run after them?" asked Zibeon.

"Father, I couldn't even lift my finger! And then . . ." he gasped.

"Then what, what?" cried everyone in unison.

"Then one of these monsters came up to me and hit me with its horrible tail," mumbled Anah, as tears started to soak the dressing.

"And?"

"And then I ran away. I ran as fast as I could. I thought I was a dead man!" sobbed Anah. His brothers looked at each other, blinking.

"I've heard about these monsters," Shoval said. "I think they are called *yemim*."

"Nonsense. These *yemim* are of the old wives' tales," said Zibeon with confidence. "My son is making it all up."

"And did I make this up also?" asked Anah, pointing to his face.

"I don't know how you got that," shrugged Zibeon. "I bet if we all go there, we'd find the missing donkeys and the people who took them. But it's getting late now—so let's go first thing in the morning. I want my animals back."

***

At sunrise, Seir's sons, grandsons, servants, and many troops left toward the sea. Anah showed them the exact location where he saw the *yemim*, but there were no signs of either the monsters or the donkeys.

There were only the donkey footprints, which extended to the edge of the sea and disappeared there. The Horites scratched their heads, and since then none of them went anywhere near the sea.

***

When Timna told this story to Eliphaz, he just laughed, "What silliness. Your nephew probably sold the donkeys to someone and faked the injury. I don't trust your relatives, sorry."

"But Eliphaz, all my brothers have seen the donkeys' footprints . . ."

"I'll believe it when I see it. Never heard of *keephas* or *ducheephath*. Maybe they exist somewhere, but I still think Anah made it all up."

Timna said, "There's something else . . ." She looked down on her stomach.

Eliphaz's feet started bouncing. "Are you sure?"

"Yes. If it's a son, I want to name him Amalek."

"Fine with me."

"Thanks. But can you do me a favor? Let's tell your father about the *yemim*. Please?"

Having heard the story, Esau said, "My son, fantasy or not, we should at least look into this. Can't you understand how great we would become if we had a way to control these monsters, if they are real?"

Eliphaz sighed. "Father, you're right, as usual."

"Huh. Then here's your little punishment: find me a magician who can summon them."

***

Esau, Eliphaz, and a dozen armed servants spent days on the mountain road leading south from Mount Seir to a town in

Midian. At last, they approached the town, where a boy came up to them and volunteered to show the way to the magician's home.

It was the best-looking house in the area, with round columns supporting a large entrance portico, which reminded Esau of Darimai's home. The back of the house disappeared into the mountain. There were no fences, no guards, no bells, and no locks on the door. The men looked at another and then at the youth, who shrugged his shoulders.

Esau grunted and got off the camel. He and Eliphaz walked into a dim foyer lit only by a few candles; the windows were covered with heavy black drapes. Plastered whitewashed walls contrasted with the drapes and the furniture, which consisted of a couch and a few chairs, all upholstered in black. Their young guide led them behind a black fabric curtain, then another one.

The dark-skinned magician was cooking something in a stone furnace. The youth put a finger across his lips and invited them to sit on rough-hewn wood benches.

As they waited, Esau glanced around. Quite a change from the austere elegance of the foyer to this workroom filled with various jars and implements. The room looked like a cross between his Hebron cave and the physician's shop. Except darker.

The magician threw something in a boiling pot and softly chuckled when blue smoke filled the air. He removed the pot, placed it on a stone bench, and turned to his visitors, who were rubbing their eyes.

"Welcome. How did you find me, Esau?" said the host.

Esau cleared his throat and said, "Peace be with you. We've been told we could find you here. But how did you . . ."

"The time and the purpose of your visit have been revealed to me. That's why I've sent my apprentice to meet you." He pointed to the beaming boy.

"What is your name?" asked Esau. "Nobody could tell us."

"It's because my name is hidden."

"Then how should we call you?"

"The magician."

"Fine," said Esau, blinking fast, "so can you summon the *yemim* for us?"

"It depends . . . it's not easy. But first, may I ask what are you planning to do when you see them? They don't listen to human commands, you know."

"Right. Can *you* control them?" asked Esau.

"No, nobody can. They just . . . exist."

"But what are they? Where do they live? Why did Anah see them?" Eliphaz pitched in.

The magician raised his hands and grinned.

"Maybe they'll listen to *me*. I should at least try," said Esau, glowering at his son. "If they don't, so be it. Can you do it for us or not?"

"As I said, it's not easy. Takes a lot of preparation."

"I got it," frowned Esau. "So how much do you want to make them appear in some spot near Mount Seir?"

"No, it would have to be here," said the magician, "and that would be 1,000 silver pieces."

Eliphaz coughed, as his father said, "That's for a one-time appearance, or can we see them anytime we want?"

"You may keep them for as long as you want. Just pronounce, *'yemim*, vanish,' and they will be gone. But as I said, I think you'd be wasting your efforts."

"We'll see. A deal then. In two weeks—here?"

"Yes, thank you."

"But wait," said Esau. "How can we be sure you can do this magic?"

"You can't. Would you like a demonstration of something simpler? How about I make your son able to fly for a minute?"

"Hmm. That would do."

Without asking Eliphaz for permission, the magician placed both hands on his head and mumbled some incantations. "Go try," he said.

Esau patted his son on a back and pointed at the entrance. Eliphaz gave him a terrified look and staggered outside. Once there, he flapped his arms a few times, as the servants looked in amazement. Nothing happened. Esau started to laugh.

Eliphaz then closed his eyes, stretched his arms above his head, jumped—and lifted himself above the ground. He tumbled in the air for a while, trying to find support with his hands. Then he straightened his arms above his head again and took off.

He circled above the magician's home and the awe-stricken servants. Then the magician motioned for him to return to earth, and Eliphaz did so, shaken but grinning from ear to ear.

"Enough for you?" asked the magician. "See you in two weeks."

***

The Horite soldiers hastened to build a massive corral for their future guests, while Esau and his party traveled back to Midian with 120 donkeys in tow. This time, they found their way without any help.

The somber magician met them at the door, and the Edomites carried a heavy wooden chest inside. Rather than counting the money, the magician stood over the chest with his eyes closed for a minute and nodded. Everybody followed him outside to a nearby field.

After his many incantations, a strong whirlwind arrived. Tree leaves, branches, even a few *sudras* torn off the heads of the unsuspecting guests started to swirl above. Esau glanced at the surrounding palm trees—they were standing still.

At last, the *yemim* appeared from somewhere just beyond the field and started to walk toward the horrified men. Their appearance fit Anah's description: half men, half beasts walking on human feet. They halted less than fifty paces away from the Edomites, grunting and growling.

Esau stepped forward and extended his arms toward the monsters. He yelled, "*Yemim,* come closer!" and they did so, some of them defiantly shaking their heads, some swinging their spiny tails. Esau yelled, "*Yemim,* stop!" and they did so, glaring at him. He yelled again, "*Yemim,* mount those donkeys!" and they did so, too.

Riding at the head of the unusual caravan, Esau waved to the astonished magician and set off. The Edomite servants kept a good distance away.

***

Thousands of the Horites lined up the mountain road to gaze at the show of a lifetime. The trembling mothers hugged their smaller children, as the older ones hid behind their skirts. The monsters were snapping at the gawkers but did not attack anyone.

A boy of about two ran out, trying to catch the tip of a huge green tail, but his father snatched him just in time to avoid being hit. A stray dog that attempted to do the same was not as fortunate.

The servants led the caravan into the corral, with a drove of sheep already inside, and closed the gates.

"They better be tall enough," muttered Esau, looking at the walls three times his height. "Now we need to figure out what to do with these *yemim*. Hope they won't kill one another—or any of us—in the meantime."

Chapter 30

Sitting on the roof of his home, Esau was enjoying the gentle midmorning breeze that ruffled his short white beard. Preparing to celebrate his one 106th birthday, he recounted his life's adventures and his victories on the military and romantic fronts. Yes, those were the days, Esau grinned. But he lost his smile and furrowed his brows when he remembered Jacob, the only person he had not been able to defeat. And then, as always, came the nagging thoughts, the torture.

For the last time, how do I explain the beating that I and my 400 men took from the mysterious warriors during our last encounter with him? I've never heard about those warriors before or after that, and I haven't seen them in his entourage when I met him.

Were they the mercenaries hired to protect him for a day? But I am familiar with all the militaries in the area, and none resembles those fierce horsemen. Were they angels, as I've wondered ever since? But I don't believe in angels.

Why not? I've mulled over this question many times, and each time arrived at the same answer. If I accepted that angels existed, I'd have to accept that God Himself existed. And in that case whomever He chose to favor and protect would be saved from harm. So isn't it futile then to try to get rid of my brother?

These arguments make perfect sense, but I cannot accept them without becoming *him*. There must be some flaw in this logic.

For example, let's suppose for a moment that God exists and He protects my brother. Surely Jacob is not perfect? Surely there must be the times when he angers God? Would Jacob be still protected then—or vulnerable to an attack?

And what of my own blessing to live by the sword? True, I could not overcome Jacob's angels—if those fierce warriors were indeed angels—but should I not be able to overcome any mortal? Including my brother and his sons after they have sinned in some fashion? If I could only find such a time, when the odds of victory were in my favor . . .

Esau was still immersed in these thoughts when Eliphaz touched his shoulder.

"Father, I've spoken with some traveling merchants, the Ishmaelites. They just returned from Hebron, and they delivered the news about your brother. His wife Leah died."

Esau lifted his eyes. "And why should I care? I don't plan to marry her anymore. But wait . . . Why don't you invite them over for a meal? I hope they don't smell of tar and oil the way they usually do."

"No, father, these Ishmaelites trade in spices."

The merchants confirmed the news about Leah and reported that Jacob and his sons moved to Shechem for a period of mourning.

"Why Shechem? Haven't they devastated the town, killing all the males there?" asked Eliphaz.

The merchants explained, "The pasture land around Shechem is much better than around rocky Hebron. Jacob's sons spend most of their time in that city anyway."

"So?"

"Jacob decided to stay with his sons for a while, so that all of them could mourn together."

"Hmm. All of them gathered in an empty city, huh?" Esau cracked a faint smile and glanced at his son.

"Yes, my lord. Everyone but Joseph, who is in Egypt."

"What's he doing there?"

"His brothers sold him into slavery, and he ended up in that country."

"Oh? Nice brothers! But thank you. You may eat everything on the table. Hope your trade goes well," said Esau and walked out, trying to digest the news.

So Joseph, supposedly the only man strong enough to overcome me, is now away, somehow sold into slavery. By his own brothers, no less. If that's not a sin on their part, I don't know what is. And just thinking about it—how funny is that?

He said, "Eliphaz, this is our chance to finish this business once and for all—something you should've done long ago. It is for a day like this that we've kept the *yemim* here. I'll tell Aduram to prepare for battle, and you tell the rest of my sons. Hurry!"

General Aduram reported that the army of 4,000 men—the force Esau and Ardon had trained and equipped—was ready. The army and the *yemim* left for Shechem the next morning.

***

Only a few hundred people, mostly women, remained in Shechem. There was plenty of space, but Jacob and his sons—the Israelites—crowded into a small plot of land they had purchased for 100 *kesitahs* from the family of the local chief called Chamor.

One of Jacob's sons noticed a dust storm approaching. It was still far away and could have missed them altogether, but they decided to move into the city to wait it out. Once inside, Jacob counted his servants—there were 200 of them.

Out of the blue, women's cries filled the air. Has the storm arrived so quickly? But a peek from the shuttered windows revealed that arrows were raining down the city. They were under attack!

Jacob wondered out loud whether the Canaanite kings wanted to avenge their dead—again. They had tried it before, the day after Shimon and Levy killed all the males in the city after the rape of Dinah.

On that occasion, an enormous army of the Canaanites banded together outside Shechem, poised to strike. Jacob and his household were saved only when an unexplained panic befell the assembled multitude, and the would-be attackers melted away without a fight. Was the history repeating itself?

Jacob's servants climbed atop the twelve-cubit-high city walls. But it was not the Canaanites, but the Edomites who surrounded the city—thousands of them, clad in red armor and glinting helmets, clanging their weapons.

Jacob asked his children, "What do you think—could Esau be reasoned with? Would he perhaps accept money that he likes so much in lieu of our blood?"

Nobody said a word, and he climbed atop a rampart himself. He noticed Esau at a distance and exclaimed, "My brother, what is the meaning of this? Last time we met I assured you of my brotherly love. I still only want peace between us!"

But Esau just scowled and turned away.

Yehuda called out to his father, "Why waste words? They've come here with only one goal!"

"You are right, my son," sighed Jacob. "We don't have a choice. Get your bows and arrows; aim at the officers first!"

Jacob searched for the best target. Far away stood a man in a general's uniform, and he made the shot.

Aduram fell over with an arrow in his chest, gasping for air. His bronze helmet rolled off, exposing his bald head. Esau yelped and started running toward the wounded general but quickly reconsidered and turned around. But it was too late.

Another arrow sent by Jacob hit him in the lower back, just missing the spine. Esau screamed and collapsed face down in the dust, bumping his temple against a rock. His sons covered him with their shields and carried him to safety, a distance of two bowshots away. They stood around him in silence, waiting for the medic to arrive, watching blood trickle down his leather tunic.

"Father, let me assume the command," offered Eliphaz.

"No!" hissed Esau between the howls of pain. "You and your brothers stay here. If both you and I are dead, say goodbye to the Edomite kingdom, you fool!"

Esau called for Nymeer, a relative of Oholivamah. He had been following Nymeer's career ever since the boy volunteered to be among the 400 warriors.

Stern-faced Nymeer, a rugged and imposing man, leaned over Esau still lying on his stomach. Esau squeezed out to him, "Take over. Prepare for the attack. From all directions at once. Announce a reward of 100 silver pieces. To anyone who kills a member of Jacob's family. Try to lure them out from behind the walls. If they go for it, let me know. We have a surprise for them. Go!"

As the officers rushed to their troops, Esau felt alone, even with his sons still standing next to him. It's out of my hands now, he thought. What a relief. I did all I could to defeat him, and here I am, probably dead soon. This wasn't supposed to happen! He closed his eyes and tried to will away the pain.

***

With the Edomites converging on the city, Jacob and his sons had to spread their meager forces even thinner. They divided themselves into four teams, with fifty servants in each, and assumed the positions along the four walls.

Jacob walked alone atop the wall, seeking out the new army commander and not finding one. For some reason, the assembled Edomites hesitated to advance.

Judah said to his troop, "We cannot win the battle by simply defending the wall—too many of them, and we don't have enough arrows. Let's counterattack instead, since that's the last thing they'd expect. Follow me!"

He descended down the rope and raced toward the Edomites; his brothers and servants followed. Arrows and stones started to fly all around them, but they quickly covered the distance to the enemy. Esau's troops did not expect the attack, and only the frontline soldiers raised their spears.

Judah and his team were swinging their blades with abandon. At first, they only aimed at the unprotected skin, but they soon discovered that the shiny red armor was no match against heavy blows of their sickle swords. Yet they also realized that the first Edomite casualties made little difference in the fight—there were still almost a thousand of troops facing them on the south side alone.

Judah's brothers manning the other walls followed his example, and the battle was raging all around Shechem. But with the element of surprise lost, the Edomites encircled the four tiny groups of Jacob's fighters and started to push them back. Soon each of the four teams was pinned down in front of the locked gates.

Suddenly, thundering steps shook the ground, and the army backed away. Through the clouds of dust moved something much more menacing. The Israelites gazed at the approaching *yemim* with slackened jaws, as the growling monsters headed straight for them. Jacob's sons looked around—there was no escape.

Jacob looked at the *yemim* and frowned. He took his bow and aimed at one of the monsters but then put it down. Instead, he raised his hands and pronounced the name of God, the awe-inspiring name that nobody was allowed to say. But he did.

The moment he said it, the *yemim* disappeared—vanished in the air. He ran along the walls of the city. Not a single one remained.

The Israelites cheered, as their enemies hesitated. But not for long. The soldiers put away their long spears, took up the swords, and surrounded them again. Pushing and shoving, the Edomites crowded around the defenders, reminding one another of Esau's reward, ignoring the desperate commands of the officers ordering them to gain the high ground and climb the walls.

The brothers were still dressed in the white clothes of the mourners, now soaked red. Though lacking military training, they were killing their teeming enemies by the dozens. But there was a limit to their endurance, and the attackers kept coming, with fresh soldiers climbing over the dying. At the end of their rope, the sons of Jacob cried out for deliverance, mixing heavy panting with halting prayers.

All of a sudden the sky darkened, as the long-anticipated sandstorm arrived.

The metal helmets of the Edomites could not protect their eyes from the clouds of swirling sand, and the soldiers had to make a choice between fighting with their eyes closed or falling back.

By contrast, Jacob's people wore simple *sudra* head covers, which they lowered over their eyes. To their amazement, they later recounted, they could see through the fabric—and also regained their depleted strength. Now they had the upper hand, killing the soldiers with ease, and they slew many hundreds.

Lirron, one of the Horite commanders, was the first to turn and run. The rest of the soldiers followed suit, dropping their weapons, shields, and armor along the way. The rout continued even when the sandstorm was over.

Jacob and his sons chased Esau's army all the way back to Mount Seir, stopping only at nightfall. Jacob was planning to finish the battle the next morning, to subdue Esau once and for all. Sitting by the fires, the Israelites looked at one another in disbelief at the turn of events. Not a single one among them was injured.

Meanwhile, the sons of Esau carried him home on their shoulders. They tried to stop the bleeding but discovered that a loin wound was difficult to treat. They had to tear apart his skin-tight leather tunic in the process.

Lying on the blood-soaked sheets, Esau was coming in and out of conscience all night. Of his wives, only Machalat stayed with him, ignoring his cries for Anadil.

***

Eliphaz and Nymeer spent the night debating the next steps. Neither of them saw a practical way of reversing their fortune.

After some arguments they decided to keep Lirron in the army for the time being, recalling that the only reason Esau had appointed him a junior commander was his pedigree. Lirron came from a large and wealthy Horite family that rivaled Seir's—a family they could not afford to alienate now.

Late at night, Eliphaz visited with Seir and his sons. The princes sat with their feet wrapped around the chair legs, fiddling with their clothes.

Seir was incensed. "I gave you the money you wanted for the weapons and armor. I agreed to your foolish attack, even though Jacob is not my enemy. I gave you my soldiers—whom you've trained—and now his forces are besieging my city?"

"We could still organize the defenses," offered Eliphaz without looking at the chief.

"If 4,000 of our best troops could not overcome them, how are the dispirited remains of the beaten-down army supposed to win? Are you the one who's going to order them to fight? After they ran all the way back here, losing their vaunted red armor and weapons along the way?"

Eliphaz was silent. And so the verdict was sealed.

***

The next morning, as Jacob's sons and servants prepared for the final attack, the bedraggled remnants of Esau's army came out with raised hands, prostrated themselves on the ground, and begged for peace.

On that day Jacob and his sons signed a peace treaty with the Edomites and the Horites, both of whom accepted Jacob's power over them. As his subjects they agreed to pay an annual tribute.

Jacob remembered that among the ten blessings his father had given him were the words, "You shall be a master over your brothers, and your mother's sons shall bow down to you." That part of his blessing was now fulfilled.

CHAPTER 31

Esau was lying down, sulking. The pain started to subside a bit, and Machalat prodded him to get up and stroll every few hours. He hated using the wooden crutches his sons had made; all he wanted to do was to stay in bed, replaying in his mind over and over the events from a week ago.

Eliphaz walked in and sat down without uttering a word. Esau glanced at him and murmured, "My son, how did we come to this?"

"Perhaps we shouldn't have gone after Jacob."

"We did what seemed right at the time. The odds were in our favor."

"Yes, father, they were. So is Jacob invincible?"

"You tell me. Did our people kill any of his at all?"

"I haven't seen any of them dead," admitted Eliphaz.

"Well, here's your answer. This time he didn't even need those fierce warriors."

"So is it possible that he was right all along and we were . . .?"

"Everything's possible," snapped Esau, "but it's a bit late for me to become a pious scholar, don't you think? He has his path and I have . . ."

The sounds of some distant clamoring interrupted Esau, and Eliphaz helped him to the window. Beyond the acacia woods, in the square facing the royal palace, a boisterous crowd of the Horites was gathering. Korach came in and confirmed that the locals were on a verge of a riot.

"What do they want?" asked Esau.

"They are angry that Seir has levied a tax on them—they've never been taxed before," said Korach.

"To pay a tribute to Jacob, I presume?"

"Yes, father."

"One thing after another!" Esau exclaimed. "If this blossoms into a full-blown riot, how are we going to put it down, when I'm like this?"

"Our defeated army is in no mood to fight—certainly not against its own people," said Eliphaz. "If anything, the soldiers probably hold a grudge against us for losing the war."

"Is Seir in his palace now?"

"I think so, father."

"This could get very serious, very fast. Eliphaz, round up all our relatives and servants and tell them to rush here."

"All of them? Women and children, too?"

"Yes. We don't know what the Horites are up to. Then go to Seir to feel him out. Enter the palace from the back, so the mob won't see you." Esau paused and added, "And after that bring all the Horite commanders to me. Korach, you stay around."

Eliphaz left. After visiting the relatives, he located Ardon, and both of them went to see the chief.

Chief Seir and all the princes were assembled in the throne room. One look at their downcast eyes and the heads tucked into shoulders told Eliphaz all he needed to know.

He bowed and said, boring into the chief's eyes, "My lord, we have a disgruntled crowd outside. They seem to object to the tax that was levied on them."

Red-faced Seir shrieked, "Yes, that's what they object to! The tax your father forced us to impose because of your foolish war! They are going to stone us soon!"

"My lord, I just came back from my father. We are working on a plan to quiet things down and will present it for your approval soon. But first, he wanted me ask if my lord has already decided on a course of action."

"We have not." Seir pulled on a strand of his white beard, as his eyes darted around the room. He regained his composure and declared, "We are looking forward to hearing your plan."

Turning to Ardon, the chief asked, "Meanwhile, are we safe here in the palace?"

"Yes, my lord. I have stationed additional guards at the front and around the building."

Eliphaz and Ardon bowed and left Seir's presence. Ardon and a pair of his guards hurried to Esau's home, while Eliphaz went to gather Nymeer and the other commanders.

***

Esau addressed the Horite commanders, "My brave officers, these are difficult times. With Aduram dead and myself wounded, I must rely on General Nymeer and on you to maintain order. We must keep the soldiers away from the mutineers. Any signs of unrest in the barracks?"

"No, my lord," answered the commanders in unison.

"Good! As you can see, I am not yet fully mobile, so I will be issuing my commands through Eliphaz." Esau dismissed the officers.

He called for his sons and Ardon and told them, "I've had enough of dealing with Seir and his pathetic tribe. After this crisis is over, we'll take over this place once and for all. We will get rid of our most committed and capable enemies, intimidate the weakest, and expel the rest. Only then will we and our families be safe here." Everybody nodded.

"But first we must take care of the mob. Let's tell them we want to negotiate and invite their leaders to Seir's palace. They won't leave it alive."

After the men were silent for a little while, Eliphaz wondered out loud, "Isn't it easier to disperse the crowd by force?"

Esau bit the upper lip and flashed his eyebrows. "Didn't you say that the army was in no mood to fight? What if they switch sides? My commanders have assured me that the army is still with us, but can we trust them?"

Korach asked, "Why not tell the Horites that the tax would be repealed—that they've won—and send them home? Then round up the instigators overnight. I bet not too many would return to the square the morning after."

Esau smiled to himself: this young man is in the right state of mind. He said, "Yes, that's another possibility. But they might ask for Seir's guarantees. Then a lot would depend on what he does. Another unknown."

Ardon pitched in, "If we assure the Horites that the tax would be repealed, what if Seir then asks how are we going to pay Jacob? We still owe him a tribute!"

"Tell him I'll pay the tribute out of my own pocket," said Esau. "I have more than I need, as I've told Jacob in the desert, remember?"

Seeing puzzled looks all around, he added, "Can't you people take a joke? Look, if we win this fight, there would be plenty of Horite property to plunder—er, confiscate—toward the tribute money. If we lose, none of this would matter!"

Eliphaz and Ardon left for Seir's palace, accompanied by two of Ardon's palace guards, one walking in front and one in the back. It was still midday, and there were few shadows in which to hide along the way. They took a longer but more secluded path to avoid the mob at the entrance.

At last, the palace was in sight. They were almost there, at the back door, and they started to breathe a bit easier.

All of a sudden, an arrow pierced the torso of the front guard; he screamed and fell backwards. Then the guard in the rear shrieked and fell, with an arrow in his back. An ambush!

CHAPTER 32

Eliphaz and Ardon stood back to back, holding their swords, scanning the area, trying not to gaze at the two moaning guards. After a pause, the soldiers wearing red Edomite uniforms stepped out from behind the trees with loaded arrows. Seven of them.

Eliphaz roared at their officer, "Lirron, what is the meaning of this? You were the first to run in the battle with Jacob. Do you wish to be remembered not only as a coward, but also as a traitor?"

"No, I am a patriot and the new army commander," answered Lirron. "*You* are the intruders and traitors. I will not allow you to ruin Mount Seir, my home. If you surrender now, you would be my prisoners. You'd be treated well. Otherwise, you die here."

He twitched his head upward, and his troops adjusted their aim, as if they needed to look any more menacing. Eliphaz and Ardon put down their weapons. The Horites tied their hands and shoved them into a nearby barn. Lirron left two soldiers outside and left.

***

The palace guards were fidgeting with their weapons, shifting on their feet, and glancing around, as the crowd in front of them continued to swell. Their commander was supposed to be back from his meeting with Esau hours ago. Some of them were furtively wiping their hands on their distinctive red-and-green uniforms.

Back at his home, Esau was tossing, too, waiting to hear from Eliphaz and Ardon. Have they walked into Seir's trap? He kept asking Korach to look out the window, but there was nothing outside but the agitated mob beyond the woods.

***

The location of Nureen's room—on the second floor in the rear of the palace—afforded maximum privacy. It was also directly above the back door, which many of her lovers had used. But today being in the back put her at a disadvantage.

She opened the curtains to listen to the sounds of some commotion out front and chanced to see Eliphaz and Ardon being brought into the barn. She recoiled and covered her mouth in surprise.

Nureen tiptoed downstairs, listening for any suspicious sounds. The palace was quiet; the guards stood motionless in the corridors.

She came up to the closest one and asked, "Who is in charge today? I need to speak with him."

The young guard straightened his stance and said, staring straight ahead, "Commander Ardon is in charge, my lady. But he is not here."

"I know that," said Nureen, louder now. "I just saw him being captured. Summon the most senior guard—now!"

The guard's eyes opened wide. He choked, "Right away, my lady!" and ran out.

When he returned with an older man, Nureen explained what she saw. She took the two of them to her room's window and pointed out the barn where the prisoners were held.

"My lady, have you seen any soldiers going into that barn, other than the two sentries outside?" asked the older guard, touching his nose.

"There aren't any soldiers inside. Seven of them brought Eliphaz and Ardon, and five left afterwards. I counted them, don't know why."

The guards waffled, and the older one said, "My lady, we have orders not to leave the building, except to reinforce the men at the front door."

"What? You won't go out a few steps to rescue your own commander?" Nureen's eyes were harsh.

"Well . . . yes, my lady. We cannot venture out there. Commander Ardon was very specific about that. What if it's an ambush? If some rebels are hiding nearby to kill us and enter the palace?" The older guard grasped his wrist behind his back.

"You are just cowards! Fine, I will go there myself and lure these sentries to the back door. You just gather your people and kill them."

"But my lady . . ."

She snatched the young guard's dagger and sliced his left palm with it. He squealed, and the older man frowned at him. Nureen dipped her fingers in his blood and smothered it on her face; she then ripped a sleeve off her dress. The guards watched this with their mouths open.

"Run! Go get your men!" she ordered, and they left in haste.

When they returned with reinforcements, Nureen opened the back door and rushed toward the barn, screaming, "Soldiers! Help!"

The two young sentries turned toward her, clutching their swords.

She cried out to them, "My husband needs you! The palace is attacked! I've been attacked! Run inside and help! Gather everyone!"

"My lady, we have orders to guard this . . ." one started to say.

She yelled at them at the top of her lungs, "GO! NOW! Save your ruler, you idiots!"

The soldiers looked at each other, jaws dropped. They glanced at the barn and hurried toward the open door of the palace.

Having ended the two young lives, the palace guards stood peeking outside.

"What are you waiting for?" shouted Nureen.

"I'll go," volunteered the young guard with a wounded hand.

Others kept back, their arrows drawn. The young man dashed to the barn and threw the door open. Soon he emerged with Eliphaz and Ardon, and all three raced to the palace. After a brief exchange with the palace guards, Eliphaz hurried back to his father.

Nureen went upstairs without speaking with anyone. She looked at herself in a polished copper mirror and cringed. She washed the blood off her face, changed her dress, and collapsed on the bed, staring at the ceiling.

***

Back in command of the palace guards, Ardon made his way to the chief. The sounds of a heated argument escaped into the corridor as he entered the throne room. Seir and his sons turned toward him without saying a word.

At last, the chief asked, "What took you so long?"

Ardon replied, "Apologies, my lord. My master Esau proposes that we invite the crowd's leaders to meet with us here and to let them air their grievances."

"Invite them here? Isn't it risky?" asked Lotan.

"Nothing to worry about, my lords. They would leave any weapons at the door, as is the rule of the palace. We will be right here to protect you."

"And where is Eliphaz?" asked Seir.

"He is still conferring with my master Esau. He should join us shortly." Ardon cleared his throat and rubbed his eye.

Seir exhaled through puffed cheeks. "So you want me, the chief of the Horites, to speak with some mob agitators?"

"My lord, it is either that or we should send the army to disperse them—your choice, my lord." Ardon paused and added, "If my lord chooses to send the army, it might still be useful to trap their leaders here."

Seir glanced at his sons, who shrugged their shoulders. "Fine. Invite them, but search them well before they enter. Your guards shall stay close to us."

***

Esau noticed that Eliphaz was carrying somebody else's sword, and his son explained what had happened.

Lirron? Who would have known? But then again, the Horites are all treacherous. Yet we need to rely on them for now, since we are too few in number . . .

"Father," Eliphaz interrupted his thoughts, "what shall we do now?"

"It depends on whether Nymeer is still in charge of the army. Perhaps Lirron acted on his own accord. But if the Horites are united against us, we have a problem. A big one!"

"Of course, father. There are only a few scores of us but thousands of them. And we are the ones who have armed and trained them! I suppose the fact they've lost most of our expensive Ubulla swords during the retreat is a good thing now."

"I suppose so, if they are against us. But we must find out who's in charge there."

"Father, but how would we do that? We can't just go there and ask!"

"No, of course not. None of us can show our faces in the army barracks. Wait . . . why don't we ask Timna to go?"

"Timna?"

"Yes. Call her."

Timna and Eliphaz walked in, and she said, "My master Esau, I am eager to help."

"Timna, you've come up with a great plan to rescue us from Seir's clutches before. Did my son explain the situation we face today? If yes, what are your thoughts?"

"Sure. I'll go to the barracks with my servants and ask if anybody has seen Eliphaz. They might not even be aware that he has been freed. It will become clear who is in charge and whether the army officers are united against you or not."

"And if they take you hostage?" asked Eliphaz.

"I am a royal princess of the Horites. Why would they want to harm me?"

"They might take you to help them bargain with your father," said Esau. "If they do, we'll rescue you."

Turning toward Eliphaz, he added, "It's worth the risk. Take Korach and a few good archers and follow her. If you see anybody trying to harm Timna, kill them. And before you go, remind all our people downstairs to arm themselves and stay there. They must be prepared for action."

Timna and two of her handmaids left. Eliphaz, Korach, and three servants followed.

*****

Ardon stepped outside the front door of the palace and announced to the crowd, "Our lord Seir wants to know what troubles his subjects today. What are your grievances?"

The crowd clamored louder. An old man in front shouted, "We don't want the tax that was imposed because Esau had lost the war with his brother!"

Another protester screamed, "And we don't want Esau, either!" The crowd erupted in approval.

Ardon addressed the mob again, "Our lord Seir cares deeply about his subjects. He invites five of your delegates to present your grievances to him in person. Select five people you trust."

The crowd did not seem to know how to react. People started buzzing and arguing with one another. Ardon waited, struggling to suppress a chuckle. At long last five people stepped forward, but they were in no hurry.

One of them yelled, "We want guarantees that we won't be harmed. Let Chief Seir himself swear to that!"

"Fine," said Ardon and went inside.

Seir was not amused at the prospect of leaving the protection of his palace and promising something that was not going to happen.

"What if one of them shoots me?" he demanded.

Ardon assured him, "My lord, we will guard you well. You'll be safe."

The chief shuffled outside the entrance, protected on two sides by the palace guards with raised shields.

"Your representatives will not be harmed," he proclaimed in haste and disappeared behind the door.

The five mob leaders followed him inside, looking around with suspicion.

Chapter 33

Timna surprised the soldiers guarding the army barracks, as the royals had never visited them before. When she asked for General Nymeer, the guards dithered. She raised her voice, and the men showed her inside, shouting, "Royal princess! Stand at attention!"

Timna and her girls went through a long corridor to a room in the rear. The soldiers stood up and stared at the ladies passing by. An officer ushered Timna into the room, as the word "treason" was spoken at the end of some sentence.

Eight senior Horite commanders were sitting around the table, some with flushed faces. After wavering for a few seconds, they stood up at attention.

An older stone-faced man with a somber bearing addressed her, "I am Nymeer, a general of the army. It is an unexpected honor to see you here, princess Timna. What can we do for you, my lady?"

All the officers were peering at her during the introduction, except for the one who was staring at the general.

She said in as dignified a voice as she could muster, "I am looking for Eliphaz, my fiancé. He is nowhere to be found. I thought that perhaps he was here with you."

"My lady, he is not here," replied Nymeer. "We don't know where he is."

Timna took a deep breath, braced herself against the table, and blurted out, "I've heard that some soldiers have arrested him. I wanted to see if this was done with your blessing, General Nymeer."

Nymeer's eyes widened and blinked rapidly. He looked around the table, his gaze lingering on Lirron for an instant, and replied, "Soldiers? Certainly not mine, my lady. Do you know where they took him?"

Timna continued her desperate gamble, glaring at Nymeer, "Yes, I know where they took him, and I can show you."

The commanders glanced at one another and then at Nymeer. They started fiddling with their uniforms and fidgeting in their seats.

Nymeer coughed and answered, "My lady, then let's go there right now and free him!"

Timna said, "Thank you, general. I'll lead the way. But we have to be very careful, as I've seen some rebels lurking around the palace. And then there is the angry crowd in the square."

As the officers shuffled out, Lirron took five of his most loyal warriors and hissed, "Stay close—and follow my lead."

***

Hiding in the thick myrtle bushes outside the barracks, Eliphaz and Korach were getting restless. Korach breathed out, "Eliphaz, how would we know if Timna was taken prisoner? How long should we wait?"

Soon they had their answer. Timna and her maids, accompanied by scores of Horite officers and troops, left the building and marched in the direction of the palace.

Korach whispered again, "What do you think they plan on doing? Confront Seir?"

"Only one way to find out," said Eliphaz.

After trailing the Horites for a few minutes, Eliphaz signaled for his small group to stop. "I know what she's doing," he said. "We need to run to the palace. RUN!"

Dropping their stealth, they sprinted through the trees, cut through the crowd at the palace entrance, and brushed aside the front guards.

"Get me Ardon! Hurry!" barked Eliphaz.

"My master, he is in the meeting with Chief Seir and the mob's leaders," answered the senior guard.

"Get him out of there!" ordered Eliphaz. "Gather all the interior guards at the back door!" The man vacillated, and he had to scream, "NOW!"

The senior guard tiptoed into Seir's room and whispered into Ardon's ear. Ardon excused himself and left the room, following Eliphaz upstairs.

The guards assumed the positions in and around Nureen's room. Eliphaz told Nureen what was going to happen, and she seemed both alarmed and delighted.

A large group of Horite soldiers and senior army commanders arrived, with Timna leading the way. They proceeded at a slow pace in a defensive formation with raised shields. Timna pointed to the barn, and several soldiers went inside, then the rest of the group.

"Shoot at Lirron when he comes out!" ordered Eliphaz.

"So that's Timna's plan," said Korach. "Smart."

The Horites returned from the barn. Lirron seemed to be arguing with Timna.

Eliphaz addressed his archers, "Hold! Lirron is too close to her." He took a bow and aimed at Lirron with great care. "Shoot only on my command."

He was startled when an arrow flew from the palace and hit the barn. He swirled around and howled, "Who did this?"

A young guard was covering his mouth, his eyes bulging out, his lips quivering, "Sorry, sorry . . . so sorry!" He was cradling his left hand.

Lirron crouched, then grabbed Timna and hid behind her. The soldiers raised their shields, looked toward the palace, and backed away. Soon they were out of sight.

Eliphaz grabbed the young guard by the throat and nearly lifted him in the air. His eyes were ready to incinerate the youth.

"Please let him go, he's just a boy," implored Nureen.

Eliphaz continued to squeeze the youth's neck. He sighed and let go, throwing him to the floor.

Nureen cried, "It's my fault."

Eliphaz stormed out of the room without looking at her, muttering, "Forget about the chicken neck—that's not the problem now. We're all sitting ducks."

***

Shaken by the events, Ardon returned to Seir's meeting with the five mob emissaries. He again excused himself and motioned with his eyes toward the delegates; Seir did not inquire further.

Eliphaz entered the room, and the chief addressed him, "I hear that my people are upset and insulted by this tax we have imposed on them. But your uncle Jacob expects a tribute from us. Is there some other way of paying for that? Does your father have any ideas?"

"I spoke with him today about this. He is certain we can find the money for the tribute."

Seir's face brightened up, and he rubbed his hands. The chief and the delegates filed outside, where he addressed the crowd.

"My fellow Horites! I have guided you for decades, and my heart has always been with you. I have heard your concerns today. Your troubles are my troubles, and your hurt my hurt. We have therefore decided to rescind the tax we imposed earlier. We are looking for other sources of funds to pay Jacob, something that does not involve getting money from you. My beloved brothers, go home in peace!"

"The pompous old fool will do anything to avoid a confrontation," Eliphaz whispered to Ardon. "But he doesn't yet know about Lirron. We'll see how he resolves that one with diplomacy."

Soon after, the stunned people in the crowd started to cheer, then yell and hug one another. They lifted up the five envoys and bounced them up and down. Soon they left the square to celebrate, while gloomy Eliphaz and Ardon remained at the entrance.

***

One crisis defused, the Edomites could focus on dealing with a far larger one. Surrounded by his sons, Esau considered their options. It was early evening, and the dark shadows from the candles highlighted the exhaustion on their faces.

"Timna and her girls are now hostages, as we have feared," Esau said, his eyes losing focus. "And we still don't know about Nymeer and the other commanders."

"We saw the officers, including Nymeer, walking with Lirron to the barn. But it wasn't clear who was following whom," reported Eliphaz.

"Then we should assume the worst—that the entire Horite army has turned. Tell everyone downstairs to be ready and if they must sleep, sleep in their clothes. Double the sentries. I suspect the rebels will show up at my doorstep in the morning if not sooner."

Esau fell silent. He shook his head and continued, "My sons, it pains me to say this, but we cannot overcome them by ourselves. However good we think we are, we need help."

Korach joined in, "But father, the Horites are disorganized— they are cave dwellers, after all! We've seen only a small garrison in the barracks. What if we attack now, before they could mobilize?"

Esau replied, "Yes, if we knew for certain it was true, this might work. But we don't. And it's dark out. The chances of getting ourselves into an ambush are high; the chances of winning, unknown."

"Father, you weren't this cautious when you were younger!" exclaimed Korach.

Esau glared at him. Turning to Machalat's son Reuel, he said, "Take two men and ride to your uncle Nebaioth the Ishmaelite. Ask him to come to our defense. If I ever needed his help, it's now. Hurry!" Reuel left in haste.

"And you, Eliphaz, go tell Ardon to prepare Seir's palace for a possible assault. He should not let the chief out under any circumstances. Detain him by force if needed."

"But why, father?"

"Don't you see? We cannot have Seir joining the army against us. If that happens, we are finished. We must frame these events as a mutiny against the chief. Then the Horites will see us as Seir's protectors."

"And you, Korach, keep a watch on the army barracks. Perhaps you'll learn what's going on there. Since you are so brave, go alone, and be extra vigilant. Don't get into any fights—I need you alive, you hothead!" A faint smile crossed his lips.

Esau fell silent and concluded, "My sons, I wish we didn't have to travel back and forth through the woods like that. I realize it's dangerous, but there is no other way. We can't fly." He turned to Eliphaz and chuckled.

Chapter 34

Leaning across the table toward Lirron, Nymeer blared, "I know we came under attack from the palace, but why did we bring the princess back here? How is it her fault? Release her! Now!"

"General, we need her. She is our only protection against an assault by Esau's forces," replied Lirron in a calm voice, as the officers' room fell silent.

"What forces? Are you afraid of his sons? Of a few palace guards? We still have thousands of troops!" roared Nymeer.

"General, have you forgotten the near-riot earlier today? People have made their choice clear: down with Esau and down with his stooges!"

"Which stooges are those? I hope you don't mean Chief Seir! Lirron, you are talking treason—again! Our lord Esau is the commander of the army! As a general in charge, I order you to desist from this treasonous talk! And release the princess. Also, explain why you've had the audacity to arrest Eliphaz and Ardon earlier without my permission."

Lirron stood up and approached Nymeer, who also rose from his seat. The two men faced each other.

Looking Nymeer in the eye, Lirron grinned, "General, you are absolutely right . . ."

He swiftly pulled out a knife and stabbed Nymeer in the abdomen.

". . . I do have the audacity—to become the new army general!"

Nymeer's gasped and covered the wound with his hands. Lirron stabbed him again under the chin, pushing the knife upward into the skull.

Blood gushed from the wounds and from Nymeer's mouth, blending with his uniform. He collapsed, his widened eyes still looking at the assailant. At Lirron's signal, the guards standing at the door—his relatives—dragged the dying general out of the room.

The rest of the commanders did not utter a sound, sitting with their shoulders hunched. They gazed at Lirron, just as Lirron examined each of them.

"I think he was trying to say that he wanted me to take over. Don't you agree?"

The officers remained silent.

When the guards returned, Lirron ordered, "Keep Timna and her girls in a holding cell and have her watched at all times!"

Lirron addressed the officers, "Our first order is to march on Seir's palace, get rid of Esau's guards there, and replace them with ours. Then we crush the head of the Edomite snake at his home. Should be simple enough. Who disagrees?" The commanders looked at the floor.

"Then it's decided. Go assemble your family troops and meet me in front of Seir's palace. I know it is dark out, but we have no time to lose. I'll bring the crowd back to the square to support us."

Lirron called for his son Jayeel, who was a soldier, and told him, "Go gather people from our clan. Have them assemble in front of the barracks. Also, let them help you bring back the mob."

"Father, they might be quite drunk at this point," Jayeel said.

"What could be better? They might need money now. Tell them I'd pay one *kesitah* to anyone who comes back to the square and chants against both Esau and Seir."

***

When Eliphaz arrived at the palace, he found Ardon and relayed Esau's orders to prepare for a possible attack. Both men frowned.

"If Lirron has taken over the army, the chances of us prevailing over the entire force are nil," fretted Eliphaz.

"At least let's try and defend the palace for a while," said Ardon.

"What about Timna?"

"We could try diplomacy—let's ask Seir."

The chief looked at them and shifted on his throne. "Nobody tells me anything. What's going on? I understand Lirron took my daughter hostage. Explain!"

Eliphaz said, "My lord, Lirron has betrayed us. He is trying to take over the army. His men have ambushed and kidnapped me and Ardon earlier in the day, but the palace guards rescued us. Princess Timna tried to help us arrest Lirron, but things went wrong, and he grabbed her."

Seir curled a strand of wispy white hair around his thumb and sunk his fingers into the cheeks. "What does it mean, 'trying to take over the army'? Who's in charge of it now? With Esau wounded, should it not be Nymeer? How can a junior commander take over?"

"My lord, we don't know who's in command there. We propose that you send one of your sons to the barracks to find out. Perhaps the prince could prevent Lirron from turning against you, if it's not too late. Whoever is in charge there has no reason to harm him. Neither of us two can go, of course."

Seir considered the offer. "What if they take my son hostage, too?"

Eliphaz responded, "My lord, it is a dangerous mission, but all of your sons are brave. I'm sure they understand the stakes involved. We are desperate. If there is a conflict between the commanders, we should try to help whoever is on our side. It's either that or waiting until they come for us."

None of the princes volunteered. They continued to argue until Seir said, "Let Zibeon go. He is related to both you and me, so he's the best person for the job." Zibeon, who was sitting among his brothers, bowed and left his father's presence without saying a word, taking two palace guards with him.

Eliphaz left the room and considered what to do next. Walking the corridors, he found himself in front of Nureen's door. After some hesitation, he knocked. Nureen greeted him dressed in a beautiful and revealing silk nightgown.

"My lady, I've never had a chance to thank you for helping save us," he started, but Nureen pulled him inside without saying a word. She stood in front of him, searching for something in his eyes, her face glowing in the candlelight. He did not need any further persuasion to embrace her.

***

Zibeon and his men arrived at the army barracks late in the evening. The sentries recognized the prince and saluted. When questioned, they told him that the soldiers from Lirron's family had assembled and left; the sentries did not know where.

"I've come to see my sister, princess Timna. I understand she is being held here for some reason," announced Zibeon.

The sentries were hedging. "We have orders not to let anyone inside," said one of them.

"And that includes a royal prince?" Zibeon tightened his fists.

The soldiers called for the officer in charge, who came in and saluted.

Boring into his eyes, Zibeon roared on, "Whom exactly are you serving here? Must I bring my father himself to see his daughter?"

"No, my lord . . . I have orders, my lord, but I'm sure *you* can enter. No need for Chief Seir to come here," cowered the officer. He escorted Zibeon and his two guards to Timna's cell.

The prince greeted the women through the copper bars of the door. Peering into the filthy cell, he asked, "My sister, are you well? Why are they keeping you here?"

Having received only a nod from his sister, Zibeon grabbed the officer by the collar and croaked, "On whose orders is the royal princess kept here like a common criminal?"

The man waffled. The two soldiers guarding the cell stood motionless on each side of the door looking straight ahead.

"I demand an answer! Do I detect treason here?" Zibeon continued to thunder.

The officer mumbled, "I don't know, my lord . . . I just have orders . . . don't be angry with your servant, my lord . . ."

Zibeon glanced at his two palace guards and yelled, "Follow me!"

He drew his sword and put it against the officer's stomach, pinning him against the cell door. His men did the same to the soldiers.

"Answer!" howled the prince.

Timna tiptoed to the door with a knife in her hand. Straining, she stabbed the pinned officer in the back. She watched him gasp and stiffen and stabbed him again, sinking the knife deep into his side.

The officer staggered to keep the balance but slid down to the floor. Both his soldiers were felled by the sword.

Zibeon found the key from the cell on one of the guards and let his sister out. Timna threw herself on his shoulders and kissed him.

"Are you hurt? Where did you get the knife?" he asked.

"I'm fine, and I always carry a knife. Do you think they had the audacity to search a princess?" Timna laughed.

"Any more soldiers inside?"

"No, I think they've all left, other than these stiffs here."

They opened the rear door without making a sound. Two sentries were gazing into the darkness, their backs exposed. Zibeon's men promptly dispatched them. Timna picked up a sword and ran her finger over its blade.

"You know how to handle it?" chuckled Zibeon.

"Not really, but it's better to have one than not."

"Keep it away from your legs—it's easy to slice yourself if you are not careful."

The three men and three women stepped outside, leaving their torches behind. The prince and the princess were not accustomed to finding their way in darkness, but the palace guards and the maids could navigate the moonlit night.

"Hey, stop!" they heard a soft voice and halted. A figure emerged from the trees—it was Korach!

"You have freed her! How?" Korach's eyes were glistening.

"A long story," snapped Zibeon. "Take my sister and her maids and bring them home to Esau. They'll explain what happened. Lirron's troops must be on their way either to my father or to yours. So you go warn your father, and I'll go warn mine."

"Oh, I know where they went," said Korach. "I've seen them leave—toward the palace. I overheard them repeating their orders."

"Which were?"

"First, to take out the palace guard—they think it's our main force. After that, attack my father."

***

By the time Zibeon and his two men approached the palace, Lirron's troops had already surrounded it. Only a few dim lights inside the mansion were visible, and its inhabitants seemed sound asleep.

Zibeon frowned, "The guards don't suspect anything, do they?"

His companions clicked their tongues. The three of them hid in a small patch of myrtle bushes, surrounded on three sides by open space—a perfect vantage point from which to observe the action. With soldiers creeping about, they spoke in whispers.

Zibeon asked, "What do you think? We could walk or run toward the front door and hope Lirron's archers would miss in the dark."

One of his guards answered, "Or maybe we could shoot a few arrows toward the palace. This should alert the front door. Or we could just yell something and run away . . ."

"Or we could get out of here and go to Esau," said another. "Ask his people to attack Lirron from the rear . . ."

The sounds of muffled footsteps interrupted the discussion. Were additional troops coming? The palace guards at the front door still did not sound an alarm. Were they even awake? Alive? Zibeon and his men held their breath.

The arriving troops bypassed them, pouring into the open areas in near-silence, and Zibeon and his guards exhaled. But then some new sounds alerted them again: somebody else wanted their hiding spot.

"I suppose there is a disadvantage in being at a vantage point," Zibeon tried his best to cheer them up.

The three men exchanged glances, tilted their heads toward the palace, and stood up. Blending in with the other armed men creeping about, they made it within fifty paces of the front door. But now they were exposed—they had to dash from there.

As they sprinted to the door, the palace guards raised their bows. Yelling at the top of their lungs, the three men continued running.

"Don't shoot! Palace guards here! Prince Zibeon's here! Palace guards here! Open the door!"

The guards at the front door hesitated to shoot but tracked the three running figures. A barrage of arrows started to stream from the darkness, and soft thumping sounds filled the air. One of the palace guards collapsed. The others opened the door and dragged him inside, in time for the runners to join them.

The screams woke Eliphaz and Nureen from their slumber. Eliphaz threw on his uniform, waved to her, and ran downstairs, where Zibeon told him what was happening.

Eliphaz asked Zibeon to awaken and assemble Seir and his sons. Seeing Ardon giving orders to the guards, Eliphaz came toward him, and the two of them exchanged silent looks. They had discussed what to do if this time would come to pass.

***

Korach led Timna and the maids, stepping on the ground with great care, fearful of the sounds of their own breathing. By now their eyes were used to darkness, but any animal shuffle, any creaking tree branch made them halt and listen.

After a while, they started to disregard the night noises and almost convinced themselves there was nothing to worry about. That's when they heard the unmistakable sounds of steps, heavy steps ahead of them. People were plodding toward them on the same path. The four of them halted.

The footsteps were getting closer, as the Edomites stood with bated breath, listening and peering into the night. One of the maids tried to escape into the woods and stepped on a dry branch, which broke with deafening noise. Timna grabbed her by the sleeve, and they all froze in place, trying to calm their hearts. The three women looked at Korach.

"We can't move off the path, and we can't stay here," he said under his breath. "We have to move back, fast."

"Not all the way back to the barracks, I hope?" asked Timna.

"No, no. Remember this huge acacia tree where we turned off minutes ago for a quick stop? Back there. That's the only place along the whole path where the soil is bare. We need to find it again."

They found the tree, turned off the path, passed through a clearing, and hid in the bushes behind it. In a few minutes a large group of soldiers came by, their raised spears softly glowing in the silver light.

A brief command, and the soldiers stopped, then spread out to relieve themselves. Some of them lumbered toward the hiding spot, as the horrified women held on to one another, struggling to breathe.

When the soldiers ventured too close, Korach led the women deeper into the woods. Without the benefit of Esau's training, the maids kept stepping on tree branches, stiffening in fear each time.

The soldiers loudly wondered who or what was making the rustling sounds, and a couple of them went to investigate. The maids hugged Timna and hid their heads in her dress.

But the officers called the soldiers back, and the men retreated. Soon the troops were gone, and the exhausted maids sunk to the ground.

Once on the path again, they picked up the pace, shaking their heads. At last, they approached Esau's home, breathing a sigh of relief, even allowing themselves to speak in soft voices.

Korach asked, "What is it with you people? How can Lirron start a rebellion against his own chief? Isn't Seir his father, or something?"

"Actually, no. Lirron is . . ." Timna stopped cold, pointing to the soldiers standing in front of them. It was too late to turn around.

Chapter 35

Five soldiers were blocking the path, leaning on their spears, as if they had been standing there for hours. Their faces were shrouded in shadows, but they seemed quite young—and snickering. None of them looked like an officer.

"Keep moving," Korach whispered.

"Who's in charge?" he asked in as stern a voice as he could muster. No reply. "I am escorting a royal princess to safety. Come with me, I need your help," he tried.

The soldiers didn't stir, and one of them exclaimed, "Wait, I know you! You are Esau's boy!" He scowled. "And the ladies!"

"No, no! We have a message from Commander Lirron to Esau," Korach continued his desperate bluff. The soldiers just scoffed.

Not losing any time, Korach drew his sword and rushed forward. With a quick thrust he slashed the neck of one soldier and, before the rest of them could react, stabbed another.

The three remaining Horites surrounded him. They dropped their spears and grasped the swords.

Korach was fighting all three at the same time, swirling between them. He rolled on the ground toward one of them and sliced his leg, in one of Esau's favorite moves. As the man lost balance, Korach rose behind him and ripped into his back.

Two soldiers were still standing, ignoring the cries of the wounded that filled the night's quiet. Korach was swinging his blade with abandon, but he started to slow down and pant, licking his parched lips. He did not react in time when one of his enemies raised his sword behind him.

But somehow the attacker halted with his arm extended in the air and slumped to the ground. Without looking back Korach sprinted to strike the soldier facing him, but the Horite dropped his weapon and raised his hands.

He cried, "Don't kill me! I am Jayeel, Lirron's son! His only son!"

Korach placed the tip of his blade against the man's throat. For a few seconds he observed the trembling lips that begged for mercy—and let go. He ripped out Jayeel's red sash and tied his hands with it.

When Korach turned around, Timna was standing over a Horite soldier, holding a sword. She raised her eyes as he shuffled closer to her. Korach smiled, and she lifted one corner of the mouth, too. The maids stood huddled together, holding each other's hands, but there was no time to calm them down.

"We have to run!" Korach screeched through his dry mouth. "If there are any more of them around, they surely have heard."

They dashed towards Esau's estate, pulling Jayeel along.

***

"Do you have any idea how valuable this youth is?" Esau exclaimed. But then his face darkened. "This means that our war with the Horites has begun."

He slapped Korach on the shoulder. "You've done even better than I had expected. How did you manage to dispatch five of them?"

"Four, actually. Timna killed one."

"Oh? She's truly becoming one of us." Esau's face lit up again. "Just curious, what was the most difficult part of the fight?"

"At the end—with the two of them. I was tired, and my vision was getting blurry. Battling one man, I lost track of the other. Glad Timna was there."

"That's what I've been teaching you: a fight with two opponents is the toughest one. I'd rather battle a large group, where people tend to get in each other's way. Two skilled men attacking at the same time are the worst. And from what you've told me, those Horites were skilled. I'm not surprised—we've trained them!"

***

"Eliphaz, as far as I can make out in the darkness, the palace is completely surrounded," observed Ardon, peering from a front window of the second floor.

"Not surprised. But you know, this window right here would be an ideal place to shoot from. That is, if we could somehow lure Lirron into the square. The rest of them would disperse after that, I suppose."

"He is not so dumb . . ."

". . . and he is also a coward, so he won't show his face out in the open, I know, I know. We can only dream, Ardon."

They went downstairs, and Eliphaz reported to Seir, "My lord, the troops of traitor Lirron have encircled the palace. Also, the mob has returned. They sound pretty drunk, and this time they are chanting against both Esau and you."

The chief grunted. "I knew Lirron could not be trusted." His eyes were moist, and his face looked limp. "His family always envied and hated mine. Now he sees his chance to use this unrest to his advantage—or perhaps he is the one stoking it."

Lotan lifted his head, "If we could only send a message to our own clan, many would come to our defense. But we are sealed off, according to you."

"Yes, we are," confirmed Eliphaz and turned to Seir. "My lord, is there anything we should know about the palace? Something that could help us defend it?"

"Well, it's only a house, not a fortress. But I've built it to be as sturdy and well-fortified as I could. Its stone walls are one cubit thick, and its oak doors are half that. These doors have cost me a fortune! The windows are very narrow, so the rebels cannot get inside through those. But you already know that," Seir chuckled.

"Anything else, my lord?"

"I suppose, there are only two ways to get in—break down the doors or climb onto the roof. No secret tunnels here, if that's your question."

"Or they could just burn us down," Lotan added.

"We'll fight to the last man," promised Ardon, rubbing his face. "We'll place some guards behind both sets of doors and on the roof."

"I'm sure you will. And how many men do we have, exactly?" asked Seir.

"Thirty-six palace guards plus us here," said Ardon. "And at least a thousand of them."

Silence filled the room.

***

The dawn was breaking, and Esau kept looking out the window. Deep shadows still covered the woods in front of his house, so he could not tell if anyone was hiding there. A multitude of people seemed to be milling around the palace. Or were these the trees reflecting the first rays of sunlight? He motioned for Korach to come closer.

"You said that they were planning to go first after Seir, then us. But shouldn't they have sent some troops here as well? Somebody needs to keep us from coming to the chief's defense, if they know anything at all about war."

"Look—here they are!" Korach pointed to the mass of soldiers marching in their direction. Many hundreds of them. They both inhaled through clenched teeth.

"Korach, where did Lirron get so many men? If he has persuaded the other Horite families to join him, he could muster thousands! This could spell the end of us."

Korach shrugged his shoulders. They could only watch as the soldiers surrounded the house.

One of the officers yelled, "Esau, there is no escape! Surrender or be killed!" and retreated behind the raised shields.

Esau did not dignify this demand with an answer. He was observing the chaotic movements of the Horites, sensing some disarray among them. Was it because the son of Lirron was supposed to be their commander—and he wasn't there? It's curious how Lirron selected a mere soldier over the ranking officers to lead the charge. Of course, Lirron himself has never commanded an army, either.

Korach interrupted his thoughts. "Your orders, father?"

"Help me put on my battle armor. Then take the son of Lirron to the roof and keep him hidden from view. On my command make him yell his piece—with conviction!" Esau clicked his tongue when he saw his ruined leather tunic lying in the corner.

He shouted through the window, "Horites, a message for you! Watch the roof!" He hobbled away from the opening.

In a few moments Korach and Jayeel rose up on the roof.

"Soldiers! If you are searching for your commander, I'm here! I am a prisoner of Esau! Do not attack him if you want me to live! Tell my father to remove the siege from here and from the palace! These are my orders!"

Korach pulled him down behind the parapet and patted him on the back. They returned downstairs to Esau.

The Horites stalled. Esau noticed a messenger running toward the palace. Good. Now we just have to wait.

***

Throughout the morning, the Horite troops were cutting down trees and chopping off the branches, leaving cubit-long stubs on the trunks. The defenders knew what was happening: the soldiers were making the trees into ladders and battering rams. The stubs would be used as the ram handles or the anchors to secure ladder rungs. The work took place out of range of Seir's bowmen, allowing them to observe all the preparations while being powerless to interfere—a common tactic on the part of the attackers during a siege.

Unnerved Seir, protected on both sides by the guards with full-height shields, proclaimed from the roof, "My brothers! We have fought many wars together. You know that I am a fair . . ." A volley of arrows shot in his direction interrupted him; all fell short.

Undaunted, Seir continued, "Killing me is not the solution. I am the only one who can unite us! To prevent us from fighting one another! Do not follow the treasonous commands . . ." He stopped and retreated after more arrows flew his way, landing closer this time. One just missed the top of his head.

The Horites received a messenger who soon went back with a large troop following him. The *kesitah*-clutching mob was still loitering in the square, and Lirron's men dispersed it.

The torturous spectacle of the attack preparations continued. While the soldiers behind the palace square were completing their ladders and battering rams, the men surrounding the palace were digging small pits, setting fires inside them, and boiling pitch over the fires. Other soldiers protected the diggers and themselves with large wooden shields.

Standing atop the roof, Ardon pointed at the warriors wrapping pieces of cloth behind the arrowheads and grumbled, "Eliphaz, I remember the havoc these fire arrows wreaked during our attack on the Egyptian caravan. That was before your time. Now we'll be on the receiving end . . ."

Everything quieted down, save for the crackling noises of the fires. The Horite archers stood ready at the edge of the tree line and all around the palace. An eerie calm enveloped the lifeless square.

***

Lirron was staring into a corner of his black field tent, slouching on a portable bench. He sighed, drummed his fingers on top of a small unpainted desk, and sighed again.

He asked his closest lieutenant, who was standing at attention, "Our original plan isn't quite working, is it? We wanted to isolate Seir and get rid of his Edomite guards, then go after Esau, remember?"

The officer answered, "Yes, sir. We've assumed that we'd intimidate the chief and he'd simply surrender. But so far there is no sign of that."

"So what are we going to do with Seir if he doesn't give up?"

"Up to you, sir."

"Still deciding. You don't understand how difficult that is . . . You see, killing Seir would make me an eternal enemy of his tribe. Are we ready for a civil war with a larger clan?"

"Maybe there wouldn't be a war, sir, if we're smart."

"Even if no open war breaks out, his people are vengeful. Do I want a life of looking over my shoulder? Having somebody taste my food? Everything would be so much easier if Seir had just surrendered and abdicated. How can we make this stubborn old man do that?" Lirron took off his helmet and ran his fingers through the long messy hair.

"Not sure, sir." The officer stared straight ahead, but a corner of his mouth briefly twitched.

"Hmm . . . one other thing. Does the capture of Jayeel change our plans at all?"

"No, sir. We still need to take the palace first."

"And after that?"

"We'd keep Esau besieged. Sooner or later he'll surrender or maybe negotiate a peaceful exit in return for your son's life."

"But what about Jayeel being there in the meantime?"

"He should be safe, sir. Too valuable to kill."

Lirron took a deep breath, straightened his back, and ordered, "Fine. Take an additional unit and assume the command of the troops facing Esau. Follow that messenger. We have more than enough men here."

***

The attackers kept shouting Seir's name, threatening to burn down the palace unless everyone inside surrendered. The princes looked at their father, all of them crowded on the roof away from the edge.

The chief said, "Lotan, my son, what do you think we should do? Look at the sea of red armor around us—the armor I've paid for!"

"I see that, father."

"They are not listening to me, so why don't *you* try to negotiate with them one last time?"

Lotan started speaking from the rooftop, as his father had done, but his words drowned in the chants "Surrender! Surrender!"

"It's no use," admitted Seir.

Meanwhile, Ardon directed the guards to fill every available bucket and vessel with water from the underground cistern, to be placed around the roof and the courtyard along with the piles of soil and thick blankets. Next, he had them remove from the exposed areas all wooden furniture and anything else that could burn. There was little else they could do.

***

At long last, the flaming arrows started to hail on the palace from all directions. Most of them fell into the courtyard and were quickly put out. But the barrage went on, and some of the arrows hit wooden posts, stationary wood benches, and interior roof ladders.

Because the flaming arrows were much heavier than the regular arrows, they were difficult to shoot, and the attackers had to get very close. The palace lacked any exterior defenses, so the soldiers could also throw burning logs and sticks, ignoring the mounting casualties. Soon, multiple small fires were glowing on the roof and in the courtyard.

Lirron's archers aimed at the windows. Wood shutters covered some of them, and they soon caught fire. Other openings were unprotected, to allow the defenders to shoot back. The attackers' arrows flew through those, igniting the curtains and furniture inside. Among a pandemonium of people running around with buckets and blankets, acrid smoke started to seep into every room.

The raiders used their battering rams on the front and back doors, as the ladders went up the sides of the palace. When the defenders tried to push the ladders away from the roof, they became the targets of the archers on the ground who picked them off one by one. Ardon and Eliphaz had already lost nearly one-half of their palace guards in this fashion. With the battle just beginning, this did not augur well.

CHAPTER 36

Nureen and two maids crowded together in the far corner of her room and covered their faces with the sleeves of their dresses. They lifted their eyes toward the sounds of somebody hacking away at the shutters.

After a storm of splintered remnants flying into the room subsided, a soldier appeared in the window. Standing on a ladder, he aimed a flaming arrow at the cowering women. They froze in fear, gripping one another even tighter.

Someone on the roof pushed the ladder away, but not before the soldier released the arrow. It missed the women and pinned the tapestry instead, punctuating a loud scream coming from above.

Rubbing their eyes, the maids rushed to grab some blankets, but two more arrows whizzed past them through the now-unprotected window. The girls shrieked and ran back into the corner, as Nureen rushed to close the opening of death.

She grabbed a heavy wood bench and dragged it toward the breach, tearing the sleeve of her favorite purple dress in the process. As she struggled to lift one end of the bulky piece and pivot it against the window, an arrow struck her in the chest, thrusting her to the floor.

***

Ardon was trying to direct the defense of the palace, fight the fires on the roof, and shoot at the attackers. He and four of his remaining men kept pushing off the ladders going up on all sides. While he was busy at the front of the palace, a tall ladder rising outside Nureen's window caught his attention, and he raced across the roof. An arrow nicked him in the thigh; he just cursed and limped along.

Grunting, Ardon shoved the ladder away from the building, but a fire arrow hit him in the abdomen. Then another. He screamed, teetered on the edge of the roof for a few moments, and fell on his back.

His cloak caught fire, and he tried to put it out with his bare hands. One of the palace guards started dragging him away but was cut down by the attackers streaming onto the roof. Ardon cried, powerless to stop the Horites rushing past him and the flames from creeping toward his white beard.

***

Three blaring sounds of a ram's horn pierced the thick cacophony of the battle. Every Horite knew what this sound meant: retreat! Through the haze, the last defenders watched Lirron's soldiers scurry away and then reassemble in the square with their backs turned toward the palace.

Some cavalry was advancing toward them.

One of the surviving palace guards recognized the banner of the Ishmaelites. The expressions on the exhausted men's faces alternated between desperate hope, caution, ecstasy, and fear. On which side would the horsemen fight? Would they fight at all?

The riders paused in front of Lirron's warriors and continued to creep forward with lowered spears. The Horites were not used to fighting armed horsemen and had no cavalry of their own. Ignoring desperate commands of their officers, they started to back away little by little, until some of them came into the range of Seir's bowmen. Without a command to shoot, the survivors exacted their revenge for the fallen brothers-in-arms. The soldiers crowded into a massive defensive formation, with raised shields on two sides.

After a few minutes, the messengers holding white flags started to shuttle back and forth, and a passage to the palace was cleared. Most of the horsemen remained in place facing Lirron's soldiers, but a few dozen rode toward the smoldering building. Some of them dismounted and went inside; the rest guarded the entrance.

Seir and his sons waited with bated breath.

"I am glad to see you, Chief Nebaioth! Have you come to save us or . . .?"

"Yes, yes, we came to help, Chief Seir." Nebaioth extended his hands, palms up. "I received an urgent plea from my nephew Reuel. He said Esau and you were under attack by one of your own." Nebaioth glanced at Reuel standing at his side and continued, "We left as soon as we could and rode through the night. We saw the fighting at your palace and rushed here first. Hope it's not too late."

"Chief Nebaioth, I am astounded at this turn of events. We have fought one another before, and we have been neither friends nor allies—but this will change now! I cannot even begin to express my gratitude! Were you to come half an hour later, it would have been all over for us. We'll be grateful forever!" Seir puffed.

"Chief Seir, I'm happy to be of help." Nebaioth coughed and rubbed his eyes. "You need to get out of here. Not sure where . . . Is Esau still at his home? Reuel told me he had been hurt in a battle."

"Yes, yes. His home must be surrounded by the enemy now. But we haven't heard any sounds of battle coming from there."

Nebaioth cleared his throat and continued, "Chief Seir, here's the thing. I don't have enough men with me to defeat this massive force standing there. I didn't expect so many. We'd have to negotiate with them to get them to withdraw . . ."

"But you have enough for them to be worried?"

"I hope so."

"Lirron, their commander, has many additional troops at Esau's estate."

Nebaioth said, scratching his forehead, "Then we definitely have no choice but to talk to Lirron. Meanwhile, are there any of your own tribesmen whom you could call upon to help?"

"Yes, but my clan is spread out all over the mountain. We've been cut off and couldn't summon them."

"Then I suggest you do it now, while a passage is cleared for us. Have your sons take some of my horses and ride to gather your men."

***

The lengthy talks between Lirron on one side and Nebaioth and Seir on the other have not yielded an agreement. Without Esau, nobody could find a way out, so any further discussions had to include him—and thus be held at his home.

According to custom, the parties hosting the negotiations provided hostages during the meetings, usually their sons. Nebaioth and Seir each designated two of their sons, and they expected Esau to name two of his. Lirron insisted that one of them be Esau's firstborn.

Waiting to be sent to Lirron's camp, Eliphaz took the three guards who were injured the least and went through the palace to help the wounded, count the dead, and observe the damage. Twenty-two people were dead and almost everyone else wounded. Eliphaz himself was unhurt, save for some burns and bruises. By his reckoning, Lirron's troops lost at least 100 men whose corpses were still lying around.

The damage to the palace was disheartening. Although the front and the back doors were battered but not broken, the roof was in shambles and in one place caved in. The exposed wood structure of the building was burned-out or charred—and all this carnage resulted from a battle that lasted less than an hour.

When they knocked on Nureen's door, a maid answered. Nureen was lying on the floor, covered in blood, with an arrow in her chest. Another maid was trying to stop the bleeding.

Eliphaz pushed away the maids and kneeled over Nureen. He glanced at the wound, at the puddle, and at his men, who shook their heads. All of them knew that the arrow that had not fully penetrated through the body was impossible to remove without causing further damage. Eliphaz had seen many people shot in the chest like this; none survived.

He looked at Nureen's face. She was still conscious, and her wide-open brown eyes longed to escape the pain. Much of her elegant purple dress was now red, and her well-cared-for hair was matted. She greeted him with her usual faint smile.

Eliphaz held her hand, fighting the tears, with the palace guards looking on. As Nureen slid into the world of dreams, she whispered, "Take care of Timna."

One of Seir's sons announced that it was time to go. Eliphaz gazed at Nureen for a while longer and whispered a farewell. He reached the door and turned toward her for the last time. She was looking at him.

As his feet moved downstairs, tears moistened his burned eyelashes.

"Eliphaz!"

"Eliphaz!" Someone was calling. Seir.

"I am sorry, Chief Seir, I was overcome by thoughts," Eliphaz managed to utter.

"Yes, there is much to think about now. But we must go."

The soldiers escorted Eliphaz to Lirron, who looked at his tattered, burnt, and bloodied clothes and asked, "You have fought a lot today. What do you think happens next?"

"I don't know," said Eliphaz. "I really don't."

***

Lirron, Nebaioth, and Seir arrived at Esau's home with some of their troops and advisers. At Lirron's command, his soldiers backed away from the house. Esau sent his son Reuel to Lirron's camp to join five other hostages, who were held at a clearing visible from Esau's window.

The talks continued for hours. It was getting late, and no one was eager to extend the ordeal through the night.

"The only way to achieve a lasting peace is for Seir to abdicate in favor of me, the new rightful chief," insisted Lirron.

"Dream on," snapped Seir.

"Chief Nebaioth, you don't have nearly enough strength to defeat me," said Lirron. "You should just leave the Horite business to the Horites, before your people find their graves on this mountain. And we would eat their horses."

"As I recall, your people didn't seem too brave when they saw mine," parried Nebaioth.

The stalemate dragged on until the loud sounds of trumpets reached the room. Outside, Seir's tribesmen flooded the entire area as far as eye could see. Some of them wore red uniforms, others did not, but all of them were armed.

Lirron's soldiers formed a ring around the hostages and crowded together, looking at the house of Esau. One could almost hear their anguished pleas for direction.

Lirron turned pale. "I will never surrender. Never!"

"What brave words—coming from a coward who was the first to run away from Jacob!" sneered Esau, tossing his head. "Tell you what, Lirron. Do you know what I would've done if I were younger?"

"What?" squeaked Lirron.

Esau grinned and continued, "I would've killed you and your advisers right here, in this room. Your soldiers wouldn't have heard a thing. And I would've waited until dark and sent my men to rescue the hostages. We know where they are," Esau pointed to the window with his thumb. "And then I would've killed all your officers and take the troops prisoners."

Esau noticed with satisfaction that Lirron's knees started to shake. "Should we bring a chamber pot?" he scowled. "But since I'm older now, I can see a way out of this without spilling blood. And here is my best offer you're going to get. The exile."

"The exile?" echoed Lirron.

"Yes—leave Mount Seir forever. Take your families and possessions and go. Anyone who wants to leave with you could go, too. All of us here will guarantee your safety, but you must depart tomorrow. Do you accept?"

Lirron looked at his advisors, who shrugged their shoulders and lowered their eyes. One of them nodded.

"I agree," said Lirron in a whisper, looking at the floor.

"I didn't hear it. What was that?"

"I agree!" screeched Lirron.

"Good. Let's get it done. We'll let you go, and you release the hostages," interjected Seir. Esau gave him a side-glance.

"And after that tell your people to start packing—tonight! Go cave-to-cave if you must," said Esau.

"We'd need to take our weapons with us," Lirron mumbled.

"Not the new ones! You can take your old sickle swords from the armory, if you wish," Esau concluded with a firm gaze. There was nothing more to discuss.

CHAPTER 37

The evening ceremony of hostage exchange capped the day's events. Four pairs of men, including Lirron and his son, stood along the sides of a square.

When signaled to do so, they started to move at a measured pace toward the middle. Having met there, they continued to their tribes' positions under the watchful eyes of the four sets of archers. The exchange went without a hitch—nobody was in the mood for any more fighting—and Lirron's troops left through a gauntlet of Seir's tribesmen.

As this incredible turn of events sunk in, as it became clear that the siege was finally over, a mood of jubilation took over the Edomites. The Ishmaelites and Seir's subjects joined in with shouts, hugs and back-slapping all around. Eliphaz ran upstairs and embraced his father.

"I'm proud of what you've done, son," beamed Esau. "I can see you taking my place soon. But where is Ardon?"

Eliphaz shook his head, "Sorry, father."

Esau gulped, and his body slackened. "He fought with me for longer than you are alive! He was a good man, a strong man . . ."

"Yes father, he was," Eliphaz lowered his head.

". . . and he never married, in order to be near me. How did he . . ."

Timna poked her head through the open door. "You are alive, my love!" she exclaimed and ran toward Eliphaz, skipping like a little girl. He hugged her without saying anything, and she clung to him, putting her head on his shoulder.

Esau now recognized some of Nureen's features in her face. The two of them will do just fine.

He announced that the celebration party was postponed until Lirron's tribe would have left Mount Seir with all their possessions. He reminded those who could not wait about the fate of Chedarlaomer's army that engaged in a premature feast.

***

Lirron arrived at the palace square and briefed his officers on what had happened. He ordered the exhausted soldiers still standing there to disband and start packing, ready to reassemble for the departure in the morning. His troops left without looking back at Seir's people and the Ishmaelites shadowing them.

Many of the departing Horites were grumbling, reminding one another how a few hours earlier they had been on the verge of capturing the palace. A dozen of them crowded together, walking, muttering, and looking over their shoulders.

"My brother died in the assault. And what do we have to show for it? Umm?"

"Lirron is a coward. He just proved it—again!"

"Yeah. Because he lost his nerve when the cavalry arrived, we have to leave our homes?"

"So let's get rid of him. We'll figure out what to do later."

One of them pointed to a soldier walking alongside and asked, "Hey, who's this? He might've heard us."

"Oh, that's Magbai, Lirron's cousin."

"What?"

"Don't worry—he's harmless. He probably hates Lirron more than we do. Lirron keeps him a common soldier, can you believe it?"

The mutineers hurried toward Lirron, blending with the red river of other distressed men.

Magbai stroked his chin and started running. He got to Lirron before the plotters did.

"My master, I have something urgent!"

"Don't you see I am speaking with Jayeel? Wait your turn!" barked Lirron with a dismissive glance.

"It's a matter of life and death!"

Lirron rolled his eyes. "What could it be, cousin? Speak!"

"Soldiers are coming to kill you!"

"Which soldiers?"

"Here they are," the cousin nodded toward a group gaining on Lirron from behind. Everyone in that group kept their eyes on Lirron, while the other Horites were looking straight, plodding in gathering darkness.

"Guards!" yelled Lirron.

He had sent his personal guards some distance ahead, to speak with his son in confidence. Now the guards had to race back. The mutineers also dashed towards Lirron, pulling out their swords as they ran. The one who got there first raised his weapon to strike.

While Lirron stood in place with gaping mouth, Jayeel drew his sword and lunged in front of his father. He parried the strike of the first attacker, but the sword of the second one pierced the side of his body. Jayeel gasped and fell, as Magbai struck the second assailant.

At that point the guards arrived. The mutineers stood no chance against the best-trained and the most experienced warriors in Lirron's army, and soon all twelve of them were dead. But so was Jayeel. The guards picked up his body and carried it with them; all Lirron could do was to follow.

***

Apprehension ruled the next day. Neither Esau, nor Seir, nor Nebaioth were certain that Lirron's people would leave, but they did. By noon, the caravans of camels and donkeys laden with their belongings descended from the mountain and spread out in different directions. Many cave dwellers owned no animals and had to carry their possessions on their backs.

"Eliphaz, do you know where are they going?" asked Esau.

"I've heard that some of them were upset with Lirron and did not wish to follow him. Still, most people will probably go north with him to the Ammonites and the Moabites. Some will go south to the Midianites."

"So if we venture out in some future war, we'd be seeing them anywhere we go?"

"It looks that way, father. But at least this mountain is now ours."

". . . and Seir's," added Esau. "Don't forget about him. For now, we still have to tolerate his authority. But not for long."

That evening, once the last of Lirron's people have left, it was time to celebrate. Esau invited Seir and his family into his home, and they partied through the night. Esau caught himself a few times searching for Ardon and Dekel amid the crowd. He kept thinking how much he missed them. And Anadil. All three would have enjoyed the party.

In the morning Esau and Seir pledged their allegiance to each other, and the chief returned to his battered palace to start rebuilding.

CHAPTER 38

The familiar road to Hebron did not reveal anything new. The same hills, the same dust, the same heat. During twenty years since Esau became a full-time resident of Mount Seir, he traveled this road many times to visit his blind father. But this was the last such visit: his father just died at the age of 180.

A messenger who brought the announcement also told Esau that to his last day Isaac had not given up on his wayward son. The old patriarch continued to hope that Esau would repent and join Jacob on the path to righteousness.

Making his way past thorns and thistles, Esau kept puzzling over why. Wasn't one pious son enough? Wasn't my life full of triumphs—without any prayers? Everything I've accomplished, I did on my own.

After expelling Lirron's clan, I have subdued the remaining Horites and lived in peace with them for a while. But I didn't forget about my main goal. When we became strong enough, I provoked a confrontation with Chief Seir—the old fool was infirm by then—and killed him and most of his family. We seized all their land, and at last Mount Seir has truly become the field of Edom—my field.

I have many children and grandchildren, and all of them have followed in my footsteps. Each of my sons—Eliphaz, Reuel, Jeush, Jaalam, and Korach—is now a duke and has a clan of his own.

I've kept an eye on Korach since he was a little boy. He has become a great warrior in his own stead. His martial glory spread throughout the land of Canaan, above all of my descendants. Good boy. Yet Korach could never understand why I disliked my brother so much. He simply doesn't care.

It was Timna's son Amalek who outdid me in his hatred of Jacob. He has this burning desire to kill all the Israelites—even I haven't felt like that. He will avenge my tears.

***

The brothers met again in Hebron among the thousands who came to pay their last respects to Isaac. All the kings of Canaan and the lands beyond attended Isaac's funeral, honoring the man known throughout the world for his holiness.

The funeral procession departed to the cave of Machpelah, where Abraham and Sarah had been buried. Barefoot Isaac's servants and family members carried his coffin, weeping. Even Esau could not keep his eyes dry the entire trip and had to wear the hood of his black shawl.

After the funeral, he came up to his brother and said, "I understand that our father has left his vast fortune to the two of us. He didn't specify how to divide it."

"That's true," answered Jacob. How do you want to go about it?"

"I'll let you divide the inheritance into two parts —however you want—but I will choose which part to take. A deal?" Jacob agreed.

The next time the brothers met, Jacob said, "I have done what you requested."

"Good. So how did you divide it?"

"I've placed all the material possessions that our father had accumulated during his lifetime—servants, slaves, gold, silver, cattle, herds—into one part."

Esau stared at him in disbelief. "Then what could possibly be in the other part?" he asked.

"Only one document: the title to the land of Canaan written by God Himself. The Promised Land. It also includes the cave of

Machpelah, which our grandfather Abraham had bought from the Hittites. Where we have buried our father. The choice is yours!"

"It's a clever division," admitted Esau. "But I'm not sure which part is more valuable. Give me some time to think it over."

***

Once again, Esau decided to seek counsel from his cousin, the only person he respected outside his family. Riding to the desert of Paran, he kept debating.

By becoming the king of the entire Canaan, I would at last fulfill my lifelong dream of outshining King Nimrod. But is a single document, even the title to the best land in the world, worth my father's great wealth?

Nebaioth nodded when Esau explained his predicament. "Esau, the title to the Land would give you great honor, but no more than that," he said. "As you well know, strong Canaanite kings reign there now. How do you propose to get rid of them? Even for a mighty man like you, the conquest would take a long time."

"I've got the time," Esau replied. "Why not cap my life's victories with this great adventure?"

"You've got the time? Look, Esau, you are about 120 now, right? Even if you manage to defeat all the local kings in your lifetime, for how long would you bask in your new glory?"

"Hmm. So you think it's better to take the riches now and enjoy them?"

"That's what I would do."

Esau followed Nebaioth's advice. The two brothers signed a contract stipulating that Jacob and his descendants had acquired the title to the land of Canaan, including the cave of Machpelah, for all eternity. Esau received all the material possessions of his father.

Chapter 39

Esau was sitting on the roof of his house, looking at the woods from his favorite ornate red chair. Eliphaz came up from behind and stood in silence for a little while before clearing his throat.

"Dinner is served, father," he said, but Esau just waved him away.

"Don't you want to eat? You've been sitting like this the entire day, staring outside. What bothers you, father?"

Esau looked up. "Use your imagination."

"Father, not again! We've gone through this how many times? Yes, you are 147 now. So what? You still have at least thirty-three years until you match your father's lifetime, right? And in any case, you've had a long and fulfilling life. Isn't it what you've always wanted?"

Esau bobbed his head and smirked. His dignified look, with a long white hair and beard, betrayed little of the fiery appearance of his youth.

"Father, you are still in great health . . ."

"Stop cheering me up, son. Last night I had a dream that the end of my life was near—does this satisfy you?"

"Well, we all have to go someday, no?"

"It's not that. You know that I like to think things through. So I keep pondering not only when I would die, but also where I would be buried, and who would bury me."

"You do? I've always assumed we'd all be buried here on Mount Seir in the kings' cemetery."

"Oh, no! I must rest near my father, in the cave of Machpelah in Hebron."

"But didn't you sell its title to Jacob?"

"Of course I did. But I have to lie near my father, title or no title. I will find a way to be interred there, I will!"

Korach rushed in. "Father, your brother is dead! In Egypt! The news just arrived."

"Thank you, my son." He turned to Eliphaz. "See? I knew something was up."

Esau remembered Rebecca's remark that she would lose both her children on the same day. But how could it be? I am still very much alive, he thought, full of energy and strength, while my brother is no more. Much good all the studies and prayers did him in the end! Was the fact that I've outlasted Jacob the final proof that I am greater than him, that I am indeed The Mightiest, immune to prophesies and superstitions?

Korach did not wait for him to finish his musings. "The messenger said something else. Important, father! Look at me—he's ready to leave!"

"What?"

"He said that a great funeral procession is carrying Jacob's body out of Egypt. All the Egyptian nobles are there. And much of the army—countless chariots and horsemen in battle attire."

Esau stirred. "Going where?"

"The man didn't know. He had heard, however, that the Canaanite kings had their suspicions about the burial. They wondered if that could be an Israelite ploy to conquer their lands with the help of the Egyptians. Why else would they need such a massive army to accompany them? The princes of Ishmael had the same misgivings."

"Hey, I do too!" exclaimed Esau. "Eliphaz, this may be it! Our last chance! Assemble the men in haste—we are going to meet with the Canaanites and the Ishmaelites. Together, we could stop this invasion."

He turned to Korach and said, "Ask the messenger to tell the kings that we'll meet them at the southern border of Canaan."

***

The combined forces of the Canaanites, the Ishmaelites, and the Edomites filled a large valley between two stony mountain ranges. The kings and the army chiefs assembled in a sprawling tent, which provided some respite from the blistering sun. Having already made the plans for the attack, they were happy to be distracted by the shapely dancers swirling around. Esau and Nebaioth were sitting side to side, remembering the old times.

Everyone was on edge. Why were the Egyptians so late? They should have been there last night by the Canaanites' reckoning.

At last a signal arrived that the procession was coming. Vast clouds of dust concealed its true size, adding to the tension among the waiting troops. But the chieftains blinked when they saw the funeral caravan up close.

Nebaioth nudged Esau, "It's a great army, but the Egyptians don't seem to be aiming for war. They are in their travel, not battle formation."

Esau stroked his beard and said, "Yeah. And behind them I see my nephews. They are armed but not in a fighting mood either. Look: they are carrying my brother's coffin barefoot, sobbing and wailing."

"And nobody is alarmed to see us."

"True. Maybe it *is* just a funeral, after all."

"Esau, I wanted you to know that I've met your brother. He was a great man, a righteous man. I bet all of us here know that."

Esau just grunted in reply.

Nebaioth touched his shoulder and said, "I realize the two of you did not see eye to eye, but you can't deny that he had performed some real miracles."

"He did? Like what?"

"Well, remember when his sons sold their brother Joseph into slavery?"

"Oh yes—they sure did!"

"Well, it turned out to be for a reason. Joseph acquitted himself rather well in Egypt. He was the only one who was able to interpret Pharaoh' dreams, right? As a result, he rose to become a viceroy, second only to Pharaoh himself."

"I know that, so?"

"Esau, the Pharaoh's dreams were about the coming seven years of drought that would devastate the entire world. Joseph took steps to gather grain during the seven years of plenty that preceded the famine. He's been selling the grain to everyone in the world ever since—to us too! That grain has fed both you and me."

"Yeah, yeah. So how does Jacob fit into this?"

"Well, Jacob and his family had to move to Egypt to escape the famine. When he arrived, your brother met Pharaoh and blessed the Nile. And after that the river started overflowing again! Because of his blessing the drought stopped after only two years rather than the preordained seven. That's why the Egyptians revere you brother—he saved them! He saved us all!"

Esau was silent. With a hand on the hilt of his sword, he approached the procession; Nebaioth and the Canaanite kings followed. What they saw captivated them.

The coffin and its bier were made of pure gold and were decorated with diamonds, which sparkled like a second desert sun. The pearl-incrusted posts supported the canopy of golden threads. Fifty of Jacob's servants walked in front of the bier spreading myrrh, aloe and perfume along the road. The Egyptians rode a respectable distance away. It was clear: there would be no war that day.

The dazzled kings and princes felt compelled to honor Jacob by joining the procession, weeping and mourning. When Nebaioth pointed to a royal golden crown of Joseph, Egypt's viceroy, sitting on top of the coffin, they took off their own crowns and placed them upon the bier. Somebody compared the sight of the sparkling crowns encircling the coffin to a threshing floor surrounded by a hedge of thorns.

Esau went along, biding his time. Nobody could tell him where the procession was going, and he did not see how he could overcome this massive army by himself, now that his putative allies were of no help. You just can't rely on people.

***

The sons of Jacob and the Egyptians held a great memorial service in a place called Goren ha-Atad and observed a seven-day mourning period there. Esau realized that the only place where the procession could be going was the cave of Machpelah in Hebron—*his* cave of Machpelah.

He knew that the cave was rather compact, with only four burial vaults. The remains of Adam and Eve, Abraham and Sarah, and Isaac and Rebecca occupied three of them. Only one-half of the last compartment remained empty, because Jacob had already used the other half to lay Leah to rest.

If they inter Jacob in the last remaining space, there would be no place for me, Esau understood. Will Jacob even after his death cheat me out of the burial spot near my father? I have to do something—anything—to stop the Israelites.

But what, exactly? I could put up a fight, Egyptian chariots or not. If I make a surprise attack, perhaps I could hurt them enough to get them to back off. And perhaps this victory would be my finest hour, once and for all cementing my place in history as The Mightiest, the conqueror of massive armies.

He glanced at the multitude of the Egyptian troops who filled the road as far as eye could see and then at the long faces of the men in his modest force. No, that was just a delusion.

Meanwhile, the procession arrived at the cave, and the sons of Jacob opened its door. They unhitched the coffin, preparing to lift it. On the spur of the moment, Esau decided to try diplomacy. He blocked the entrance with his body and raised his arms.

"Stop, my dear nephews! You cannot bury my brother here. The last resting spot in the cave is reserved for me! I am the oldest son of the holy Isaac, and you cannot deny me the eternal rest near my beloved father."

The sons of Israel kept looking at him in silence with unflinching stares, until Joseph said, "May I remind you, my dear uncle, that you've sold your share in the cave? Along with the title to the entire land of Canaan? After the death of Isaac, you've chosen to take all his material possessions instead, do you recall that?"

Esau did not back down. He stood with his feet apart, staring back at the Israelites. "All I recall is that I've sold my birthright. Not the right to be buried next to my father!"

"No, you did sell us the rights to the cave as well," Joseph insisted.

"Then where is the bill of sale attesting to that?" Esau demanded.

He knew that none of the Israelites standing in front of him were present during the sale—thus nobody could testify that it had taken place at all! Jacob's sons looked at one another in confusion. A bill of sale?

Joseph replied, "It's in Egypt, where we now reside."

"Then go get it and show it to me, if you really have it!"

Esau felt a stroke of luck. His nephews did not seem to want a fight at the funeral, and they went along with his arguments! But surely all this multitude will not wait here in the desert for many days until somebody finds that piece of leather. Will they leave?

He observed with enjoyment as the sons of Israel huddled together, with Joseph extending his arms to them, palms down. By their looks and gestures Esau understood that his hunch was right: They did not want to commemorate their father's last hours above ground with fighting. They were prepared to meet his demands for the sake of keeping the peace!

Joseph asked his brother Naphtali, "Please run back to Egypt and retrieve the document for us."

"Why me?" asked Naphtali.

"Because you are as swift as a deer! Remember your father's blessing on his deathbed? They say you can walk on corn husks without crushing them!"

Naphtali grinned and raced out, accompanied by some of the Egyptian cavalry. The opposing parties settled into an uneasy calm.

Esau was thinking, how long would it last? How long would they allow Jacob's coffin to stay above ground? Keeping a coffin unburied for a long time was considered a sign of disrespect for the deceased. Indeed, both the Israelites and the Egyptians were becoming more and more restless in the furnace that was Hebron.

"We can't continue standing here waiting," one of the sons of Jacob observed.

"Glad the Egyptians allowed us to take our weapons for the journey," said another.

"Now is the time to use them!" exclaimed the third.

They approached Esau and his men standing at the entrance to the cave and tried to force them out of the way. They drew no weapons—it was just a lot of pushing and shoving, which Esau and his warriors were able to resist. Both sides prepared for the real battle.

When the fighting started, it lasted for more than half an hour. Hundreds of men were swinging their swords around the cave in a messy free-for-all.

The sons of Jacob killed forty Edomites without losing a single man, but they still could not dislodge their enemies and they could not harm Esau himself. The elderly Edomite patriarch was too good of a fighter. He stood on a dry patch of land surrounded by a puddle of blood with his white beard unsullied.

The confrontation came to a reluctant halt, with nothing decisive accomplished. The Israelites retreated to catch their breath.

Esau beckoned to Joseph, who was standing a good way off, surrounded by the Egyptians. Draped in a purple royal mantle, he was the tallest and the most handsome man in the group.

Esau called out, scowling, "Join me in combat! One on one. We'll see how good you are!"

Pharaoh's advisers were tugging at Joseph's clothes, trying to keep the frowned man from leaving. Three of them blocked his path, as Esau continued his taunts.

"If you are the same Joseph who was born to defeat me, here is your chance!"

Addressing Joseph by the name Pharaoh had given him, the Egyptians implored him, "Tzafnat Paneiach, you are our viceroy, our lord. Pharaoh had commanded you not to get involved in any fighting. Not only would that be an affront to your position, but we cannot risk having you hurt in battle. Our entire kingdom depends on you—we'd be lost without your wisdom!"

Clenching his teeth, Joseph stayed put, peering at Esau. In a few minutes, the Egyptian army commander came asking for a permission to attack the Edomites.

One of the Pharaoh's advisers glanced at Joseph and said, "Our lord viceroy orders you to stand down. This is not our fight. No need to start a war with Edom over a cave."

The commander hesitated, and the courtier whispered in his ear, "After all, if Jacob isn't buried here, he'd be buried somewhere else. So what if the procession turns around and goes back to Egypt? Surely it would be better to have the grave of a holy man in our country, rather than here, in the land of our enemies?"

***

Chushim, the son of Dan, was at his assigned task—guarding the Israelite women and children with the only weapon he had, a club. He was a strapping man but deaf and mute, and he did not understand what caused the delay in his grandfather's burial.

"What's going on? Why all the fighting?" he asked, as best as he could enunciate.

"Esau does not allow us to proceed with the burial until Naphtali comes back from Egypt with the bill of sale for the cave." After a few tries and gestures Chushim understood.

He mumbled, "So are we going to stand around here? And my grandfather will lie in shame, unburied, all this time?" He tried to find the answer in his brothers' eyes, but they turned away.

With flared nostrils, Chushim paced up and down for a few moments and left. Keeping his gaze on the prostrate bodies, he crept towards Esau, who was still standing at the entrance to the cave looking around with satisfaction.

Savoring his victory, Esau did not pay much attention to a lone Israelite edging closer. It was his last mistake—with a swift blow, Chushim hit him on the head with his club.

As blood started trickling out of Esau's fractured skull, his body remained upright. He gave the attacker a blank look and tried to unsheathe his favorite blade, but Chushim grabbed someone else's sword and with a mighty swing severed his head.

People gasped, as the head of Esau rolled inside the cave and stopped at Isaac's grave. Some say it is still there to this day, "in the bosom of Isaac."

And so Jacob's burial took place after all.

Having lost the head of their tribe, the Edomites now had no choice but to retreat. As they prepared to transport Esau's headless body back to Mount Seir, his soul was ascending through the vortex of time and space.

From the celestial heights, he got a glimpse of his descendants' future lives and those of his brother. He saw the riches of Haman, the glory of Rome, and the infamy of Germany. To his dismay he also noticed that the sons of Israel were still around as far into the future as he could behold. Not only have they refused to fade away, but they prospered despite all the adversity that his heirs inflicted upon them. Some of his own progeny—Obadiah and numerous others—have converted to the faith of Abraham and became well-known prophets and rabbis.

He remembered the final blessing his father gave to Jacob: "Those who curse you shall be cursed, and those who bless you shall be blessed." In the final moments of his last journey Esau realized that he never had a chance in his fight against the sons of Israel.

The End

MAIN SOURCES

The Torah: Chumash Bereishis, Kehot Publication Society, Brooklyn, NY, 2004.

Rabbi Moshe Weissman, *The Midrash Says*, Benei Yakov Publications, New York, NY, 1980.

Sefer HaYashar (*The Book of Jasher*) J.H. Parry & Co., Salt Lake City, 1887, accessed at http://www.succatyeshua.nl/upload/files/The%20 book%20of%20Jasher.pdf.

Jewish Encyclopedia, 1906, accessed at http://jewishencyclopedia. com/articles/5846-esau.

Multiple articles at www.Chabad.org.

ABOUT THE AUTHOR

Alexander Newman was born in Russia, which he fled 40 years ago. An engineer by profession, he has written three popular nonfiction books published by McGraw-Hill, one of which is in the third edition and translated into Chinese. This book is a culmination of his lifelong interest in epic biblical stories and the daily life in the ancient times. In addition to extensive research, he has visited Israel to gather precious details that make all the difference in a novel. He has been drawn to the biblical conflict between Jacob and Esau for a long time, because it is so similar to the struggles in our own lives. He and his family live in the Boston area, at the edge of a forest.

www.ingramcontent.com/pod-product-compliance
Lightning Source LLC
Chambersburg PA
CBHW032122180726
48284CB00002B/659